BOOK OF HOURS

THE BEGUILEMENT OF BROTHER ALPHAIOS

J. S. ANDERSON

Lucky Bat Books

A Lucky Bat Book

BOOK OF HOURS:
The Beguilement of Brother Alphaios

Copyright © 2013 by J. S. Anderson

Cover Design by Guilherme Gustavo Condeixa

ISBN 978-1-939051-46-2

LuckyBatBooks.com

10 9 8 7 6 5 4 3 2 1

to Liz,

and this journey toward grace

ACKNOWLEDGEMENTS

First and foremost, my thanks to my dear friend and now wife, Liz Waters, with whom this imagining began and matured into a novel. The straightforward guidance and encouragement by Editor Peter Gelfan were essential and gratefully accepted. The enthusiasm of the late Fr. Thomas More, S.J., for the character of Brother Alphaios came at a seminal moment. Also, thanks to Fran Marian and Barry Webb for their close and critical read of an earlier draft. Any errors of fact, history, syntax or otherwise are mine alone.

J. S. Anderson

A MERE TWENTY-TWO DAYS after his ascension to the Throne of St. Peter in May of 1555, Pope Marcellus II lay on his deathbed. He would not survive into the evening.

Physical exhaustion would be ruled the official cause of death, but rumors already busied the back rooms of Vatican City. Poison was the most favored, for Marcellus was only fifty-four years old and hadn't been frail or sickly. To the contrary, he'd been a vigorous man, known as a champion of the Vatican Library, and before that as an unrelenting papal emissary during the throes of the Counter-Reformation. In that role, fueling the current whispers, he'd won the enmity of no less than Charles V, Emperor of the Holy Roman Empire. It was only weeks before that the emperor had openly opposed Marcellus's rise to the papacy.

Other treachery could not be ruled out. Only three cardinals were present in Rome for the conclave, and until just before his election, Marcellus had never even been made a bishop. If one were to set aside God's own influence for a moment, Marcellus was hardly a consensus pope.

The Vatican's most skilled physicians surrounded the papal bed, but whatever the cause of his illness, the state of medicine was not in Marcellus's favor. He was beyond any human help when his personal secretary eased away from the holy bedside, his place taken by someone more anxious to witness this death.

The secretary slipped into the pope's private chapel and genuflected. Standing once more, he glanced over his shoulder and then gathered into his arms the richly illuminated book of hours that lay open on a pedestal. He then turned and left the papal apartment through the attendants' quarters.

Later, some would say they'd seen the secretary approach the opening to the necropolis upon which the vast new Basilica of St. Peter was being built. No particular evidence of this came to light, however, and the searches were futile. The only complete agreement ever reached was that the pope's personal secretary had disappeared, and with him an extraordinary book of hours for which no written record existed, not even in the meticulous Vatican Library.

Three days later, Pope Marcellus II was laid to rest. It would be another 417 years before the book of hours was seen again.

In 1972, workmen came across it in a long-forgotten storage room along the Grand Canal in Venice. Though carefully wrapped, time, water and worms had severely damaged its covers and many of its pages. Its poor condition, along with disputed claims of ownership and the vagaries of scholarly research, would relegate it to obscurity for nearly forty more years.

Now, the book of hours had emerged once again.

CHAPTER 1

ON THE OPPOSITE BANK of the river, a wall of buildings rose straight into the air, impossibly vertical, inconceivably high. Brother Alphaios pressed his face against the window so he could absorb it all.

The taxi moved at high speed along an elevated highway beside cranes loading and unloading cargo ships. It was carrying Brother Alphaios from the airport to the ruined book of hours and his temporary home in America.

Beside him, Prior Bartholomew seemed to sense his excitement, for he paused in his questions about acquaintances in Florence. "It's amazing, isn't it? And seeing it at night, you'd think the world couldn't have so many electric lights."

"That's where we're going?"

"Looks intimidating, doesn't it? Even more here than from the doors of the monastery. You'll get used to it." Bartholomew fell silent, and Alphaios tried to take in all he was seeing.

The great masses of concrete, steel and glass spoke of pure math and engineering, unsoftened by the gentler arts he was used to in Rome and Florence. In those ancient cities, engineering had long been subservient to art and architecture.

The rise of the city into the sky was so immense it seemed geologic in scale.

Far too soon, they swept under a steel bridge with two levels for automobile traffic and another for trains. They followed a sharp upward curve and then were on the bridge itself. Alphaios watched the city blink by through girders suspended from enormous cables and bonded by millions of rivets.

Moments later they descended into a canyon so deep that he could no longer see the sky. Endless lines of cars and trucks struggled to occupy the same narrow spaces. The city growled, squealed, howled, banged, and thudded. It was noisy, but more than just loud. It sounded strident, as if it were some great, chained beast straining to pull forward its own impossible weight.

Around them armies of pedestrians advanced in all directions. Now Alphaios shrank back. For the first time in his adult life, he felt awkward, naïve in his simple rust-brown habit, rope belt and blocky ankle-high shoes. He began to wonder if it had been wise for Cardinal Ricci to send him here.

After twenty more minutes of stop-and-start traffic in the vast canyons, the taxi turned into a narrow, tree-lined street of attached brick buildings, four stories tall. Prior Bartholomew gestured toward one of them.

"Here we are." He leaned forward to pay the driver. "Let's get your package."

Everything Alphaios had brought with him was in one small box: a few items for personal care, a worn Bible and a clutch of paintbrushes of exceptional quality. He owned nothing more and would need nothing more, for he would be a guest here until the book of hours was completed. He took the box from the driver and followed his new host.

The prior led him to a set of steps with black curlicue handrails. There was no sign, and except for minor variations in the color of brick and architectural features at its windows and cornice, the building was virtually indistinguishable from any of the others on the street. It didn't look like any cloister he'd ever seen.

"This is it?"

"This is the library—I thought you'd like to see it before we go to the monastery. Your book of hours is here."

Alphaios's universe lurched. "The book isn't in cloisters?"

"We have no scriptorium, Brother. It was either bring the book and everyone working on it into the monastery, or have you do the work here. We have the room but not the tolerance. We chose the library."

Cardinal Ricci hadn't told him he'd be working outside the cloister. And in this overwhelming colossus of a city?

In all his years as a monk—from his teenage years as a novice in Greece, even during his training and work as an illuminator in Rome and Florence—he had spent little time outside the comforting walls. Mostly, it had been unnecessary, for the cloisters in Italy possessed hundreds of illuminated books that had kept him occupied.

In addition, first as an apprentice and now as master, he had long had the opportunity to study books held by other exceptional collections, both public and private. The reputations of the two monasteries for scholarship and restoration were so great that manuscripts which would be lent nowhere else were made available to them. Even so, there were limits. In order to study the most priceless of books and paintings, he had occasionally traveled to the Vatican Library in Rome and the Uffizi and other libraries in Florence. But he'd always been accompanied on such trips, and those cities were nothing like this.

Prior Bartholomew pushed a button on a numbered pad beside the doorframe. "We'll have only a few minutes." After a buzz and a click, the prior opened the door. They entered a small foyer that was unadorned except for a wooden coat rack and black-and-white checkered floor. Somewhere a clock ticked.

"Ah, there you are." A slight man approached from the base of a handsome, curved stairwell. He looked to be in his mid-thirties and was dressed in brown slacks and a form-fitting, honey-colored sweater. "Prior," he said with a handshake and small bow. "This must be our illuminator. Brother Alphaios, is it?"

"Yes." He wasn't sure what else to say.

"Inaki Arriaga, Chief Archivist." He grinned. "Actually, the only archivist. Come in, please. You've had a long trip. Let's take a moment in the sitting room." He led them through a set of French doors into a large room well appointed with couches and armchairs. "So, Brother, you speak English."

"Thanks to a small talent for languages and some American brothers. Is the scriptorium here?"

"We haven't called it that, but it's a good name for our restoration room."

"And the book of hours?"

"Yes."

"This is a library. What do you call it?"

"It doesn't have a name. We prefer not to exist in the public eye."

"Who owns it? Is it the party who bought the book of hours?"

"I can't tell you that, either. I can tell you Cardinal Ricci has arranged to make the copy, but of course you already knew that."

"What else do you have?" Prior Bartholomew asked.

"Some primitive maps and documents pertaining to western civilization. Letters among royalty and former heads of state, and the originals of quite a number of notable histories. We also have religious holdings from the Middle Ages, but nothing else quite like this book of hours."

"If you can't tell people what you have," Alphaios said, "how can scholars use it?"

"Sometimes they can't. If we learn of important scholarship that our pieces might help, we make them available through other libraries and museums. But this collection, this library, stays private—completely confidential." He paused and looked at Alphaios. "Cardinal Ricci has assured us of your full discretion." He looked at the prior as well. Both men nodded their assent.

While the secrecy of the library was unique in Alphaios's experience, it was no surprise that it so carefully guarded its collection. Even under the most careful circumstances, irreplaceable documents were known to have been lost, stolen, or damaged beyond repair.

"I hear it's in poor condition."

"It's amazing it survived at all. We don't know how long it was shut up in the storage room in Venice, but there's no known trace of it between 1555 and 1972. It was presumed lost or destroyed centuries ago, but the book is beyond restoration as a complete work. Parts of it could be repaired, but nothing was ever started."

"I've done some very difficult restorations," said Alphaios. "It's quite unusual to forgo that in favor of a copy."

"On a number of pages there's simply nothing to restore. Unless you count smears and mold."

"Then we restore what we can, and accept that it will be incomplete."

The archivist seemed surprised, and paused to look squarely at Alphaios. "The cardinal's made it clear he wants every page to appear just as it was in the original. Even those where no text or pictures are left."

"And how do we do that?"

The archivist's eyebrows lifted, and he gave Alphaios a wry smile. "The difficulty has been made known to him. He says he has faith in us."

Faith? In place of pigments and ink? Alphaios frowned, but before he could form a response, Prior Bartholomew spoke.

"Where did it come from?"

"There's still considerable mystery about is origin, which as Brother Alphaios can tell you, is quite unusual. Even more so, there are no apparent exemplars for any of the book's decorations. They all appear completely original."

No exemplars? Alphaios wanted more. "What else is known?"

"'Known' is the wrong word. What we have is informed speculation. It was a lavish undertaking. It may have been made in a monastery, either for its own purposes or commissioned by a wealthy landowner. Though it was made much earlier, it's been suggested that Marcello Cervini, the Vatican librarian, acquired it for the Holy See sometime in the mid-1500s. Unfortunately, no records have been found to support that contention. And we don't know where it might have been before that. In 1555, Cervini became pope—Pope Marcellus II. It's said he took just one book, this book, with him to his papal apartment. He died twenty-two days later. He was only fifty-four years old."

Alphaios reached up and rubbed the side of his neck. Perhaps Marcello Cervini simply was not the vessel the Lord wanted as his Bishop of Rome.

"Upon his death," the archivist continued, "it vanished. It wasn't seen again until it was discovered in the palazzo. How it got there?" He shrugged. "Its discovery was a big event in the book world. Some scholars examined it and took steps to preserve it against further deterioration. Then a court decided that after more than four centuries it belonged to the owners of the palazzo and not the Vatican. At which point it was largely forgotten."

"I'm told the cardinal and Pope Gregory are friends," Alphaios said, "and the book is to be a gift. Why this one in particular?"

"More than friends. They've known each other since boyhood and stayed close throughout their careers. Pope Gregory's from Tuscany, near the hill town of Montepulciano, where Pope Marcellus was born. In 1501. Both went to university in Siena—centuries apart, of course. Cardinal Ricci knew that Gregory's ancestry traced back to Marcellus's sister. So, wanting to give his friend the greatest possible gift when he became pope, he tracked down our book of hours. He gathered the funding and the experts, sent you to us, and here we are."

Alphaios felt the weight of history settle across his shoulders. It was not age or beauty alone that gave the book of hours great value. It had a mysterious past as well, and a familial connection to the pope himself.

The others must have felt it, too, for there was silence in the room.

It was broken by Alphaios. "It will be a gift for the ages."

Arriaga and Prior Bartholomew nodded solemnly.

"Can I see it?"

"I'm afraid we don't have time for that," the prior said.

Alphaios turned to look at him, disappointed. Now that he was here, he wanted to examine the manuscript immediately.

The archivist glanced at the prior and back again. "To-morrow, I gather. I'll show it to you then. Will you come at the same time?"

"I'll come after the noon meal and work on it in the after-noons. I'll have duties to perform at the monastery as well."

Arriaga nodded, then accompanied the men to the front door, released the lock, and bid them goodbye. Prior Bartholomew led them to the corner, where he hailed another taxi.

 CHAPTER 2

AFTER A SHORT RIDE, they stopped in front of a pair of oversized doors in a high, windowless gray wall that ran nearly the length of a city block. At its far end, Brother Alphaios could see the façade of a church with a tall steeple, Gothic in style. Constructed of red granite, it was blackened by age and acids in the air.

The noise of the city faded as soon as the big doors closed behind them, overtaken by the sound of falling water. At the center of a courtyard, a disproportionately large, ornate fountain splashed water from bowl to bowl. To his right was the side of the church he'd noticed from the street. His eyes found the top of its steeple but were driven even further upward by the lines of other buildings that towered over it. It seemed that only a half-acre of sky was left.

Built around the courtyard was a colonnade with a sloped roof. This was the cloister, a feature so central to monasticism that the word had become the very term used to describe such life. It was this walkway the monks would use to go to and from the church for prayers and to shield themselves from weather. This cloister was plain, absent of any of the hand-carved columns and lush gardens that made such structures in Italy so beautiful, so peaceful.

The prior lowered himself onto a stone bench, the only one being warmed by the sun. Tall, slender and white-haired, he sat in high relief against sunlit granite made more brilliant by the shadows around it. He wore the same habit and cincture as Alphaios.

"Let's take a moment—the world outside is exhausting. Whenever it seems there couldn't be more noise, new sounds get heaped upon the old ones."

The courtyard didn't show much benefit of sunlight. There was no grass, only gray, uneven paving stones. Some small, inexpensive concrete statues had been placed near meager shrubs, and there was one thin, sparsely leafed tree.

Was his life here to be lived in shade? This was far different than the pastoral, sun-drenched monasteries from which he had come. This would be a colder world, and though it was not an especially cool day, he felt a chill.

Bartholomew gestured toward the fountain. "That was added in the twenties, a gift from a wealthy patron. Truth be known, he intended it for his country estate. His wife found it too risqué, so he had it moved here." Alphaios now saw three beckoning nudes woven into its design. The prior gave a small smile. "Some of the brothers still find it embarrassing, but its music counters the noise from the street. Besides, it's too expensive to replace."

The sound of the water rattled off the stone walls of the courtyard. It was not so much music as replacement noise. It was steadier and less random than the sounds from outside, but still intrusive; the prior had to raise his voice to be heard.

"The walls used to be eight feet high, then twelve. They were raised to eighteen feet back when car and truck horns replaced the shouts of the carters. People think the walls are to keep them from looking in, but they're mostly to keep the noise out. So, we make a bargain with God: Less of His glorious sunshine in return for fewer disturbances from other of His fine creations." He paused and his mood seemed to shift. "But then, it's not external disturbances that test us most, is it?"

He stood up reluctantly. "You'll be staying in the residence. I'll show you to your cell, and you'll have a while to rest. I'll send Brother Harold for you. He's the guest master. He'll introduce you to our community and bring you to vespers and the refectory for supper." He gave a slight smile. "Be kind to Harold. He has precious few guests to tend anymore."

The smile faded. "Just a note, Brother Alphaios. You're here at Cardinal Ricci's request, and we welcome you as a brother. I must ask you, though, to accommodate yourself to our way of life. We protect our routines jealously. My job is to guide the spiritual health of this community, and that means comity among our brothers. The cardinal, as great as his influence is, knows I will protect this fiercely."

Alphaios was a monk of the same Order of St. Ambrose, had lived most of his life within its rhythms, and intended to continue doing so. But might he not be as welcome here as he'd thought? "Of course, Prior."

They entered the residence, climbed the stairs to the second floor, and entered a long, dim hallway. The walls were of stone, the floor of polished dark wood. A few gray pieces of statuary rested on wooden pedestals and in alcoves along the walls. It was the first quiet space Alphaios had encountered since his departure from the monastery in Florence, and it wrapped around him like a comforting blanket.

The prior spoke quietly now. "The brothers know why you're here, of course. I took the matter to chapter when I received the cardinal's request." He stopped before a door. Like all the others in the corridor, it was of the same dark wood as the floor, and rounded at the top. "This will be your cell."

Alphaios bowed his head. "Thank you, Prior. I pray I won't disappoint you or Cardinal Ricci." He opened the door and went into the small room. It held a narrow bed, an upright chair and a small writing desk. As in the corridor, the walls were of stone. A crucifix hung above the bed, and a dark picture of a monk over the desk. Through the small window came little light. He looked through its wavy glass and could just make out a corner of the courtyard.

The room held everything he needed for his contemplative life. Perhaps he could hope, though, for a sliver of sunlight from time to time.

Alphaios closed the door and sat down sideways on the chair, one arm dangling over its back. Prior Bartholomew would expect him to spend his time in solitary prayer, and in his own way, he would. He would reflect on the long trip from Italy, and especially on the extraordinary sights he had seen that day.

As an artist, as an illuminator of ancient books, he was accustomed to using—and sometimes deliberately misusing—linear perspective and human scale. In the past, St. Peter's Basilica in Rome had been his standard for immensity. But today, this American city had redefined for him the very concept of architectural scale. What surprises would future days bring?

For the moment, he was simply happy for quiet, though he became aware of a distant thrumming. It seemed to come from the floor. Did the machinery of this great city intrude even here?

He was still on the chair sometime later when he heard a quiet knock at his door.

Brother Harold was a short, slight man with round spectacles. He wore the same rust-brown habit as Alphaios and Prior Bartholomew, but over it a white scapular fell from his shoulders to the hem of his habit; it was open on the sides, gathered by the rope at his waist. Though derived from a kind of apron meant to symbolize humble service to God, it gave him a formal look. In contrast, Alphaios's scapular was meager and rested under his habit. Though just as symbolic as Harold's, it consisted only of two tiny squares of cloth tied to a length of cord and worn around his neck.

The guest master also bore a full head of dark hair. Unlike Alphaios, he did not have the traditional tonsure, a shaved circle of skin the size of a small plate at the crown of his head.

"Good afternoon, Brother. We have a few minutes before vespers. May I come in?" He spoke in a formal manner, practiced.

"Of course." Alphaios offered Brother Harold the one chair. The guest master chose instead to sit on the edge of the bed, adroitly leaving the place of greater status to Alphaios.

"Welcome to St. Ambrose. Let me tell you a little about our cloister. We were founded on this site in 1832 and have carried on without interruption. The city has grown up around us, but our life has changed very little. You should know we guard our privacy with great care. Any intrusion at all from the outside is unwelcome."

Alphaios nodded.

"Cardinal Ricci has provided a sinecure for your stay here. We've been told your task may take considerable time. With that in mind, we've decided to have you live here in the residence rather than the guesthouse."

"I don't know anything about finances," Alphaios said. "Only that Cardinal Ricci arranged for me to come here to work on the book of hours."

"We have no other brothers who are externs. You'll be expected, of course, to participate in the holy offices and share in the daily assignments."

Harold's reminder that he would be working in the city again set his heart racing. "I would expect no less." He'd been serving meals, cleaning kitchens and lavatories and floors for much of his adult life. As the newest monk in this monastery, even though its guest, he could expect to be given some of the least desirable tasks. It mattered little—he'd done them all, many times over.

"Tomorrow we'll get you a fresh habit. After the divine office of sext and then the noon meal, Prior Bartholomew will show you to the library. You'll be walking, of course. Now, let us join our brothers."

There was a side door to the church under the cloister roof. They joined the other monks in a line until a signal was given and then proceeded into the church.

The Order of St. Ambrose was not a pastoral order. While the church was open for personal worship, there would be no public services and no parishioners: the needs of the public were incidental to the spiritual journeys of the monks. As a result, Alphaios was not surprised to see that the apse, the area of the church behind the altar, was nearly as big as the nave and separated from it by a carved wooden screen. Here was the choir, the area where the monks gathered for the holy offices. It was the spiritual center of any monastery. In the dim light, he could see three long rows of handsomely carved, dark wooden seats on each side, high wooden separations between them. They all faced a central lectern.

He let himself settle into the moment, and an ocean away from home, found comfort in the familiar ritual.

At suppertime, the monks again formed a line and, in silence, entered the refectory, on the first floor of the residence. As Alphaios expected, they sat at tables around the perimeter of the large room, facing its center. The monks were silent during the meal, except for one who stood at a lectern and read aloud for their spiritual guidance. The supper was heavy and salty to his taste. He was not surprised to catch several monks stealing glances at him, some in apparent welcome, others appraisingly. There were two sets of unfriendly eyes, however, that stayed on him throughout the meal.

Strange to his ears were the sounds of sirens, punctuated by a klaxon horn. No one else seemed to notice.

Two hours later, the monks gathered in the cloister again, this time for compline, with its prayers for the dead and one's own soul should he not awaken. It was night, but the windows in the buildings around the monastery were ablaze with light, leaving the courtyard strangely luminous. Deep shade in the day, bright lights at night? He took a position at the end of the queue, centered his mind, and followed the monks into the church.

Not long into the service, he noticed the singing of the monks was uncommonly beautiful. He closed his eyes and listened appreciatively to each note of the ancient music. He was sorry when they finished.

At the end of the service, as they exited, Alphaios detected pride in the glimpses of some of the monks and wondered if they had been performing for him. If so, he didn't begrudge them. His own voice, though practiced, was toneless compared to theirs.

He returned to his cell. As he settled into bed, he gave a moment of sardonic thanks to Pope John XXIII, for it was after Vatican II that the order had combined matins, the traditional 3:00 a.m. prayer, with lauds, which was conducted at the more humane hour of 5:00. No matter that the change was born not of consideration for the monks' comfort but instead to increase the productivity of their working hours.

He fell asleep, conscious still of the sensation, the tiny vibration of distant mechanical life that seemed to rise from the ground upon which this strange new world had been built.

CHAPTER 3

THE NEXT MORNING, when solemn silence came to an end after angelus, Brother Harold sought him out again. This was a work period.

"Counting you, we have twenty-seven monks and a retired priest cloistered here. Father Michael." He led Alphaios toward a long three-story building with large windows. The courtyard was in full shade with a stiff breeze even in this protected area. Alphaios shivered and hunched forward.

"The buildings around us create funnels for the wind. You'll get used to it." Yet he too gathered his garment closer about his neck.

They entered the building. "Our primary support comes from making shoes for our brothers. We ship them around the globe."

Alphaios was more than familiar with the monastery's shoes. They were black, blocky and utilitarian. Their style had not changed in more than a hundred years. Made of heavy leather and rigid soles, the uppers were known to outlast heels and soles five to one. It occurred to him that while he was new here, the shoes he wore had come home.

Though the shoes were sturdy, their laces, famously, were not. He suppressed a grin. Many monks, upon getting a new pair of shoes from St. Ambrose, did not wait for the laces to break before finding strings or leather thongs to replace them.

"When the monastery was founded," Harold said, "we got our hides fresh from the slaughterhouse and had our own tannery. But when the city grew around us and became homes and offices, our neighbors couldn't stand the smell. The land the tannery was on was sold in 1895."

In a large workroom on the second floor, perhaps a dozen monks were cutting, sewing and fashioning leather into shape. They used hand tools and foot-driven treadle machines. Except for the irregular tapping of cobblers' hammers and noise from the street, the room was quiet. Dozens of finished pairs of shoes sat on a table near cardboard boxes, ready to be labeled for shipping. Though several monks looked up at him, no one stopped work or spoke. He didn't expect them to; when monks were not observing solemn silence, they had "simple silence." Conversation could occur in order to function, but otherwise, quiet spiritual reflection was expected.

As he watched them, it struck Alphaios that these monks showed no great enthusiasm for their enterprise. This was not a labor of love, but of necessity or just habit.

He had long ago accepted the order's teaching that worldly tasks were important only to the extent that they sustained spiritual pursuit. The communal tasks he had shared for years were quite acceptable. But though he had never admitted it aloud, he would dread a life of thoughtless, repetitive labor. He knew he was a fortunate monk. Not only did he find monastic life satisfying and centering, but he was able to practice a craft that gave him great joy.

If asked, he would find it difficult to articulate how his artistic life differed from his spiritual one. Through the years, color, waves of color, seemed to have infused both until they were inseparable. Beauty of the kind he pursued seemed to him as devout as prayer.

From what he could see around him, it seemed likely that many of his brothers here would find it difficult to accept this view. He would need to keep it to himself.

"Sts. Crispin and Crispinian," he muttered, referring to twin brothers who were said to have given up their wealth and nobility in the third century to convert to Christianity. They had become preachers and cobblers for the humble. When they refused to denounce their faith before civic authorities, they were beheaded, martyred. They had become the patron saints of shoemakers.

"I'm sorry?" said Harold.

"St. Crispin and St. Crispinian. Which one is for the left shoe, which for the right?"

The joke brought a disapproving frown from the guest master. Apparently there wasn't much humor here regarding shoes. He would need to tread softly.

As they continued through the long building, Alphaios saw many unused rooms; it had once been a much larger enterprise. This was what Prior Bartholomew had meant about having space.

At the far end of the building was the laundry. He was relieved to draw a fresh habit from the communal supply and change his clothes.

Harold led him outside into a sizable open area, and both again drew their shoulders forward against the chill. They were behind the refectory, where the fountain could not be heard and the noise of the city was palpable. A patch of ground that might have been a garden now consisted only of a few struggling plants and brittle brown stems. A handful of red and purple leaves speckled the ground. "Brother Timothy fights a losing cause," Harold said. "Poor soil and little sunlight. Yet somehow he manages not to despair."

"I will like this Brother Timothy."

Past the garden was a small cemetery fenced in rusting ornamental iron. The graves were marked by flat stones but otherwise unadorned. One was recent; the ground over it had not yet fully settled. Harold knelt before it for a moment and crossed himself. He made no comment.

When Brother Harold left him, Alphaios returned to his cell, grateful for its warmth, to await sext. In just a few hours, he would venture back into the huge, chaotic city. And he would see for the very first time the medieval book of hours that had brought him to this new land.

CHAPTER 4

WHEN THE PRIOR opened the big doors again, Alphaios's heart was already racing, his senses alert to what might come.

He could not have said which struck him first, the discordant noise or the constant motion. Both seemed to invade the courtyard instantly, as if they had been waiting for the opportunity.

Prior Bartholomew stepped into the stream of pedestrians, and Alphaios followed. As his companion turned to close the door, Alphaios looked for assurance from the small sign that would tell him he was home again.

Monastery of St. Ambrose
1200 Broad St.
PRIVATE. NO VISITORS.

To his left, as far as his eyes could see, the street was lined with extraordinarily tall buildings, each one pressed hard up against the next. To his right, the same. The canyons stretched so far into the distance that the air began to make the buildings indistinct, just as mountain ranges appear beyond mountain ranges.

While he was accustomed to feeling small and humble in God's great and constant presence, here among these creations of mere mortals he suddenly felt tiny, lost.

"This way." The prior guided him to the left. It was a cool day but the sun was high, and for the moment its warmth and brightness reached the street. Sweaters and jackets were open, scarves hanging free.

They walked along the high wall and in just a few moments reached the front of the church. A central bell tower and spire dominated its tall, narrow form. It was classic in line but heavily ornamented with crenellated gables and decorations of uncertain shape and meaning. It didn't match the plain dignity of the church's interior nor reflect the simple life within. Might it, like the fountain in the courtyard, have been the gift of some well-meaning patron?

"Help me, Brother, help me."

Startled, he lowered his eyes to the voice. There were four heavily dressed men sitting on the church steps. They wore tattered winter coats and grimy caps, and all had bedrolls or other bundles of some sort. They sat apart, though, and gave the impression they were not a group, but that each had arrived here without particular design.

"Help me, Brother, help me." The voice came again, its source a man leaning against a railing. He was looking at the prior, but his tone was mild, even casual. It projected no sense of urgency. It sounded like a mantra, carrying with it no expectation of an answer. The man did not even shrug when they passed by without acknowledgment.

"We'll cross Broad Street here," the prior said. They joined a crowd waiting for the traffic signal and moved with it across the street. The noise was everywhere, a living part of the life that surrounded them.

Once on the other side, they continued straight, along the cross street. Within moments they were in deep shade. Alphaios shivered. Ahead, the next intersection was bathed in sunlight, and he found himself eager to get there. It was the same for the next several blocks—chill, then warmth, then chill.

Though in their habits they were dressed very differently from anybody else around them, they did not seem to draw special attention. Eyes moved across him and occasionally met his own, but he found no judgment in them nor even any particular interest.

What he'd taken for regimented movement yesterday now appeared much more individual. Some people moved quickly, purposefully, as if they had a schedule or destination. Others paused to talk or hug or sip hot drinks from paper cups. There was an astonishing variety of races and forms of dress and apparent wealth. No wonder people were taking little note of him.

The buildings, many of them quite handsome, were mostly in shades of gray. Even with some newer ones showing the blue or green of tinted glass, the effect was monochromatic. Of natural color, there was little except for the fresh fruits and vegetables at curbside stands; it was apparently not a hospitable environment for nature's own spectrum.

Just about everywhere he looked at street level, though, were the bright and urgent colors of commerce: neon signs, awnings over shops, posters for movies and musical events, flyers for sales, political and social messages, magazine covers at newspaper stands, brightly painted buses and taxis, and pictures in restaurant windows so garish as to make the food they intended to sell look completely unpalatable. The clothes worn on the street and in window displays were in palettes much brighter than he had seen in Italy.

He welcomed these manufactured colors of the street. His own ancient vocation of illuminating books to illustrate or augment their written messages served largely the same purpose. Color was one of the fundamental needs of the human soul, and in turn, an expression of it.

After they had gone several blocks and were crossing yet another street, Alphaios glanced to his left, then looked again. In the distance was a single tower so high it dwarfed even the giants he found so astonishing. He studied it again each time they crossed a street.

Throughout human history, it was to the glory of gods that men had erected obelisks and driven towers and arches toward the heavens. Cathedrals and mosques had represented men's highest aspirations, the best of what they had to offer. What values, then, had created this huge city, what captains had accomplished such heights? Once the spire of St. Ambrose Church had risen into the sky, a bright message to all. Now, were he to peer out his window, he would see walls as high up as he could look, dwarfing the spire. In this city, worldly accomplishment seemed to diminish all else.

After several blocks the buildings grew shorter and interspersed with more ordinary structures. He would have liked some comments on what they were passing or where they were going, but the prior looked straight ahead, seemingly intent on shutting out the very experience Alphaios wanted to absorb.

Prior Bartholomew suddenly turned right, and Alphaios thought he recognized the narrow street they had been on yesterday. His memory was confirmed when the prior stopped in front of the row house. "Here we are," the prior said. "I'll count on you to find your own way back. Do you remember the route?"

Bartholomew's discomfort reminded Alphaios of his own apprehensions. He again became anxious but didn't want to show it. "Eleven blocks, 1200 Broad Street. I'll find my way."

Alone, he climbed the steps and pressed the button.

CHAPTER 5

S EEING THE BOOK OF HOURS for the first time was both sobering and exhilarating. The pages the archivist laid before him were only remnants, but they were glorious remnants—pieces of a large book as lavishly and beautifully decorated as any Alphaios had ever seen.

Arriaga had been right—many of the pages had been ruined, some to the extent that they contained nothing recognizable at all. Though it had been thoroughly cleaned and stored in archival conditions for the last forty years, he could still detect the musty scent of age and a sour mix of fetid water, decayed animal skin and organic pigments.

Spread out in front of him was a damaged bifolium, a large leaf of parchment that had been folded in half, thereby producing four pages. The two pages facing upward bore gothic script with tiny paintings inside embellished primary letters, as well as finely decorated borders. The one most spoiled caught his eye: woven into what was left of its border were paintings of mountain wildflowers that were delicate and seemingly real and appeared to float above the page. This artist had been unusually skilled.

He lifted the edges of the bifolium and turned it over. Here had once been an extraordinary, full-page painting. Its left, outward side was ruined, gone. What remained was vivid in color and meaning. The painter's work was exceptional, the subject the expulsion of Adam and Eve from Eden. The point of view was from a moderate height, looking down. On the far side of a high stone wall were lush green trees, flowing water and abundant fruits all highlighted with the warmth of gold leaf and the sparkle of crushed silver. Were the picture intact further to the left, Adam and Eve would be seen emerging fearfully from a gate, covering their nakedness as best they could.

In a treatment he'd never before seen, the painting simply stopped at the wall. There was only bare parchment across the foreground, which was perhaps the lower third of the page. There was no baking desert outside the wall, no wolves or jackals waiting, no fires of hell, no hint at all of what was to come. The effect was electrifying, even in this fragment. What awaited Adam and Eve, and what would be most terrifying to them, was emptiness, the complete unknown.

If these pages were any indication, at one time this book had been the equal of the most famous illuminated manuscripts ever created.

Alphaios stood at a high, standing worktable in what he already had designated the scriptorium, the large restoration room at the back of the library. It had exceptionally high ceilings, and tall, south-facing windows for natural light. No adjacent buildings obstructed the early afternoon sunlight, which in this city seemed nearly miraculous. Sharply inclined desks awaited the scribes who would letter the manuscript, along with heavy wooden cabinets with thin, wide drawers in which to lay the sheets of parchment. The room was orderly and free of dust.

He wasn't able to see the entire book. Arriaga was bringing individual leaves from their drawers for his inspection. Both men wore white cotton gloves.

"It's never been reassembled since it was cleaned in 1972," Arriaga said. "It was inventoried and organized by section. It's mostly in gatherings of eight, but there're some odd counts at the end of sections. And the calendar, of course." Gatherings— or quires, as Alphaios knew them—were groups of bifolia that were folded in half and sewn together to form sections of a book.

Like most ancient books he'd worked with, these pages were made of parchment, or vellum. They had started out as calf or sheep skins, which were processed, stretched and scraped to provide thin, durable writing surfaces. The only other widely used medium of the time, papyrus, was too brittle to sustain frequent use in book form.

"What are the dimensions?" he asked the archivist.

"Quite large. The pages are twenty-three inches by fourteen. Nearly the same as the twelfth-century *Lambeth Bible*. The *Bury Bible* is twenty by thirteen and a half. By comparison,

Très Riches Heures du Duc de Berry is only eight-and-a-half by five."

Alphaios knew hundreds of books of hours had been created before the invention of the printing press in 1446. They were highly individualistic in design and content, reflecting their periods and regions, the wishes of their patrons, and the various talents of scribes and illuminators.

With a practiced eye, he studied each bifolium Arriaga placed before him, especially the miniature paintings and border illustrations. Most medieval books of hours, though handmade, drew upon previous works for the content and composition of pictures. In fact, patterns had been created for the most popular illustrations, and medieval booksellers used them to customize books to suit their buyers. As a result, many books of hours contained recognizable pictures, consistent even to color and incidental decoration.

In this book, Alphaios could find no familiar paintings or borders. This confirmed for him the remarkable conclusion the earlier scholars had reached: there were no exemplars for this book, no prior manuscripts used as models for its making. In turn, it verified for him that no copies had ever been made from this book. It was completely original, entirely unique.

Even in its present catastrophic condition, its size, beauty and originality made it priceless. It was breathtaking.

He realized now why the decision had been made to create a copy. Restoring it all would be impossible. Yet creating a faithful copy would be nearly as difficult. No, not a faithful copy, an exact copy.

He looked again at the last several bifolia Arriaga had brought him, holding them up and slanting them to the light. Not one of them bore the signs of erasures, which were accomplished on vellum by scraping away at the surface of the page with a penknife. This was a remarkable feat. Perfect bifolia were notoriously difficult to accomplish.

He turned his attention to the lines of text. No phrases were underlined with dots, a common way medieval scribes had of saying to their readers, "These words were a mistake; ignore them." He saw no abbreviations, a form of shorthand for busy scribes. There was a high level of uniformity in the calligraphy, which was unusually large, with no more than fourteen lines on a page. This was clearly a book designed for a lectern. Whether it was intended for daily use or as a showpiece might never be known.

Alphaios looked at Arriaga, who raised his eyebrows but said nothing.

He picked up a page that time and water had stained beyond any recognition except for one small section of border in what had been the gutter. The gutter was at the spine, where sections of the book had been sewn together.

"Exact copy," he muttered to himself, shaking his head. Aloud, he said, "Can you give me the numbers?"

"OK, here we go. Three hundred and thirty-two pages in all, including the calendar. Twenty-two full-page paintings, sixteen of them illuminated with gold or silver or both. One hundred and twenty-two pages with miniatures in the text or borders or both, sixty-eight of which are illuminated with gold or silver. Four hundred and eight decorated versals. No page is without decoration of some kind. Twenty-eight pages are completely unreadable. Of those, we can calculate and distribute the missing text on twenty-four, but have few clues about decorations or their size. As to the other four pages . . ." He held up his hands and shrugged.

Alphaios rolled his head back and closed his eyes. This would be an immense task, the most complicated and delicate he had ever taken on. And if that were not enough, this book was to be a gift to Pope Gregory. Hundreds of years after it had been created, this book of hours would enter—no, re-enter—the history of the Church. He could not allow an imperfectly scribed page nor accept anything less than perfection in his own work. He felt lightheaded.

He put the ruined sheet of parchment back down on the worktable and turned to Arriaga. "Tell me about the arrangements."

"I'll put these away, and we'll go up to my office." Arriaga continued to speak over his shoulder as he opened drawers and slipped the bifolia into their places. "Our vellum will be coming from a workshop in Connecticut. Calfskin, because of the size. The first shipment of twenty skins is already here. Good quality; there's a rejection rate of twenty percent, which is about as good as it gets since we accept only the largest and best hides."

"What about color?"

"Thickness and color are good, with only mild coloring on the grain side. The supplier cuts them to dimension. I'll see they're chalked for use. You'll double-check them before they go to the scribes. If you see any flaws that get by me, go ahead and set them aside."

Arriaga was ready to go upstairs and beckoned Alphaios to follow. "As for the quills, they'll be coming from Kentucky— goose feathers from live birds, only from the five outer pinions of the wing, of course. Probably what they used originally. They'll be hardened and skinned, then shipped here. The scribes will cut their own tips, of course."

Alphaios would himself be using quills in addition to his brushes. Quills were slightly curved, and those used with comfort by right-handed scribes came from the left wings of the birds. Left-handed scribes were not unknown, but rare.

He agreed with this approach. Although modern pens could be more precise, the authenticity required of this manuscript demanded quills. That, in turn, meant finding or mixing their own ink. Modern ink was too thin.

"Have you tested the inks?"

They arrived in the archivist's large but crowded office. Alphaios chose a straight-backed chair by a round wooden table stacked high with books and papers. He turned it toward the archivist's desk and sat down.

"The black ink they used was iron gall." This widely used ink was a mixture of iron and tannic acid from wasp galls found on oak trees, which was then thickened with gum arabic. "No surprise there. There's also vermilion, of course, as well as unusually large amounts of blue and green lettering. You're the color expert, but I thought we'd get our inks from your monastery in Florence. At least the black. There isn't a better source. You can make the other colors here if you think it's needed to get the right hues."

"That'd be best."

"As to the paints and brushes, that's your province. Will you be mixing your own paints?"

Alphaios nodded. He would have to duplicate ancient and unique colors, some of which had remained remarkably vibrant for centuries and some of which would have to be analyzed scientifically. "The paints can't be mixed in the scriptorium, so I'll need a room. It doesn't have to be big, but I'll need natural light, fresh air, and some cabinets. I'll make a list of ingredients for you."

"No problem. I'll have a room prepared."

So far so good. "What about the scribes?"

The archivist rubbed the back of his neck. "That's been a challenge. The calligraphers in this country are delighted at the prospect of working on such a project—until they hear of the time commitment. I've retained two thus far. They've been waiting for you."

"Good. When do we begin?"

"In ten days, Monday after next."

Alphaios was glad he'd have a few days alone with the manuscript. He wanted to know it as well as possible before starting work. In addition, he and the archivist would need to decide where they would begin. It was unlikely they would simply start on page one. This book would be done in pieces, probably as it was created in the first place.

"I'll be here six days a week. I'll come after the noon prayer." He paused. He was not an especially assertive man, but in the scriptorium, he would be both monk and master. He wanted to make his needs known. "The work table directly under the windows, where you showed me the bifolia, will serve quite well for me."

Arriaga nodded.

"I don't work under artificial light. I'm particular in this regard. On days with poor natural light, I won't color the manuscript. If there's gold or silver to be applied, I can lay the gesso for it. I'll inspect the work of the scribes or study the next decoration to be done, or help lay out a new quire. Also, you should know I don't paint more than two hours a day. I find I don't do my best work after that."

Arriaga grinned. "Cardinal Ricci told me you'd be like this. If he can accept your terms, so can I."

"I'm not surprised. He knows me by reputation. Do you have an incinerator?"

"The city won't issue a permit, so I got a shredder. There won't be any pieces of work finding their way into public hands. No souvenirs."

The cardinal had been insistent on this matter. This gift to Pope Gregory was not to be announced prematurely by any stray work. He preferred an incinerator, but could nonetheless oversee the destruction of spoiled or unwanted parchment.

"The cardinal mentioned a commission of scholars. Has it been formed yet?" Such a group of experts was essential to verify that the new book of hours was an exact copy of the original where it was possible, and historically sound where it was not. However beautiful and compelling it might be, without such a process, scholars could and would find eternal fault with their work.

"They've met once, and have seen enough pieces of the book to know the task," Arriaga said. "They're all recognized experts, so I suspect you'll know most of the names."

"Probably not. Monastic life is . . . insular. Masters and apprentices might never leave their cloister, and few know much about the world of commerce. I myself have much to learn." Though he'd said it, he wasn't at all sure he needed or wanted to learn such things. What could he, a simple monk, do with such information? For that matter, what could such information do to him? He changed the subject. "What about the binding?"

"That's a long way off, but I understand why you ask. The cardinal insists everything be done under one roof. The piercing of the pages and sewing the quires will be done by hand. You might well have a part in it. When it's time, a commercial paper cutter will be brought in to trim the pages. As for the covers, we know they were dyed leather over wood with iron clasps and ornamentation. Surprisingly plain, actually, for such a book. We have them upstairs, but they're in poor condition. We'll have to have them remade."

Alphaios nodded. "There'll be time for that. We have a lot of work to do between now and then." He stood up to leave, then turned to look at his new colleague. He swallowed, but when he spoke his voice was thick. "Inaki? You've seen many illuminated texts?"

"Yes, a great many."

"Have you ever seen a painting such as this Expulsion?"

Inaki returned his gaze for a long minute, then shook his head.

"Nor have I."

A few minutes later, Alphaios let himself out the front door and heard its lock click behind him. He stood at the top of the steps for a moment to sense the air, then descended and turned toward the busy street that was his way "home." As he joined the stream of pedestrians, he no longer felt like a wide-eyed foreigner in an impossible city. Instead, like those thousands who had amazed him just one day ago, he walked quickly and with purpose, his mind full of images and half-formed plans.

CHAPTER 6

ALPHAIOS CAME ACROSS the two nativity paintings late on his seventh day. Their power took his breath away.

He was alone in the scriptorium, taking bifolia from their slender drawers and studying them in the good light under the windows. As of yet, he'd seen only about a third of the manuscript. He was making careful notes about inks and pigments as he went, and dwelled at length over many remarkable pages.

Scenes of Christ's nativity were common in illuminated books and were usually high in drama and rich in color. By contrast, this one was strikingly intimate. It was private, and appealing in its complete lack of ceremony. But its pairing with the painting below was what made the page so audacious.

Instead of the more common gold leaf around such an important subject, the upper picture was framed by rough wooden timbers. In it, Joseph was laying a bare, newborn

Jesus at the breast of a recumbent Mary, perhaps for the very first time. There was yet no great star in the sky, no angels, no shepherds, no wise men or kings bearing gifts. The carpenter and his wife wore the humblest of clothes. Except for thread-like halos of gold over Jesus and Mary, this might have been any poor family of the time.

The walls of the wooden stable were ramshackle, and in several places the roof was broken and open to the sky. Mary reclined wearily on a faded blue robe laid over a gathering of straw, her joy unmistakable. Joseph knelt on the bare ground beside her, his arms outstretched, his face hidden from view. A single cow stood feeding at a manger not yet prepared to receive the infant.

Alphaios was transfixed. What would be in their minds? What complicated feelings, born of foreknowledge of a birth unlike any other, were pierced at this moment by pure parental love? What instinctive hopes had young Joseph and Mary at this moment, what dreams?

The artist had captured perhaps the only time ever that Mary and Joseph would have Jesus entirely to themselves.

Over Joseph's shoulder and through the open doors of the stable, a long barren hill sloped upward to a darkening sky. This was Golgotha, the hill of skulls. Though in fact the stable had been in Bethlehem and Golgotha near Jerusalem, the implication was clear.

The features of the three figures were nicely proportioned, the linear perspective correct. The brush strokes were confident, not fussy.

Below this scene, about halfway down the page, there were two lines of script with a large versal, an ornamented B. Then came a shallower painting, though it too ran the full width of the page. In this one, the keeper of the inn, sumptuously dressed, was making room in his establishment for the kings who had come to kneel at the manger. A line of royal porters carried richly decorated luggage inside even as the gesticulating innkeeper was driving poorer lodgers out. Here, the border was gilded.

Alphaios found the quiet, pure joy in the upper painting and the pecuniary self-interest in the lower in stark contrast. He pulled a tall stool forward and sat on its edge. He'd never before seen such a brash statement in a book of hours. It excited him, energized him.

Would these kings demand such treatment even as they knelt in holy supplication? Would they allow such demands to be made on their behalf? On the other hand, they were kings—why would they not?

If indeed this painting had been done in the early fourteen hundreds, its painter was not only an early master but well ahead of his time. Celebrated or reviled, such quality and boldness as this would have been well known. Yet Alphaios had never before encountered this artist. Where had he learned his craft?

He found himself hungry to do this painting. He wanted to do it now.

He left it on his worktable and went back to the drawers to get the other three bifolia that would complete this quire.

Arriaga had mentioned he wanted to start with a section that had little damage so they could ease their way into the book. Alphaios hoped this quire could be the one. After all, the scribes would be here in three more days, and they would need a place to begin.

He was studying the last page of the quire when Arriaga came into the workroom.

"Are you about done for the day?" He wore a well-fitted brown plaid sports jacket over a sage-green sweater. A supple leather document bag hung from his shoulder.

"Just finishing some notes. I've found the place to start."

"Come with me, then. We may as well get acquainted."

Alphaios looked up in surprise. The archivist had been helpful and courteous but had mostly left him alone in the scriptorium. That was fine with Alphaios; he was accustomed to solitude and liked the silence that came with it. He returned the documents to their drawers.

He expected to follow the archivist upstairs to his office, but instead was led out the library door and into the weak afternoon sun. They went down the steps and turned left, opposite the direction he had learned to take back to the monastery. At the next corner, they went left again. They were on another tree-lined street, this one a neighborhood of residential buildings and small fashionable shops. They crossed a street, and Alphaios followed until Arriaga turned and entered a gated patio. Inside a waist-high ornamental fence, black metal dining tables sat under yellow and blue umbrellas that for the moment were cinched closed. Most of the tables were occupied.

He stopped, confused.

Arriaga came back to him. "Come on. It won't bite."

"I can't go in. It's not allowed."

"What isn't? Collaboration with a colleague on a project such as ours?"

"Not that, of course. I'm permitted out of the cloister only to work on the book of hours."

The archivist gave a conspiratorial grin. "But that's precisely what we're doing." His voice became arch, contrived. "We've been thrown together to work on a long and difficult task. We need to know something about each other, and to do that, we need to talk." His voice returned to normal. "And I want a cup of coffee."

"But for us, meals are times of reflection or listening to readings." Alphaios was disconcerted and quite aware his colleague knew it.

"We're not going to eat. Just have coffee and talk." The archivist looked at him, eyebrows raised. "You've never been to a café, have you?"

"No." He was embarrassed and could feel himself blushing.

Arriaga turned and studied the patio, then weaved through the patrons until he arrived at a table for two alongside the fence separating the patio from pedestrian traffic. He picked up one of the chairs and set it down again on the sidewalk outside the fence. He sat down in the one that remained. "Come on," he called. "Have a seat."

Not wanting to be rude, Alphaios followed the outside of the fence to the chair.

"I'll have the coffee," Arriaga said, "and we can talk." Alphaios sat down self-consciously, but pedestrians curved around him, giving him little notice. Despite his embarrassment, he was amused at Arriaga's solution. It seemed creative work-arounds were not restricted to life inside monasteries.

A thin, erect man of middle height approached them. He wore a short black jacket with a white towel draped over one arm. He raised his eyebrows at the seating arrangement—or at the odd appearance of a man in a habit and tonsure.

"Nico," Arriaga said, "this is my colleague, Brother Alphaios. He's new to the city. I'll have a coffee, and he'll have . . ." He looked at Alphaios, who shook his head. Nico nodded and left.

Though the weather was cool by Alphaios's standards, the small patio was nearly full. The sun brought little warmth, but it did bring color to the umbrellas, the leaves on the trees, and the clothes of pedestrians and café patrons. An Asian couple sat near them. They appeared to be in their early thirties. She sat back in her chair, legs crossed, smoking a cigarette and looking off into some inner distance. He leaned forward, elbows on the table, in conversation on a cell phone. They were familiar with each other, comfortable.

"You don't carry money, do you?" Arriaga asked. "I'll buy the coffee."

"No. And no thank you."

"Vow of poverty?"

"And obedience."

"Tell me, Alphaios, how does a man of your talent come to live in such seclusion?"

"Without the monastery, I'd have no such talent."

Arriaga lifted an eyebrow, cocked his head and waited. Alphaios shrugged. "My vow of poverty made little difference to me. I was born in a farming village where the soil was thin and the crops were . . . indifferent."

"Greece?"

He nodded. "In the countryside, alongside the sea. My family was poor. We didn't have much land, but even those with more weren't much better off. My father repaired broken farm tools, mostly primitive, but nobody had the money to buy new ones. It was always understood I'd grow up to help in the family business, like my brother. Truth was, there wasn't enough work just the two of them."

"So what happened?"

Alphaios watched a tall man stride by. Like most pedestrians, he kept his gaze straight ahead. He wore a blue suit jacket above faded denims, a solid red necktie, loosened, and a full graying beard. Unruly Hasidic side locks dangled from under a blue baseball cap.

"We had no school in my village. My family couldn't—and wouldn't have—sent me, even if there'd been one. I'd heard of schools in the city, but they were out my reach. Yet I knew there was something beyond our meager little existence. Something larger, much larger."

He fell silent as Nico approached with Arriaga's coffee and set it on the table. The waiter withdrew to serve another customer, and the archivist set about stirring in some sugar from a tiny envelope. "Larger?"

"On the hillside that led down to the sea, and even within our own village, there were great carved stones lying about. Pieces of buildings. When I was still a child, digging in the dirt behind an outcropping of rock, I found a statue of a young girl. A maiden, sculpted in white marble. She was poised. Serene. I thought of her as some kind of gift to me alone, and I kept her a secret. She may still be there today. I didn't know where they'd come from, except from the minds and hands of a great people . . ."

He looked down at his hands to form his next words. Arriaga took a sip of coffee.

". . . and that I would learn nothing of them while repairing plows and harrows."

Arriaga watched and waited.

"In our village there was a Catholic priest, nearly as old as the stones. He told me of a monastery school in Athens. Everybody knew about Athens, of course, but few in our village had ever been there. He told me I could go to school if I accepted a religious vocation—it seems the one and only Catholic monastery in my Greek Orthodox country placed a great value on novices. It was an easy decision for me even though it meant opposing my father's wishes." He paused. "Fortunately for me, my vow of obedience came later, to a more forgiving Father."

He looked across the fence into the archivist's eyes. "Because of the monastery school, I've had the opportunity to study the work of some of the best minds of the last two thousand years. And the freedom to exercise such talent as I have. How could I possibly agree with your characterization of that as seclusion?"

Arriaga sat back in his chair and nodded slowly. He gazed into the distance for several moments. "You know what we're in for, don't you?"

"What do you mean?"

"If we do it right. If we succeed."

Alphaios shrugged. It wasn't something he'd ever considered. In his world, excellence was always the hallmark, and there was always time to do it right.

The archivist looked at him over the rim of his cup. "A lifelong reputation for ourselves and our scribes. A little slice of history for the owner of the library. And most pressing for us all, a happy Pope Gregory. If the pope's happy, Cardinal Ricci's happy."

A long silence let Alphaios know he was expected to ask the obvious. "And if we don't do it right?"

"There'll be no great gift, no public announcement, no celebration. But the pope will surely hear of the attempt, as will others—friends and foes of Cardinal Ricci alike. The response won't be public, but there will be one. While a great success will be celebrated publicly, a great but failed attempt will be mocked for a generation in the back rooms of the Vatican. And in the halls of academe. Ricci will lose stature. Opportunities that might have been ours? They'll simply go elsewhere—we won't even know we never had a chance at them. We'll quietly slide away, and won't quite know what's happened to us. The library will protect itself." He was quiet for a long moment. "Want that coffee now?"

Alphaios shook his head. "Then we must do well. It's the book itself, Inaki, that deserves it most."

A motorcycle flew past, its tenor howl echoing among the buildings. A woman moved down the sidewalk. She had tailored blonde hair and wore a full-length fur coat that reflected its rich coppers back at the sun. From one hand dangled what must have been a fashionable purse; from the other trailed a worn-out suitcase on wheels.

Arriaga stood up and waved to get Nico's attention. "All right, I'll let you go now. Thanks for humoring me."

Alphaios remained seated, his hands on his lap. "I want to start with the nativity."

"Pardon?"

"I want to start with the painting of the nativity. Have you seen it? It's in the Hours of the Virgin."

Arriaga sat back down. "Yes, but haven't studied it. What about it?"

"I like this illuminator. He isn't just a decorator, a painter of pretty pictures. He has a statement to make, one that doesn't just mirror the text. It's amazing the page even made it into the book. Perhaps he slipped it past careless superiors. I don't think so, though, because I've seen some other provocative pages as well. Maybe this whole book arose out of some theologically adventurous monastery, one that wanted to challenge Church convention." He took in a breath. "Maybe that's what drew Marcello Cervini to this book in the first place, if the story is true. Maybe that's why he didn't show it around. Maybe that's the reason it disappeared from the papal chapel when he died."

Arriaga was leaning forward, fully intent on Brother Alphaios. "That's a big leap to make from one painting."

"Two, actually. Two paintings together on the same page. Have you noticed in several of the other paintings, ones that include contemporary figures, high Church officials have been given some kind of unattractive feature? Like a goiter or bulbous nose or a shortened limb?"

"Can't say that I have."

"I'll show you. They're easy to spot once you know they're there." He lowered his voice even while knowing no one else could hear them. "There's something very unusual here. Artistically, this illuminator is one of the best of his time. So how is it he wasn't—isn't—known to anyone? He's also daring. He did the Expulsion of Adam and Eve as well. I want to get into his mind."

He relaxed back into his chair. "Anyway, I want to start with the nativity. I was checking it today, and its quire has only minor damage. Technically, the work is pretty straightforward." Arriaga said nothing. "Inaki, it's a good place to start."

"Well, then, that's where we'll begin."

Alphaios let out his breath. "One other thing. You said the Vatican stopped looking for clues when it lost control of the book. Maybe it's time they started again. Where was it made, and by whom? Why did it disappear? Did Cervini really find it, and where? We need to know a lot more than we do if we're going to recreate the pages that were destroyed."

The archivist nodded. "I've been thinking the same thing. Perhaps Ricci can prod them into it. I'll contact him and suggest it."

This time Alphaios stood up. "I have to go. Prior Bartholomew will wonder what's kept me so long." He lifted his chair back over the fence, reached out and shook the archi-vist's hand, then set off on his way back to the monastery. He looked back and saw Inaki standing by the little table, watching him go.

After compline, alone in his cell, Brother Alphaios let his mind run over the day. He grinned into the darkness.

He did not go to sleep before reflecting on the people he had seen from his odd seat at the café. He'd like to know more about them, much more. Could he?

Could he?

CHAPTER 7

SEVERAL DAYS LATER, Brother Harold approached Alphaios as he was crossing the courtyard to leave for the library. "We're in need of another sewing machine operator in the manufactory."

Alphaios was appalled. Surely he would not be asked to run a sewing machine! He'd gladly do the most unpleasant and menial labor imaginable as long as he could continue illuminating books. But the thought of operating a machine that could mangle his hands made him cringe.

"Brother Levi asked to be transferred there. Prior Bartholomew agreed and has assigned you to take his place as morning churchwarden. You're to keep the nave and choir clean and do simple repairs. It'll be your responsibility to open the church in the mornings and close it for sext. Most important, you must see that its sanctity is protected—no sacrileges committed against it."

"Sacrileges?" He was greatly relieved, but couldn't imagine what awful things Harold might have in mind.

"It may be more difficult than you imagine. You'll start tomorrow. Find Brother Levi after angelus, and he'll show you what to do. Good day, Brother."

Today, for the first time and for reasons he did not understand, Alphaios felt his heart lift when he stepped out of the big doors and into the teeming city. He knew only that before him were eleven blocks of visual adventure, and at their end a great task.

When he arrived at the library, Inaki was in the scriptorium with the two new scribes. They had agreed the archivist would provide their initial introduction to the book, and he was showing them samples that demonstrated the broad scope of the work to be done.

For his part, Alphaios was to orient them to the process of making the copy. Despite his own eagerness to actually get started, the scribes would not be given the nativity quire until they thoroughly understood the task before them and he had assessed their skills.

Inaki made introductions. Kenny was a slender man of medium height with dark brown hair and round wireless glasses. He wore a black turtleneck shirt and pressed khaki slacks over a trim torso. He carried a small professional bag—his pens, Alphaios supposed.

XM, by contrast, was big, burly and disheveled. He had long, unkempt hair and a bushy beard, and was probably years younger than he looked. He wore faded blue jeans and a rumpled black T-shirt emblazoned with "Grand Funk Railroad," whatever that was. His forehead was nearly covered by a red headband, and part of a tattoo showed below his sleeve. Strangest of all, his earlobes had been stretched far beyond their natural shape; wide silver pegs penetrated both of them.

Alphaios looked at Inaki. What had possessed him to hire this man? Inaki tried to hide a grin, but the amusement in his eyes gave him away. Well, so be it. He would know soon enough. At least the man's hands and fingernails were clean.

"OK, gentlemen, here we go. Have you worked with parchment before?"

Both men nodded.

"In bifolia?"

XM shook his bushy head. "Not me. How's it different?"

"First, unlike ceremonial documents or presentation pieces you might be used to, both sides of the parchment are used. It's therefore important to apply only as much ink as necessary. We have to protect against shadows on the reverse side. Especially against bleed-through. Also, we're going to duplicate the ink and paints used in the original manuscript, so the ink will be thicker than you're accustomed to. We'll be using quills, not pens. You'll have to learn to prepare your tips and control the flow of ink. Tell me, how closely did you look at the pages Inaki has been showing you?"

The men looked at each other, and then at him. They didn't seem to know where he was going.

"Did you look for erasures or corrections?"

Kenny looked uncomfortable. "It's the first time we've seen them."

"So you don't examine the work of your fellow scribes when it's placed in front of you?"

Kenny frowned. "Of course I do."

"Then you will have noticed there are no erasures on these pages. None. How many pages are there, Inaki?" He did not wait for an answer. "Imagine, three hundred and thirty-two pages, and not a single erasure mark. Can you do that?"

The two men stared at him.

"Our book of hours was completed some six hundred years ago by men not much different than us, under less favorable conditions. We will match their accomplishment. Is that understood?"

"Inaki told us the work would be exacting. But then, calligraphy always is." It was Kenny again. He was revealing a brittle pride that would bear watching.

"The second difference. XM, is it? The second difference is the extent of organization and planning required. Any error or deviation from the original, any at all, will result in the whole bifolium being rejected, regardless of how close it is to being finished."

Kenny's stool stuttered against the wooden floor. "But that could be four whole pages."

"That goes for my work as well. I won't decorate a single page until you've completed the text on the entire bifolium and it has passed my inspection. Any imperfect work will be destroyed as soon as it's found. When you're done and I've accepted the bifolium, let's say I make a mistake while painting it. In that case, it'll also be destroyed, and we'll all have to do it again."

Kenny looked as if he were going to protest further.

"And if Inaki or the commission finds fault, we'll do it over yet again. If Inaki hasn't informed you of the commission yet, he will."

Alphaios waited long enough to imply opportunity for questions but not long enough for the silence to ripen into a challenge. "One other thing. Don't start applying ink to a page until you've blocked out the entire bifolium and Inaki or I have approved it. It's too easy to place a line or page out of sequence. Obviously, that also would mean starting again."

XM looked puzzled. "How could a page get out of sequence?"

Alphaios took four pieces of notepaper from the drawer in his worktable. He put them together and folded them once, into the form of a small pamphlet. He numbered each resulting page, front and back, one through sixteen. He held it up in front of them.

"This is a quire. Each of the sheets in a quire is a bifolium. If I remove the outermost sheet, you'll note that on the outer side are pages one and sixteen. Its inside face has pages two and fifteen." He took off the next sheet and held it up. "This bifolium contains pages three and fourteen on the outside and four and thirteen on the inside. Fortunately, the existing book serves as an exemplar for us. Think how difficult it would be to figure out if we were to start from scratch."

The two men nodded. Perhaps they were beginning to see the complexity of the work.

"That isn't all." He reassembled the small paper quire and marked each page with a plus or minus sign. "The plus sign represents the flesh side of the parchment, the minus sign the hair, or grain side." He reached into a nearby drawer and withdrew a piece of vellum. "I'm sure you know the texture and color differ from side to side. When a quire is opened as a book, it's aesthetically important to have the same color and texture on facing pages. That's the way our book is made. So when creating a quire, one sheet is laid flesh side up, the next flesh side down, and so on." He turned the pages of the quire so they could see the marks. "Then each subsequent quire must be assembled to conform to the prior one. Do you see?"

He again received nods, but Kenny had a question. "If one little error can ruin four whole pages, why are we using bifolia? Why not just cut them in half and do two pages at a time?" It wasn't a good sign that he seemed so focused on errors rather than confident performance.

"The short answer is because we're recreating a medieval document. There weren't any adhesives of sufficient strength and pliancy for use in bookbinding at the time, so books—especially books that were meant to last—were made by building quires of parchment and sewing them together. But we do have it easier than the original bookmakers in another way. Did you notice the margins?"

Alphaios could see the scribes were put off by his questions; they hadn't expected to be schooled in an area so close to their own expertise.

This time it was XM who spoke, his grin sheepish. "OK, Brother, what's it you want us to see?"

"The outer margins on each page, outside the text field, are exactly the same width. It's another remarkable aspect of this book. Fortunately, the calculation has already been done for us. All we have to do is copy it, working not from the outer edge, but from the gutter to the far edge of the text field. Because before it can be bound, our copy of the book will also have to be trimmed."

"Man, this's complicated. You done this before?"

"I've been working with ancient books most of my life. But this?" Alphaios shook his head. "Artistically, this book is one of a kind."

He went on. "Unlike you probably do in your own work, we'll use tiny pinpricks to block out our pages instead of pencil marks. Pencil lead doesn't penetrate the surface of vellum, and it doesn't leave traces when erased. But it is not the way the original was done."

This time, there were no questions or comments. "Oh, one other thing. There is to be no food or drinks in this room, and no visitors. Ever. And I presume Inaki has told you that nothing leaves this room. Nothing at all. No remnants, no relics, no tales told. This is completely confidential work. Have you agreed to this constraint?"

Both men looked Alphaios in the eye and nodded.

"Inaki, are you ready for the next step?"

The archivist nodded, and took Kenny and XM to the area where the desks stood. All of them had sharply inclined tops designed specifically for use by scribes.

"Choose a desk. It'll be yours until we're done." As they moved among them, Inaki continued. "In the drawers are straightedges, penknives, calipers, quills, and so on. Your inkwells are full, with iron gall ink. In the wide drawers to your left are sheets of new vellum. Use cotton gloves whenever you handle either the original document or the new sheets." He pointed to a tall cabinet against the back wall. "You'll get them over there. If you need other tools or supplies, let Brother Alphaios or me know."

The men chose their places and sat down on the high stools in front of them. "Your first task is to block out a bifolium," Inaki said. "You'll have as long as it takes, so don't think you're working against a deadline. The important thing is that the mockup is sufficient to produce an exact copy." He went to a cabinet and came back with a document for each man.

"But this isn't parchment," Kenny said. "It's just a photograph."

"Chill out, bro," XM said. "Would you let someone borrow your ride the first day you met them? Not likely."

Alphaios didn't know what a ride was, but understood the point. At least XM was going to be patient. Kenny gave the other scribe a sour look but didn't say anything more.

"Yes, they're photographs," Inaki said, "the exact size of the original. Block out your work on a fresh skin. All four pages. Then go ahead and inscribe the text on the first page. First page only. If you want to get used to the quills and ink, there are some scraps of vellum in the bottom drawers. I'd recommend it. This task will take you a day or two, maybe more. At the end of today, I'll come back and have you put your work away for the night. Tomorrow you'll continue, and the next day if necessary. If you need additional sheets of vellum, go ahead and get them. When you're both done, we'll critique your work. Remember, you're making a copy."

The next day, Alphaios arrived in the scriptorium to find both scribes bent over their tasks. He was tempted to check their work, but he had pressed Inaki to let them do this first assignment themselves, to work through it without help. He needed to know what they were capable of. There would be plenty of problem solving to do in the future, and if they were good enough to stay, he wanted their minds fully engaged.

He went to his own worktable and opened the drawer. A small brass key lay there, just as Inaki had promised. Key in hand, he left the scriptorium, walked down the side hall to its end, and unlocked a door to find a small room with shelves and countertops filled with cans, boxes and jars—all the ingredients on the list he'd given Inaki. He was pleased to see a small sink. Sunlight streamed through a window above it.

He checked the drawers and cupboards for tools and supplies, then took all the containers down from the shelves and put them back up in the order he wanted. Under the counter were two large bottles of the black ink Inaki had had flown in from Florence. He nodded in satisfaction; the room would do nicely.

XM was standing beside Kenny's desk when Alphaios returned the key to its drawer. They appeared to be working out a problem. He could see at least one piece of vellum in the wire wastebasket beside Kenny's desk; he would have been surprised not to. There would be more discards, most of them far more painful than this one.

He went upstairs and found the archivist in his office, writing. "We need to talk. Can you come downstairs?"

"Is there a problem?"

"Come with me."

Inaki rose from his chair, concern on his face. Alphaios led him down the steps, but instead of turning to the scriptorium, he led the way out the front door.

"What is it, Alphaios, what's this about?"

"You're a stranger with whom I have been thrown together to work on a long and difficult task. We must know something of each other if we're to succeed."

The archivist laughed. "Well said. So it's turnabout, is it?"

Today the sun was warmer, and the yellow and blue umbrellas were up and spread wide. This time, without pause, Alphaios went along outside the patio until he came to an empty table for two. He reached across the fence, lifted a chair out and set it down on the sidewalk. "Have a seat," he said when Arriaga reached the table inside the patio.

"Do you want a coffee?" Inaki asked.

Alphaios declined, and moved his eyes to the scene around him. Small trees lined both sides of the street, their trunks encircled in ironwork. A row of stately townhouses faced them. Unlike the ones that included the private library, these homes boasted an array of colors and styles. Mansard roofs were interspersed with flat roofs, and house fronts varied among pale greens, brick reds, reserved grays and whites. Most windows were squared at the corners, but some were rounded at the top. The entrances boasted distinguished brass and cut glass, and small wrought-iron fences pretended to protect them.

He turned his attention to the sidewalk. Not more than twenty feet away was a bearded man dressed for much colder weather. Behind him was a shopping cart overflowing with bags of all sorts. Alphaios remembered the men on the church steps his first day out with Prior Bartholomew and guessed this man might be homeless as well. Some kind of newspaper had captured his attention, and he stood motionless, looking at its open pages for a long while. He had on three layers of coats, all unzipped in the warmth, a worn short-billed, padded cap on his head, and a hood over that. Except for the bright yellow lining of a second hood that fell unused onto his shoulders, his clothes were in shades of blue and gray. On his hands he wore gloves, one white, one black. What most caught Alphaios's attention, though, were the six coat zippers shining in the sun; they resembled long golden chains falling from the man's neck, half of them dangling brilliant zipper-pull pendants.

"It's a racing form," Inaki said. "For picking your bets. Horses."

"Do you see his necklaces?"

"Necklaces? Where?"

"The zippers on his coats."

Inaki leaned forward. "OK, what is it you want to know?"

"About you. How you arrived here."

"Probably by a more straightforward route than you. I grew up in a seaside village called Lekeitio. The Basque country— northern Spain. My parents were both scholars—still live there.

I followed their path and trained in ancient documents in San Sebastian. My specialty was Basque history and Euskara, the Basque language. After university, I did an apprenticeship in the National Department of Antiquities."

He shifted in his chair. "We became aware of a large collection of Euskara manuscripts that was to be probated. We wanted to have it donated to the Euskal Museoa in Bilbao. I was assigned to catalogue it and assess its charitable tax value to the owner's estate. Much to our disappointment, though, the Spanish government didn't have the authority to keep it in the country. The executor elected to split up the collection and place it for auction. Here in the United States."

Alphaios frowned in sympathy, and Inaki nodded sadly. "Euskara has no roots in any other language. It's completely unique, and Basque history is a very narrow specialty. Because of the work I'd already done on the collection, the auction house asked me to come to America to prepare the sale catalogue. It was enticing—a young man invited to one of the most vibrant cities in the world, and getting paid for it. You said you haven't been exposed to the documents market, right?"

"Very little."

"Most buyers of major art and historical documents bid through surrogates. It lets both the purchasers and failed bidders remain anonymous. That's what happened to the documents in this collection."

"So you don't know where they went?"

"Not usually, but in this case I do."

"Where? Have you ever seen them again?"

"They're upstairs at the library. I'll show them to you sometime."

Alphaios leaned forward. "The library was the buyer? So how did you get here?"

"I worked at the auction house for four more years, finally becoming the assistant head of the documents section. I learned to assess market value, the best times to schedule auctions, how to estimate prices and set reserves. I was good at it. But the whole time, truly remarkable objects were passing through my hands with little thought for anything but their revenue potential. The pace was frantic, and always with a sense of great importance. And there I was, a scholar working as a bookseller. The few times the schedule slowed down enough for me to think about it . . ."

Nico brought Inaki his coffee and left. He sweetened it and drew in a sip.

"Anyway, one day I got a phone call from a man looking for an archivist for a private collection. Very secretive, the library's existence known only to a very few. He knew my work put me in contact with many academics and other professionals. He wanted to meet and talk about who might be available. I was flattered that he wanted my opinion and agreed to join him for dinner. We met at a restaurant too fancy for my paycheck, didn't even have a sign. The only meal I've ever had like it, and not just the food."

He smiled thinly. "I learned he'd checked me out. Said my credentials were acceptable—that's the term he used, *acceptable*. He told me he'd had auctions managed by my section reviewed for any off-the-books deals that had advantaged some buyer or seller. Or me. There weren't any. He'd also had me vetted to see if I had any associates in the ETA. I didn't."

"What's the ETA?"

"A militant group of Basques fighting for national separation from Spain. They've been outlawed by the Spanish government for decades now, but they don't go away." He looked at Alphaios. "Some call them terrorists, some call them freedom fighters."

When Alphaios didn't respond, he shrugged and continued. "It was an odd feeling knowing I'd been looked into so closely. And I still didn't quite understand why I was there. Anyway, the man told me he'd been watching my work since the sale of the Basque documents. He said the library he 'represented' had purchased them for its collection. He went on to describe some of the library's other holdings. I was impressed—but still had no idea who this man was or where his library might be."

Inaki's eyes moved beyond Alphaios, and he chuckled. "Check out your friend."

Alphaios turned in his chair. The zipper man was pushing his cart along the sidewalk. Fixed to its side was a crude cardboard sign, "Home Is Where The Heat Is."

"What does it mean?"

"He sleeps on the street where he can find a steam grate. So, after several courses and a dessert I've never heard of, the man told me he intended to hire me. Said he wanted me to be the archivist for the collection and assist in further acquisitions. Made a salary offer that was really rather ordinary. His research had prepared him well, though. He told me I could conduct my own scholarship, starting with the Basque collection. I would also be able to use the library's resources—though he didn't say what those were—to access other closely held collections. I now know those resources are considerable. Anyway, I came to see the collection the very next day. A month later, here I was."

"Did you know the book of hours was here?"

"Not until after I got here. Quite frankly, it wasn't one of stars of the house. It didn't become a focus until Cardinal Ricci tracked it down and told us what he wanted."

"Do you have a family?"

"I'm married." He lifted his hand and showed his ring. "To one of those proxy buyers I mentioned. She makes more than I do. But then, I get to spend my days in history's playground, so who's complaining?"

"Now tell me," Alphaios said, "just where did you come across this XM? He's really a scribe?"

"XM's quite famous here locally, at least among a certain crowd. You can see examples of his work nearly every day. He's a tattoo artist."

Alphaios gasped. "A tattoo artist? For the book of hours?"

Inaki laughed out loud. "Take it easy, my friend. He's an accomplished calligrapher with an impressive portfolio. Several years ago, he found his skills crossed over to body art, as they call it now. I don't comprehend it myself, but many otherwise normal people do. Anyway, the work he submitted for the audition was superlative."

"But why would a so-called body artist want to be involved in a project like the book of hours?" Alphaios still bridled at the thought.

The archivist turned serious. "Not everyone gets to be a part of creating great art, Alphaios. Very few people ever get a chance to do something in their life so exceptional that they know—they know with certainty—that it will be considered an artistic masterpiece for a thousand years and more. XM knows this is his opportunity." He paused for a long moment. "It's mine, too."

Both men were quiet for a while until Inaki swallowed the last of his drink. "You're Greek. How come you don't like coffee?"

"Oh, but I do. And I miss it. I'm afraid Brother John, our kitchener, bless him, has no idea how to make it. He can stretch a pound of coffee from here until Judgment Day. I'd love to send him to one of the monasteries of Italy just to learn its godly virtues. I'd offer to teach him myself, but I'm a guest."

"Then you've got to try it here one day."

"I'm not allowed, Inaki."

"Maybe." The archivist grinned. "At least you know what you're missing."

A few minutes later, the two men left the café and Alphaios began his long walk back to the monastery.

That evening in his cell and among his prayers, Alphaios recalled Inaki's words. He had long appreciated and drawn inspiration from the great art and music and architecture that were the very apex of human capability and found himself hoping he and Inaki, and yes, Kenny and this strange man XM, were skilled enough to return the book of hours to its original splendor. But for him, it was not the book's longevity or place in history that mattered most, nor the happiness of some pope. Rather, it was the simple physical and spiritual joy of breathing in and creating great beauty.

CHAPTER 8

ALPHAIOS WENT THROUGH the cloister door and into the church to meet Brother Levi. The church had a great silence, the kind of breathing quiet one hears only in the vast spaces of old buildings with very high ceilings. The soft hiss of steam and the distant clanking of heat pipes seemed only to emphasize the effect.

The cross-ribbed ceiling was traditional and high. Tall stained glass windows with biblical depictions lined the side-walls, but they were pale, almost devoid of color. On one side of the church, the windows at the clerestory level were dark, as if covered from the outside. Above the choir was a large round window of leaded but colorless glass. Smaller but similar round windows were at the front of each side aisle, one above a statue of Joseph, the other of Mary.

Near the main door was a painted, life-sized statue of St. Ambrose in the same clothing worn by his followers today.

One hand held a Bible close to his chest; the other was spread low and open in welcome. On the other side of the door was an entrance to a tiny chapel. In it, a woman knelt on a bench before a small golden shrine to Mary and the infant Jesus.

Overall, the space was simple and plain. Like the rest of the monastery, it was largely absent the joy of color.

He found Levi waiting in the vestibule. As soon as he approached, the older monk unlocked the front doors and turned back into the nave. It wasn't a moment before nearly a score of men and women, all heavily dressed against the cold, pushed into the church. They dispersed quickly among the pews, as if each of them had a customary place. As they passed, Alphaios noted downcast eyes and sharp body odors. They did not speak to Brother Levi or to each other.

In turn, Levi greeted no one. His eyes were hard, his thin lips set in a line of permanent disapproval. He motioned Alphaios to the side aisle.

"How long have you been doing this?" Alphaios asked in a low voice.

"Thirty-one years."

Alphaios's eyebrows lifted. Thirty-one years must feel like eternity.

"I could tell you stories. You've got to be smart. Tough. I don't let anything get by me. You really have to take charge sometimes, or they'll take control."

"Who'll take control?"

Levi frowned and swept his arm toward the nave. "They will. The vagabonds who come here to take advantage of our hospitality. You don't think these people come here to pray, do you? Or tithe? Fat chance of that. Yet we have to keep the place heated and in candles. Think any of them'll lift a finger to help?"

Alphaios was embarrassed. While their voices were low, sound carried easily in the big space. He took his own voice down to a whisper. "I don't know. I haven't met any of them."

Levi did not follow suit. Surely his words could be heard by everyone. "And you don't want to, either. It used to be different. Decent, honest people would come. Now, there're only a pitiful few who'll come in to actually pray in the—"

Without warning, Levi swept around Alphaios and back toward the church door. He held his arms wide to block the path of a huge, disheveled man. "No. No. Go back. You can't come in here." His voice clattered against the quiet.

The man looked puzzled and took a step to one side. "I wanna see Jesus. Get warm."

Levi countered with a similar step. "You can't come in here. You know that."

"Wanna see Jesus."

A woman in one of the back pews stood up and gathered an oversized bag to her side. She walked stiffly to the man and took his hand. He dwarfed her. His open, broken-toothed smile was one of utter innocence. "Hi, Mary. It's me, Teddy."

The woman ignored Levi. "Come on, Teddy, we're not welcome here." She led the man through the door without further comment.

Levi returned to the side aisle and picked up where he'd left off. "Here's the janitor's closet. This one's the key. You'll find a broom and a mop bucket, and a few tools. Turn off the light when you aren't using it. Oh, and don't touch any of their body matter, blood, feces. We've got some dishwashing gloves hanging by clothespins in a jar of disinfectant. Use them. Prayer candles for the votives are in here, too. The liturgist does all the others."

Alphaios was still taking in what he'd just seen. Now blood and feces?

"Why couldn't that man come in?

"He breaks the rules."

"What are the rules?"

"Be quiet. No, we don't have public restrooms. Don't disturb others. Don't stink too bad. Leave when you're told to, or you can't come back."

"Not exactly welcoming . . ."

This earned him a sharp look. "I told you, they aren't here for worship." His voice tightened. "And watch out for Mad Old George—he tries to get in every now and then. Whatever you do, don't let him past the vestibule. You'll be sorry if you do."

It seemed strange to hear Brother Levi, elderly himself, refer to someone as Old George, mad or otherwise.

"How will I know him?"

"He'll be cursing you and the Church and anybody within sight. He's an unrepentant blasphemer. Thinks he was done some wrong years ago that he can't let go. We want nothing to do with him. This key's to the basement. The door is outside by the front steps. There's some old lumber, mortar, broken furniture. I haven't been down there in years."

Levi's vigilant glower swept the church again. "Keep an eye on the chapel. You'll need to move Mrs. Bridlewood along. Most of the time she'll be wearing a long black coat and a veil. When she gets to the kneeling bench in the chapel and starts saying her Hail Marys, she won't let anybody else near it. She and her husband paid for most of the last roof repair, there's a plaque with their names on it in the vestibule. She thinks it gives her privileges. But the other ladies complain. Oh, and keep your opinions to yourself. This is a church, not a debating society."

A man in a business suit entered. He stood in front of the statue of the monk for a few moments, crossed himself, then left as quietly as he'd arrived.

"Make sure the sanctuary is empty before you lock up for sext. Start closing up early, and check everywhere. You'll have to chase some of them out, those that don't care about the rules. Any questions?"

"None. I'll manage."

Levi handed him the small ring of keys. "See that you do, Brother."

After Levi left, Alphaios explored the sanctuary alone, taking quiet inventory of the people in the pews and the small maintenance jobs needing attention. When he was done wandering, he sat down in the rear pew closest to the small chapel.

A few people came in, prayed briefly and left, but those who had come in first stayed in their places. Though he remained alert for them, the most aberrant behavior he could find were figures slumping sideways in sleep. When at last he started to lock up for sext, the "parishioners" gathered up their coats and bags and left without objection.

He was glad that this one long morning had passed. Thirty-one years. It was nearly impossible to conceive of it, at least in the fashion he'd witnessed so far. Had Levi brought his cynicism with him, or had events here soured him? Might the sheer weight of time and repetition have made him so ungracious? True, theirs was not a pastoral order, but maybe Brother Levi had let himself become a warden in a way never intended.

But then, he, Alphaios, was completely new to this country and its ways—perhaps he should not judge his brother monk so harshly. Still, the monasteries in Greece and Italy valued their laity and were generous of heart and spirit. Though deliberately withdrawn from their communities because of spiritual vocations, they relied heavily upon the goodwill of others. Could it be that this great, noisy and anonymous city all around them could have a negative effect on one's spirit? Or maybe it was something as simple as the often-inhospitable weather.

A few minutes later he was in the choir for the divine office, bowing deeply from his waist in concert with his brothers, when he heard a hollow noise from elsewhere in the church. Moments later, a grizzled face and manic eyes appeared around the high wooden screen separating the choir from the nave. Alphaios remembered the man coming into the church at midmorning, but thought he'd left shortly thereafter.

Brother Levi caught his eye and glowered. The other monks were only momentarily distracted, and continued without pause. He'd never seen a holy office interrupted by an outsider before, and so took his cue from his brothers and tried to concentrate on the prayer.

In a few moments, the man edged further into the choir and began to mimic the monks' bows and their responses to the prayer. There was no signal that Alphaios could see, but Brother Haman left his stall and, shushing the man with his finger to his lips, led him away. A few moments later he heard the sound of the front door opening and then thudding closed. Haman returned silently to his place.

Levi scowled at Alphaios again as they disbanded.

Before he could follow the other monks to the refectory, he felt a tug on his habit. With a self-conscious grin, Haman, the shyest of the monks, guided him silently into the nave. They were midway back when Haman pointed at the center section where a long, boxed-in heat duct ran along the floor and transected the pews. "They hide in there."

Alphaios stepped toward the duct and bent down. Under the pew to his left was a nearly hidden space bracketed by the heat duct and a low structural partition of some kind. It was dark, warm and undetectable from the aisle.

He thanked Haman for the tip, and followed him to the refectory. When finally he stepped into the street after the noon meal, the sun was out to brighten his mood and warm his bones.

～

THE SCRIBES WERE WAITING for him when he arrived. They had completed their tasks, and it was time for Alphaios and Inaki to review their work.

He greeted them by name and asked them to bring the bifolia they had prepared to his worktable. He and Inaki donned white cotton gloves—more out of habit than need, for this parchment would not be saved.

Alphaios first stood a pace back from XM's work and let his eyes roam over the full document. Then he moved closer, his face no more than a foot from the surface. His eyes moved systematically across the work, first on one side and then the other. Kenny started to ask what he was finding, but Alphaios motioned him to remain quiet.

When he was satisfied with the mockup, he turned the sheet back over and repeated his actions with regard to the newly inscribed text. That completed, he lifted the parchment and held it up, studying it diagonally as the light slanted across it.

He laid the parchment down on the table and stepped back to his original position in order to again appreciate the whole.

It was some twenty minutes before he was done, and no word had been spoken since the scribe's one futile attempt. Finally he nodded to Inaki. The archivist took XM's bifolium to another worktable to examine it himself. He removed a caliper and a ruler from the drawer and began measuring and making notes. Alphaios turned to Kenny's parchment and repeated his process.

With his own work under scrutiny, Kenny settled back to wait. Perhaps now he was less eager to hear what the monk was finding.

When he completed his review, and Inaki had done his measurements, the scriptorium had been silent for nearly an hour. Alphaios turned and spoke to the scribes.

"This is a journeyman's start, Kenny. I'd say you finished your work shortly before I got here. You would have liked more time to go over it again to make sure it was OK."

"There a problem with that? You said to take all the time we needed."

"No, no problem. XM, from looking at your work, I'd say you finished late yesterday afternoon, and this morning you took time to review it. But you made no changes."

Inaki was watching Alphaios as closely as the scribes were.

Kenny bristled. "How can you tell?" The man seemed to chafe even at implied criticism. "Inaki came in to lock up. He told you, didn't he?"

"I haven't talked with Inaki since yesterday. I didn't mean my remarks to criticize. When I do, I'll be far more direct. For now, let me critique.

"Both mockups are virtually the same. The text and picture areas have been boxed correctly, and the margins match the photographs with great accuracy. Except for one area, on the last page on Kenny's parchment. Is that right, Inaki? You were measuring them."

"Well, yes. Otherwise, the measurements are quite precise."

"Kenny, you made the mistake when you were redoing your mockup. You had to start over with a sheet of vellum after you started to put ink to the text. The mistake is on the last page, so you were in a hurry."

"So I started over. Isn't this about practicing?"

"Quite right. And the fact that the two mockups are otherwise identical means the two of you collaborated."

Kenny and XM looked at each other and nodded.

"That's good. What's on the reverse side of your work?"

Kenny found and held Alphaios's gaze. "Ink spots. Bleed-through."

"Right. One of the reasons I know XM finished first is that his wastebasket has scraps of vellum he used for practice with the quills. Yours has only full sheets, meaning you didn't practice before going ahead on your text. So when you made an error, you had to start all over again. A false sense of skill with this vellum and this ink, not a poor command of calligraphy, led you to go ahead before you were ready. So you lost time."

Kenny flushed pink but stayed silent. He gave a shallow nod.

"If you exclude the bleed-throughs," continued Alphaios, "the lettering looks quite good."

"But you can't exclude them, can you? Not on bifolia."

"No, we can't. What the bleed-through means, as well as the shadowing, is either you didn't cut your quill properly, or you spent too much time and ink on each letter. Less ink will produce less shadow. As with modern ink, iron gall is a dense black. It doesn't require layering for satisfactory darkness. But the letter spacing is accurate, and the scale of the lettering is nearly correct. Right, Inaki?"

"They're about three millimeters short in height but correct proportionally, which means they're also slightly narrow. So the spacing between letters and words is too wide."

"As I said, the size of the letters is nearly correct. Even if everything else I've mentioned were acceptable, if this were an actual bifolium for the book, we'd still have to discard it."

"I get it." Kenny now seemed more willing to accept Alphaios's critique.

"Slow down. Relax into it and you will find you make fewer errors. Your effort is getting in the way of your work."

He was done with Kenny, and Alphaios could see some of the tension leave the scribe. He turned his attention to the strange man with the stretched earlobes.

"All right, XM. As I said, the mockup is good. Your pinpricks are so tiny that in some areas they almost have to be imputed. That's OK if it works for you. It's all I need to do my painting."

XM nodded.

"You have some shadows through the page under the first two lines of text, but none below that. That means you grew accustomed to the flow of ink. Your practice on the scraps served you well, and helped you adjust quickly. How many quills did you go through before you pared them correctly?

"Took me four, but I got it." He turned to Inaki. "Good quills." The archivist acknowledged him with a nod.

"OK, now to the lettering. I want you to compare line seven on your copy to the photograph."

XM peered at both documents. "I don't see no difference, 'cept maybe mine is straighter."

"You're right. Look." Kenny followed XM and peered around his shoulder. "Your text is straighter than the original," Alphaios said, "and the letters are more uniform in size and spacing. Look at this word. It is slightly high on the original, but it's on the correct plane in your copy—it's fully articulated with the rest of the line. Another example. Look at this E. In your work it is vertical, just right. In the original, though, it leans back toward the previous letter."

Kenny nodded. This time, he was the first to understand the point.

"That's a problem," Alphaios said.

XM was surprised at the apparent turn of logic. "Why? How's that problematical?"

"You are both trained in calligraphy, where making the text straight and even is a requirement. After years of practice, your eyes and hands know exactly what to do. You don't even have to think about it. Straight and even. Uniform. Unfortunately, it means you'll have to retrain your eye for this document."

It was XM's turn to protest. "I see your point, but why not correct the imperfections as we go? Make it even better."

Alphaios took a moment to construct his answer. "The book of hours is already a masterpiece of millennial proportions. Our task is not to make it better. Our task is to make an exact copy." Acknowledgement entered XM's eyes.

"As you will both see later, this will be the easy part. One other comment: both bifolia are free of penknife scrapes. That's good, as you won't get any erasures past me." He paused. "Inaki? Any comments?"

"OK, gentlemen." Inaki looked with warm respect at his colleague. "It appears our monk here knows what he's doing. The task for the rest of today and tomorrow morning, using the same sheet of parchment, is to apply the text to two of the remaining pages. The page behind where you worked, with the shadows and bleed-throughs, we'll forget. Apply what you've learned here today. If your work passes muster tomorrow, we'll begin in earnest."

Alphaios and Inaki left the scribes to their task. When the door to the scriptorium closed behind them, Inaki motioned the illuminator toward the stairs. He sat down on one of the steps and put his elbows on his knees, hands clasped in front. Alphaios remained standing.

"Ready for some history?"

When Alphaios nodded, Inaki continued. "Cardinal Ricci says the research will be considerable, but he has friends in the Vatican who've agreed to help. Turns out our friend Marcello Cervini had an impressive career. He was made papal secretary in 1534. In 1539, Pope Paul III sent him along with a delegation to meet with Charles V, the Holy Roman Emperor, and then with the King of France. From there, he was sent to Germany to serve as papal legate for the Third Diet of Speyer. After Cervini got there, Pope Paul decided the Diet was weighted too heavily against him and he recalled the legation. As we know, the diet convened anyway. Then in 1545, Cervini was made one of three presidents of the Council of Trent, another effort to counter the reformation. Once there, he took such a hard line against any reform at all that he drew the anger of Emperor Charles. In fact, to mollify the emperor, Pope Paul removed him from the Council and reassigned him to the post of Vatican Librarian. That was in 1548."

"Seven years before he became pope," Alphaios mused.

Inaki nodded. "Back at the Vatican, he became a well-known collector and increased the Holy See's collection by more than five hundred books. Keep in mind, most books worthy of the Vatican's interest would have been exceptional in content or appearance. Or both. In other words, Cervini traveled throughout Europe and was in the thick of one of the most fundamental conflicts the Church ever faced. Who knows where or how he might have learned of our book of hours?"

"If in fact he did," said Alphaios.

"One other thing. When Pope Paul III died in 1549, Emperor Charles opposed the man who succeeded him, Julius III. Then when Julius died six years later, Charles also opposed Marcello Cervini. The cardinals snubbed Charles again, and Cervini became Pope Marcellus II. The Emperor can't have been happy." Inaki paused and looked at Alphaios.

"So," Alphaios said, "at fifty-four years of age, this man—an accomplished traveler, tireless advocate for the Church, book collector and enemy of the Holy Roman Emperor—dies from the burdens of the papacy just twenty-two days after taking up the *ferula*."

Inaki gave him a lopsided smile. "So it would seem."

Alphaios frowned. "Interesting, but what does any of that have to do with the book of hours vanishing when he died?" There were two mysteries here: the book's origin and its disappearance. Were they in any way connected? The pope's untimely death was a third, of course, but what did it say about the book?

Anything at all? "The information is good as far as it goes, but what we really need to know is what was on the ruined pages."

Inaki nodded. "That's the goal, but it'll take some time." He paused for a moment. "Perhaps we can help it along. I'll contact some other confidential libraries the scholars didn't have access to in '72. Secular and religious. See if we can get a hint of our book from any of them."

The archivist nodded goodbye, stood up and climbed the stairs to his office.

Alphaios walked down the corridor to his mixing room. He opened the door and was pleased to see sunlight filling the small space. All in all, the afternoon's work had been encouraging, and he allowed himself to imagine painting the remarkable nativity. He looked at the well-stocked shelves. It was time to begin mixing his paints, and he would start with the intense blue of lobelia in the shade.

As he reached up to collect the ingredients, he noticed that a new box, flat, narrow and unlabeled, had been placed on one end of the top shelf. He brought it down to the work surface and opened it. Inside were a score or more of bills of American money, all with a 5 printed on the corners, and a handwritten note:

> *When you're ready, use one*
> *bill for each cup of coffee and a*
> *perch to watch your new world.*
>
> $\qquad$ *I.A.*
>
> *P.S. If you want to keep Nico*
> *happy, leave the change.*

Alphaios felt the heat of embarrassment rise to his cheeks, but could not resist a smile.

CHAPTER 9

TACKED TO A WALL in the housekeeping closet was a yellowed list of cleaning tasks. They weren't difficult or time-consuming, and within a week Alphaios found them entirely routine.

Determined to be more hospitable than Brother Levi, he unlocked the church doors and swung them open each morning with a smile for the waiting group. He greeted each of them with a "Good morning" or "Come in, come in, how are you this morning?"

Still, even after many days, no one in the group had responded to him in kind. He did receive a few furtive glances that he took to ask, "Are you talking to me?" Mostly, however, they crowded to the other side of the foyer as they filed past him, as if they did not wish to pay even a simple greeting as a price of admission. More likely, given their experiences with Brother Levi, they didn't trust anybody's expression of warmth.

Because the daily tasks did not take long—except for watchfulness, which was his primary chore—Alphaios started to move around the church and sit beside each person. He didn't crowd them, but sat close enough for them to be conscious of his presence, to wonder what he was doing in their space. At first, he would remain quiet and join them in their own state of reverie. Then, in a low voice, not to them or with them but beside them, he started to pray aloud. He used only prayers of hope and thanks. Acceptance might be what was needed most, so he avoided repentance, self-diminishment and even supplication.

At first, most of them just burrowed closer to the ends of their pews. Some stood up and moved away to another spot, grumbling at the intrusion. He didn't follow them, but stayed where he was, unperturbed. After all, while they may be the faithful in presence, it didn't mean they were God's Faithful. Four of them got up and left the church altogether, but he was gratified when all of them returned over the next several days. He repeated his routine with them; this time they didn't leave.

He could see Brother Levi's point about Mrs. Bridlewood. In order to capture the kneeling bench for herself, the tiny lady in black was quite willing to elbow aside other votaries. Once in place, she ignored anyone else who might be waiting. Alphaios knew the kneeling bench was not a goal in itself, but for many devout people it held a habitual place in their prayers.

Although they didn't complain aloud, several women had left the church shaking their heads in disgust. More than once

Mrs. Bridlewood left the little chapel only a short time after the ladies she had outlasted.

One morning when Mrs. Bridlewood was adjusting her coat to leave, Alphaios approached her. As she lifted her black lace prayer scarf, he could see silver hair and bright, direct eyes in an elfish face. Diminutive as she was, she stood erect, courtly in manner.

"Mrs. Bridlewood, I'm new here, but want to thank you and your husband for the gift of our new roof."

"Well, I'm glad someone still remembers." She sounded mildly offended, as if at a slight. "No one has said boo about it since it was dedicated."

He didn't know what "boo" might mean, but her tone was clear. "That's a shame, because it's a fine roof. It works splendidly." She looked at him askance as if trying to figure out whether he was making fun of her.

"Mrs. Bridlewood, we need your help with a problem."

"Young man, you may as well know right now there isn't any more money. The late Mr. Bridlewood thought people would actually honor his memory for all these gifts. He barely left me enough."

"We're not asking for money, just your help with the chapel."

She stiffened. "What do you mean? I can use it whenever I wish."

"Of course you can. It's just, well, some of the ladies take so long that others don't really get a chance."

"Well, that's certainly my experience, too, Brother . . ."

"Alphaios."

She looked him up and down. "We don't see many new monks here. You're the first I can remember in years. Yes, I know exactly what you mean. Sometimes I have to push myself in just to get any time at all."

"That's just what concerns us. Perhaps you could help come up with some kind of solution."

"Why, I suppose I could think about it, couldn't I? No money?"

"No money at all. Thanks so much for your assistance." He opened the big front door for her, wished her a good day, and watched as she worked her regal way down the front steps.

Back inside, he looked around the sanctuary. There was considerable work to be done. Cracks showed on the walls, and dark water stains spread below several of the windows. The big leaded glass panes were so covered with grime that the light penetrating them was tinged a dull yellow. He was looking at some broken tiles in the right-hand aisle when one of the regulars stood up and approached him. "Say, Brother, somepin' I could help do?"

Alphaios met his gaze. "Thanks. What's your name?"

"Jimmy Belkin."

"Well, I don't know, Jimmy. I guess I need some new tiles."

"Won' do. Tiles are too old. New ones won' fit.

"What do you mean?"

"These here are thicker'n they sell today. Smaller, too. They make 'em that way so you gotta buy a whole new floor. Won' find no color match, neither. Prob'ly why no one's fixed 'em yet— can't afford a whole new floor. I got a way 'round it, though."

"How's that?"

"Pop some good ones outta some back room nobody goes. Or from under somepin', but then the color might be too different. Stick 'em in here. Look better'n this."

"How about the housekeeping closet?"

"Sure. Might work. Gotta key?"

"That I have. Do you want to look with me?"

Jimmy nodded thoughtfully. "Sure, may's well."

Alphaios led him to the small room. The tile there was considerably darker than that in the aisle. "Just dirty. Strip it, wax it, it'll be OK. Now all you're gonna need's adhesive and some heat. Got some?

"What do you mean, heat?"

"Lady's hairdryer, somepin' like that. Gotta heat the tiles so they don't break pryin' 'em loose."

Alphaios didn't know what a lady's hairdryer was, but supposed he could ask. "Thanks, Jimmy. I'll see what I can come up with."

"Wan' me to help you when you got the stuff? I used t' lay tile."

"That'd be good. You know I can't pay you."

"Don't 'spec' no pay. Good to have somepin' to do."

"OK, then." Alphaios reached out to shake Jimmy's hand.

Jimmy looked down at his own hand, nearly black with grime. After a moment's hesitation, and with a sudden, large grin, he reached out and grasped the monk's. "OK, then."

Jimmy walked a little taller on his way back to his seat.

Alphaios did as well. It was his first breakthrough with any of the regulars. He wasn't a priest, this wasn't a parish, but he'd come to think of this small and relatively constant group as parishioners. His parishioners.

Some days later, Mrs. Bridlewood came in earlier than usual and beckoned to him from the back of the church. He leaned the dust mop into a corner and went to meet her.

"I know what we can do." She was animated today. "We can limit each person to twenty minutes if anybody is waiting." She reached into her purse and held up a small cooking timer. "It can be set whenever somebody starts to kneel. When it goes off, if someone else is waiting, they get a turn."

"You know, that sounds like a good idea. Perhaps we could make a sign to let them know."

"I thought of that too, of course." She dipped into her purse a second time and pulled out a wooden nameplate holder, the kind used on desks. "It was Mr. Bridlewood's." It looked old, but its engraved brass plate was new. Instead of a name, it read TWENTY MINUTE LIMIT.

"Wonderful. Why don't you set them in the chapel, and we'll start it today. Oh, by the way, how can we make sure people are courteous and follow it?"

"That's my job," said Mrs. Bridlewood. "You can count on me. I'll show them how it's done, and I'll remind them when they need it. I just know some of the ladies will try to go overtime."

"That's very generous of you. Thank you."

"Of course, Brother. It's been obvious for a long time that somebody needs to supervise the chapel. You monks don't come in nearly often enough to see what really goes on."

Alphaios accepted the criticism with a slight bow.

When he was done with morning chores, all was quiet in the sanctuary, the regulars in their places. He decided to go to the basement to see if he could find any surplus tiles that might have been stored there. If he were lucky, he might also find a can of adhesive. Whether or not it would be useable would be another question. Jimmy Belkin would know.

He went down the front steps and found the door. When he unlocked it and turned on the light switch, a string of dim bulbs dangled off into the distance. He stepped into the near-darkness and was just starting to get oriented when he heard shouting. It was coming from directly above him, from inside the sanctuary.

Alphaios turned, rushed out of the basement, and took the steps into the church two at a time. He swung the doors open, ran through the foyer, and came to a sudden stop.

There, standing before the altar, was a madman. He was nearly naked, dressed only in an improvised loincloth. He was waving his arms in the air and shouting curses Alphaios had never before heard or imagined. They were interlaced with words he couldn't understand; the man seemed to be speaking two languages at once.

He hurried up the aisle to quiet the man and restore order. Jimmy Belkin saw him coming and stood up. "That's Ol' George. He'll be a handful."

The man's face was gaunt and bearded, his long gray hair tangled and dirty. He was so thin his ribs and hipbones stood out in high relief. Under the dirt, his pale arms and legs were like sticks. His lips were slick, his eyes ablaze.

When the man saw him coming, he began gesticulating even more wildly. "Servant of the devil! Whore of the Antichrist!"

Alphaios stood quietly for a moment, letting his breath return to normal and deciding what to do. "Welcome to our sanctuary, my friend. My name is Brother Alphaios. Come, sit down and talk with me."

Now the man moved threateningly toward him. "Go away, man-whore!"

He could feel wetness from the man's outburst on his face. "They tell me your name is George." He sat down in the front pew and gestured toward the space next to him. "Sit down. Let's talk."

"They lie! They all lie! Abraham knows the Church is false! Isaac knows the Church is false! God of Abraham, show this spawn for the liars they are! Liars! Foul liars!" The man's face was contorted, and he was screaming at the top of his voice.

Suddenly, Brothers Levi and Samuel appeared at the man's side. Alphaios hadn't seen them come in, but now saw the considerable bulk of Brother Maynard lumber through the side door behind them. Levi was red-faced and furious. "Out!" he shouted at the man. "Leave this House of God! You profane it! I command you to go. Go!"

The man paused his ranting to look at Levi. "You! I know you." His voice was suddenly quiet, all steel and menace. "I know you for what you've always been, the devil's first spawn." Then he shrieked directly into Levi's face, "Spawn of the devil! You multiply even in the face of God!"

"Go back to the hell where you belong! You profane this place with your heresies! Maynard, get his arms."

Brother Maynard stepped behind the cursing man, seized him in a bear hug pinning his arms to his side, and lifted him off the floor. The man fought, legs flailing in the air, trying to strike anyone close. He howled in anger. Levi turned to Alphaios. "Grab his legs. Get him out of here."

Alphaios was shocked. Certainly there was another way to deal with this man.

"Alphaios, grab his legs!"

"But you can't just throw him out."

"Watch me. Now, get his legs!"

Alphaios didn't move.

"Samuel, you get his legs before Maynard gets hurt."

Brother Samuel gave Alphaios a look of disgust then waded forward, trying to dodge the wild man's kicks until he could corral his legs. Together, under Levi's cold eye, they bundled the jerking, screeching man to the back of the church and out the door. "My clothes, I need my clothes, you sons—" was the last thing Alphaios heard as the door closed.

There was a sudden but uncomfortable silence in the sanctuary.

In a moment, the two monks returned, breathing hard. As they came forward, they scanned the church for the man's clothes. Brother Maynard found them in a heap on the floor between two pews. He picked them up gingerly, held them as far away from his body as he could, and turned his face aside in distaste. He carried them back up the aisle and out the door.

Brother Levi turned his contorted face to Alphaios. "I told you what would happen if you let him in here! You were supposed to watch the sanctuary. Where were you?"

"In the basement, but only for a few moments."

"You left the sanctuary unwatched?"

"I was looking for some supplies."

Levi stared at him in barely controlled anger.

Alphaios was angry, too. He had just begun to reason with the man when Brother Levi intervened with pure physical force. "And what are you doing, my brother in Christ, physically throwing a man out of the House of the Lord? All God's children are welcome here."

"God's children? Brother Alphaios, you're responsible for this sacrilege. I'll see that this is brought up among the brothers. You can count on it. Come, Brother Samuel, Maynard. Let us leave Alphaios to his . . . duties."

A sudden creak of pews and the scuff of footsteps caught their attention. All four monks turned to the sound. The men and women in the pews, all of them, gathered up their belongings and walked out of the church. One of them stooped to pick up a small dark article Brother Maynard had dropped, perhaps a sock. In a matter of moments, the sanctuary was empty.

"See what you've done, Brother? You've managed to let one demon interrupt the prayers of the many and drive the faithful from this church. May God forgive you." Levi herded Samuel and Maynard out the side door.

God's forgiveness was likely to be easier to gain than the warming of Brother Levi's heart. Where had his great compassion for the many and the faithful been before?

Alphaios sat down in a pew and gathered himself. He was shaken by the episode, far more by the actions of his own brothers than the rantings of Mad Old George. Why had Levi felt it necessary to intervene so quickly and so forcefully? And why, if the parishioners were going to leave, did they go only after the incident was all over? He was deeply sorry they had been driven out of a house of worship.

Levi had been the master of the sanctuary for so long that he would likely find any method other than his own unacceptable. And he had warned against letting Mad Old George in at all. On Friday, Alphaios would face Levi's wrath in the chapter of faults.

He didn't care for the phrase, but it was a traditional one. The weekly chapter meetings in which the administrative operations of the monastery were discussed were also the forum for settling the inevitable differences among the monks. The communal pursuit of salvation brought with it an interdependence that often chafed.

Sloth would be the charge against him: laziness, dereliction of duty for not being in the sanctuary and allowing sacrilege to occur. Levi would be incorrect to use such reasoning, but that wouldn't stop him.

By Friday, solemn and simple silence notwithstanding, it was apparent the entire brotherhood had already heard about the incident. They had not learned of it from him, so any information they had would be one-sided.

Chapter meetings were held in the refectory. The dining benches were brought from behind the tables to the open area in the middle of the room and arranged into an oval. Out of habit or a sense of ownership, the monks sat in roughly the same area of the room as they dined. Light came from small windows high on the walls.

When the time came for such matters, Levi did not initiate the assault himself—Simon took that honor. Simon held no official posts, but it had not taken Alphaios long to learn that he liked to stir up matters among the monks in order to then claim stature as a leader in finding solutions. There was some talk that he'd long wanted to become procurator, the buyer for the manufactory, but Prior Bartholomew held that role.

"I'm sorry to inform my brothers," Simon intoned, "that an incident of profound sacrilege has occurred within our sanctuary. I for one believe it must be reconsecrated."

A buzz of voices filled the room. Reconsecrated?

"During the watch of Brother Alphaios, a madman was permitted to strip himself and to utter horrendous blasphemies before the very altar of God."

Brother Maynard followed. "And our guest, though serving as churchwarden, refused to lift a hand to end the sacrilege. Because of that, Brother Samuel incurred deep bruises."

There was more buzzing as Samuel solemnly nodded affirmation.

Simon picked up again. "Our brother admitted he was not even in the church when the madman came in. Where he was, we're not certain."

There was an expectant air in the room as the monks turned to Alphaios for his reply. He remained quiet, hands folded in his lap.

The order was fundamentally a democratic one. In matters such as this, Prior Bartholomew was more a moderator, a first among equals, than a managing director. When it became clear Alphaios wasn't going to speak, the prior turned to him. "Brother, what do you say to these complaints?"

"I fear there are more charges to be made, Prior. I'd rather not answer these, only to have my responses consumed by the heat of others. Let us hear all that my brothers have to say."

Bartholomew gave Alphaios an appraising look, then turned back not to Simon, but to Levi. "Is there more?"

"There is."

"Then let's hear it." There was a murmur of agreement.

"I myself told our brother he must prevent such incidents, and warned him explicitly about Mad Old George. At the time, I thought him amused by the rules and dismissive of my years of service. Prideful. And in fact, he disappeared from the sanctuary and failed to keep watch. He permitted this heresy to occur. Then, when Brother Samuel and I arrived to quell the disturbance, we found him merely sitting in a pew, watching this man profane the Church. In insane, horrific language I can't repeat, Mad Old George accused this Church of being a false church, the church of the Antichrist."

This comment earned Levi dark mutterings among the monks. "Not only that, he called one of us the devil's own spawn." The muttering gained volume.

"Then, when I asked Alphaios to assist Brother Maynard in removing this blasphemer, he would not. In fact, he questioned me—challenged me in anger—for following Christ's path and casting out the demon. Called him one of God's children. These actions were so grievous, my brothers, that every prayerful person in the church was driven out. They left in droves."

Levi was having the effect he sought, and many of the monks were shaking their heads in disapproval.

After a long pause, during which he surveyed his audience and let the discontent build, Brother Simon reasserted himself. "Would our guest have been so reluctant to protect God's house were he not under insidious influences outside these walls?" He let the question hang in the air. "Who can know? But the occasion of this heresy, my brothers, requires our urgent action. What shall it be?"

Several monks started to speak at once, but Prior Bartholomew quieted them down. "Brother, would you care to respond now?"

Alphaios sat quietly for several moments before speaking, gathering his thoughts and watching Simon and especially Brother Levi. He didn't have enough insight yet to understand the depth of anger coming from his brother monk.

"As best I can tell, I am accused not only of the sin of sloth, but of excessive pride and anger as well. Are those your charges, Brother?"

Levi nodded, then added with venom, "And of tolerating the most despicable blasphemies in God's sanctuary."

Alphaios let his eyes roam over the others. "Yes, my brothers, to my regret, this awful blasphemy did occur." The room was quiet now. "No, I was not in the sanctuary when this man came in and began to scream profanities. Yes, I chose not to help evict him from God's house. Yes, the parishioners all left after he was expelled."

He took a breath, then continued before he could be interrupted. "Yes, these are serious matters, so let us examine them one by one. Brother Levi did in fact warn me of this man you call Mad Old George, not to let him enter the church. I had gone to the basement to look for supplies to repair the broken floor tiles. I heard the commotion and came back straightaway. This man George was in the church and undressed when I got there."

"So you did leave the church unattended," Simon said. "You allowed him to come in."

"I did. I was out of the sanctuary for several minutes, as I said."

"Didn't Levi warn you against leaving the sanctuary unwatched?"

"I have just agreed he did."

"And then why did you do so, Brother?"

"I've stated why. I was looking for some tiles."

"Do you have some expertise in laying tile?"

"No, I don't. None at all. Jimmy, one of the men who comes in every day, offered to help fix the floor. He said he used to lay tile for a living."

Levi bristled. "We're to believe that one of those . . . people . . . offered to help?"

"He seemed quite eager to do so."

Prior Bartholomew spoke up. "Let's stick to the point, my brothers."

"The point is," said Samuel, "you left the sanctuary unattended."

Alphaios looked around the room. It was an unsettled group. "Brother Levi has served as churchwarden for many years. How many others here have served in this role from time to time?"

Several monks raised their hands. "Brother Levi, I must ask you and these brothers if you have ever left the sanctuary unattended. Perhaps because of an imminent physical need, or a sudden bout of indigestion? To resupply the housekeeping closet or convey a message? Anyone?" The same monks raised their hands again, more tentatively this time. "Not you, Brother Levi? Not in thirty-one years?"

Levi sat, stone-faced.

"This man you call Mad Old George is clearly known to all of you. For good reason, as I can see now." He smiled ruefully. "Even Brother Harold alluded to him, though not directly." Harold blushed at the mention of his name.

"Mad Old George. Because he's so well known by this name, and because he must be so guarded against, am I right in inferring that similar incidents have occurred in the past? One event alone wouldn't be enough to assign him such a familiar name. So I'd guess more than once. Three times? Four? More?"

The room was silent.

"The number isn't important. I'm not trying to lay fault, or even to excuse my own actions. I'd just like to know whether similar charges were made on those other occasions."

Several of the monks were looking at the floor or had found other objects in the room to draw their attention.

Prior Bartholomew looked at him with interest. "No, no such charges were made."

"Perhaps, then, no need was found to reconsecrate the sanctuary, as Brother Simon has proposed."

"No, not that either."

Alphaios let the silence speak for him before continuing.

"As for pride, I can dispense with that quickly. Indeed, I'm often guilty of pride, and pray nightly for guidance. Brother Levi, if my actions on my first day as churchwarden were prideful, I plead guilty and ask your forbearance."

He did not wait for a response. He knew remittal would not be forthcoming, and did not want to lose the momentum.

"Now, my brothers, I believe we must go to the heart of the matter. The question is not whether I refused to assist in removing Mad Old George, for I did. At least in the manner Brother Levi wished. Nor is the reason for my refusal the central question. The question is this: Is it acceptable that Mad Old George was physically restrained by the brothers of St. Ambrose, hauled to the door against his will, and forcibly evicted from our sanctuary?"

A loud murmur rose among the brothers.

Levi could take it no more. If custom did not require monks to remain sitting during such disputes, he might have leapt from the bench. "That's obvious, isn't it? He was profaning God and the Church itself! We merely did what Christ did—cast out the demon from our midst."

He heard mutters of support, and surveyed the monks for a long minute. "It is my recollection," he said quietly, "that

Jesus cast the demon from the man, not the man from His presence."

"You're quibbling," Simon said. "Instead, you should be thanking Brother Levi for fixing your problem. Christ could do such miracles, mere mortals cannot. Even so, in this case, casting out the man has the same effect as casting out the demon."

"For whom, Brother Simon? For that man, or for us?"

Brother Samuel was agitated. "For all the worshippers praying in the sanctuary! Because of Brother Levi, they're less likely to suffer such interruptions in the future."

"Brother Levi has made the depth of his concern well known to me." Out of the corner of his eye, Alphaios saw a monk stifle a smile. For his part, Levi stiffened. His eyes did not leave Alphaios's face.

Though bashful, Brother Haman joined in, his tone more inquisitive than emotional. "If we're unable to expel the demon, is it not then reasonable to expel the vessel in which the demon resides?"

He was ready for this question. "Who among us knows anything about this vessel we call George?"

This question also met silence.

"If we know nothing about George, then how can we say he is possessed by demons?"

"He's a madman who invokes the name of the devil in his curses," Samuel said.

"Quite the contrary, Brother. In fact, he invoked only the name of God and his prophets, and asserted that the devil lies among us. Not that I agree, of course." He ventured another small smile. It was not returned. "Perhaps he has a mental disease, an illness of the brain or personality. Or some physical condition that controls his behavior."

"That's not for us to decide," said Haman.

"I agree with that. But then how, without knowing this man at all, can we conclude he's possessed by demons? Are we qualified to do that?" Alphaios knew he was on solid ground here. The investigation and expulsion of demons was a rare event, highly controversial even within the Church.

Simon had reached his limit. "Enough, Brother Alphaios! We can see how adroit you are in deflecting responsibility. The fact is you failed to keep order. This man was cursing the Church and us as well, using the most vile language. You refused to help remove him, and Brother Samuel was injured. This man drove out other worshippers by his actions. Surely you don't think one man can be allowed to interfere so callously with the prayers of others. It would be anarchy."

"Indeed it would."

"You agree, but couldn't lift a hand?" Simon gestured dismissively. "That's most unkind of you, Brother."

"I concur that such interruptions cannot be tolerated for long. It was the means used I cannot support. In fact, I would argue that he should be invited back in."

Notwithstanding Alphaios's last statement, Simon seemed to sense an opportunity and pushed ahead. "My brothers, our prior asked our guest to assume duties as morning warden. We don't blame him, for we know of his generous nature, and in any event, he could fairly assume Brother Alphaios would be capable of such a responsibility. Having seen the result, however, I propose Brother Alphaios be relieved of this duty."

"I support my brother's comments," Levi said, his voice now unctuous. "Were I not so badly needed in the manufactory . . ."

Alphaios held his breath. It was probably inevitable. But that long first morning as churchwarden now seemed like ancient history, and he found himself hoping against reassignment. He would miss his parishioners.

Prior Bartholomew nodded thoughtfully. "The faults alleged here today are serious indeed. Yet Brother Alphaios has made a strong defense. More than that, he has posed questions that require reflection among us. For my part, I intend to use this opportunity for that purpose. We would all be well served to pray on this matter, my brothers, for there seems a particularly ungenerous spirit among us today."

Levi seemed almost bursting. "Prior, some action is required. While we consider further, can we not ask another brother to serve as morning warden?"

Bartholomew nodded again. "Brother Alphaios, in the cause of retaining goodwill among us all, I will ask you to relinquish these duties until further notice."

Alphaios's heart dropped, but he was determined not to let anybody know it. Levi was smirking. "Yes, Prior." He bowed his head in concession, then lifted it. "May I request, however, that one other question be considered?"

"Of course."

"Did the parishioners walk out of our church because of the unconstrained rantings of a madman? Or did they walk out because a man they know to be troubled and vulnerable, a man like many of them, was callously expelled from the one place they feel safe?"

Brother Levi was no longer smirking when the priest began the prayer of benediction.

~

ON THE MORNING AFTER the chapter of faults, Alphaios was assigned to assist Brother John in the kitchen. The kitchener had welcomed the help and put him to work scrubbing the pantry floor. Now he was sitting in the courtyard sun for a few moments before sext. It was the same bench where Prior Bartholomew had settled himself when Alphaios had first arrived. He watched the falling water in the big fountain and wished its sounds could soothe him. For the first time in his adult life, he found the cloister confining.

He didn't hear Brother Timothy approach but wasn't surprised to see him. It was Timothy who constantly struggled to bring a garden to life in the monastery's inhospitable soil and keep weeds from among the pavers. He was an old man, perhaps eighty, and could often be seen outside wearing a heavy cloak to keep the chill away from his bones. He moved slowly. A bend high in his spine hunched his shoulders and head forward.

"Good morning, Alphaios. May I sit with you?"

"Of course, Brother." He moved over to make room.

There was a companionable silence for a few moments while Timothy found a satisfactory position on the warm stone. Then he reached up and rested his hand on Alphaios's shoulder.

"I sought you out this morning, my young brother, to let you know my thoughts. I didn't speak up during chapter because my comments are often not well received by our more . . . boisterous brethren."

Alphaios turned his full attention to the old monk.

"Over the decades, the spirit of this monastery has gradually grown darker. The sun is hidden from us for much of our days, and our nights are surreal. Yet we cannot bring ourselves to discuss such things."

Timothy looked into the fountain for so long that Alphaios wondered if he were lost in it. "Joy that once came naturally—though I can't say we were ever a particularly happy group of souls—has been consumed by shadow. Then throw the noise and grime into the mix. We've become weary. And begrudging."

His face lightened, and he turned and looked at Alphaios. "Do you remember the first night you joined us at compline?"

"I always will, Brother. The singing was unusually beautiful."

The old monk smiled contentedly at the memory. "It was, wasn't it? We have few visitors here, Brother, and no new blood to sustain us. As the oldest of us die off, we are not replaced, and the burden on the rest of us grows. So while we wait for God's blessings in heaven, I'm afraid we've grown as stiff and dry as old shoe leather." Though his point was serious, he snorted in pleasure at his metaphor.

"Some of us, if we had the opportunity again, would choose an eremitical life." He gave Alphaios a sly glance. "Forgive me for saying so, but many of us who would not choose to become hermits would be quite happy if some others did."

It was not difficult to guess whom he meant. "Is your work going well? Your task sounds immense."

Alphaios nodded. "It is, Brother. It brings me joy."

"Good. Joy's in short supply within these walls. Now, I hope you'll also find tolerance in your heart for a bunch of old men whose world has shrunk and become colder." He stood up slowly and again rested his hand for a moment on Alphaios's shoulder. "Go in peace, my young friend. And celebrate this joy you've found."

CHAPTER 10

WHEN BREAKFAST and the morning angelus were over, Alphaios sat down on a wooden stool in the pantry. He was worrying a long string of hemp from an empty potato sack when Brother John came in. A steaming cup of coffee sat on the floor beside him.

The kitchener sat down on another stool close by. "You don't need to do that, Alphaios. You aren't in some third-world hermitage. Just go to the laundry and get a new pair."

"No thanks, John. This'll do. Reminds me of home." He cut the string with a knife and set it down on the floor. One shoe off, he hobbled into the kitchen and returned with a large mug for his friend. "Here, have some of this."

While John looked questioningly at the hot cup, Alphaios picked up his own and took a drink. "Coffee, made as the Lord intended. Go on, take a drink."

John sniffed deeply at the dark brew, and took a sip. He made a sour face, which earned him a grin. "Have it with some sugar. Here, let me sweeten it for you." Alphaios reached into a sack of sugar with a tin cup and poured a generous serving into John's mug. "Stir it up. Then tell me you don't like it."

John stirred the coffee and lifted the cup again. This time he puckered his mouth and lifted his eyebrows. "We can't serve this, Alphaios. Surely you know that."

Alphaios picked up his shoe and began to thread it with the hemp. "I know. But you and I can share a cup from time to time. Try it with milk."

John shook his head with mock exasperation. "So, Brother, you've brought another temptation to add to my mortal burdens."

"There's no sin here, Brother. This is the same coffee that's drunk in Florence and Rome. How can something that isn't a sin in one cloister be a sin in another? No, here there's only umbrage at color and taste and difference, even if they are gifts from God."

John nodded again, but more soberly. "Perhaps not, Alphaios, but it'll surely be treated as one. Here, there's no fault too petty to be called out by the righteous. Or the small of heart." He lifted his cup and took another, deeper drink. He raised it toward Alphaios as if in salute. "Or those who possess both. But for now, it's time to mix the dough for our brothers' bread."

CHAPTER 11

TODAY, ALPHAIOS was especially happy to escape the confines of the monastery. The morning had been spent in a dull chapter meeting that Brother Richard, possessed of a good heart but small mind, had stretched out interminably. And lunch had been uninspired even by monastery standards.

It was a false spring day. More rain and cold would come before winter released its grip on the city, but today he would enjoy the contrast of warm sun and chilled air. The sun was brilliant, and he could nearly finish the page that had been absorbing him for days.

He decided to take a parallel route to the scriptorium and crossed Broad, then went right for two blocks before turning again. Not far from the library, he entered a tree-lined street of well-kept brownstones which seemed to be private residences. Beside each stoop was a tiny yard surrounded by a short, ornate iron fence. The little patches of plant life were all well-tended, and in a few yards, the presence of gloves and trowels showed eagerness for an end to winter.

The street was mostly quiet until Alphaios heard a long, curved tusk of a musical note. It was the unique, unmistakable soar of the clarinet opening to Gershwin's *Rhapsody in Blue*. It was coming from a townhouse with all its doors and windows thrown open to the air. The music overfilled the house and spilled into the street. The occupant was no doubt feeling particularly sentient on this rare day and wanted to absorb both the freshening air and the music. He admired the occupant's openness to sensation, and found a perch on a step and sat down to share the experience.

Through eight changes in key, through multiple tempos and rhythms, he listened. He listened through long rolling waves of piano runs that seemed to fill the keyboard three times over, and through boisterous horns, sailing trombones and blue notes. He listened through the low muttering of the bassoon, the wah-wah-wah of muted trumpets and brassy notes finished raucously. Through elegant strings swaying like summer maples in a strong breeze.

The music nearly tumbled over itself in its run to conclusion.

He could think of no music more vibrant, more suited to a day like this. And surely the clarinet had been invented with just this rhapsody in mind.

When quiet replaced the music, he became aware he was not alone. Three others had also paused to listen, among them a well-dressed but bedizened man who noted, "Cool," as he strode away.

Alphaios sat a little while longer. He'd heard *Rhapsody in Blue* just once before, many years ago in Rome. The music was very different from that of his Grecian countryside and from European classical music, and so much more cerebral than the shards of pop music he had heard in the streets of Rome. It was a whole new idiom. For Alphaios the artist, it was like seeing a whole new spray of colors for the very first time. He remembered hoping one day he could visit the place where this brash, compelling music originated. And now, in his excursions almost every day through the city, he could see its very source.

But *Rhapsody in Blue* was somehow not complete. Even as he heard it, Alphaios hungered for just a bit more; his was a taste not quite sated, a sensation not quite completed. This must be some of the genius of the piece—a still-whetted appetite, a search for something just out of reach. That was why the music so well characterized this American city he was coming to know. He found himself wishing for more time living the city and less time shut away.

The music still filling his mind, Alphaios rose from the stoop and waved his thanks to a man who appeared in an open window.

He would begin today's work by proofing three bifolia the scribes had recently completed with text. He would compare them against the original book to make sure there were no deviations. If they were acceptable, they would go back into the broad flat drawers to await his colors. If not, he would mark them with a slash of black ink, review them with the scribes, and destroy them.

In Alphaios's experience, all hand-scribed texts, all the way from early Christianity until the invention of the printing press, showed the peculiarities of their creators. Most illuminated manuscripts were handmade copies of prior documents and revealed the personal characteristics of successive scribes as well as changes in religious teachings. Old errors became codified and new errors made, which in turn could inadvertently influence doctrine for unwary readers. Ignorant or playful monks, careless proofreaders, powerful patrons, church politics and, changing dogma all conspired over time to modify the appearance and messages of these books. Greetings and news bulletins to other monasteries, jokes, complaints, even rude remarks about abbots and bishops showed up. Caricatures of both cardinals and saints, some of them profane, could also be found.

He had learned to be especially attentive when he proofed the lower portions of newly scribed bifolia. The large sheets of vellum being used for this modern copy were expensive, and the scribes, experts themselves, exercised great care. Nonetheless, they would find it easier to discard a leaf when an error was made nearer its beginning than its end, after hours or days had been invested in its preparation; the further into the work, the greater a scribe's wish to mask an error. Of course, as this whole enterprise was to create a faithful copy, the eccentricities of the original would be copied, too. Text lines that wandered out of level, letters that crowded one another, lack of visual balance, all were to be reproduced exactly.

To the unpracticed eye, most true copy errors would be indistinguishable. It was, in fact, more likely that deliberate adherence to irregularities in the original would be perceived as mistakes than any errors newly made. But to Alphaios, any deviations from the original were fatal flaws that demanded correction. He would not hesitate to slash black ink across an otherwise meticulously prepared page if it did not satisfy his eye. Already each of the scribes, and indeed he himself, had suffered the indignity of watching hours of work ground to confetti by the shredding machine. XM had taken to calling it "feeding the dragon."

He let himself into the scriptorium to begin his work. He found Inaki there, holding a severely damaged bifolium in his gloved hands. He nodded to Alphaios and then toward a worktable where several ruined leaves lay. "These are the worst of them. They've been weighing on me."

While Alphaios had looked at each one separately, he'd not had the courage to bring them together as Inaki had done today. They stood together in silence for a long moment until he cast a sardonic glance toward Inaki. "We're very fortunate."

"We are indeed," the archivist said. "But perhaps you could shed some light on just how."

"The water didn't ruin the whole book. It seeped in almost randomly, leaving nearby pages in reasonably good shape."

"And," Inaki said, "we know it's of the 'use of Paris,' the dialect of the Parisian archdiocese. Therefore, we also know what comes before and after the damaged pages, and can determine with reasonable certainty what text was on them."

Alphaios continued the give and take—it might lead somewhere. "Except in the suffrages to the saints." The suffrages would contain references to specific saints that could provide a clue as to the patron of the book, and therefore where it was made. Unfortunately, one of the pages of the suffrages was also unreadable.

Inaki ignored the tangent. "We can use the pattern of the pages around them and draw inferences as to how the text was distributed on them. How many lines might be on a page, and where."

"And which of the four painters worked the quire," said Alphaios. "Jeremiah, for instance."

The archivist was about to respond in rhythm, but instead turned abruptly toward Alphaios. "Four? Who's Jeremiah?"

"One of the painters. I gave him the name. It isn't unusual for there to be several illuminators in a single work."

"And scribes as well. But you've concluded there were four? And named them?"

"Jeremiah did the Expulsion of Adam and Eve and the nativity. And all but two of the other most significant pages. At least of the ones that are intact. Inaki, he's truly a master. If this book had become public, he would be as well-known as Masaccio or Fra Angelica. Or the Limbourg brothers."

"What about the other three?"

"Zechariah illustrated the calendar of the saints and did its lettering. The artistry's fairly typical of the time. What makes the calendar so extraordinary is the quantity of gold and silver, and of course its size. It wasn't uncommon for calendars to have been created separately, and that's the case here. Zechariah's hand isn't found anywhere else in the book. Outside the calendar, Zephaniah did the decorated initial letters, the versals. They're beautifully drawn. Let me get some examples, and I'll show you."

Alphaios went to the drawers, drew out several intact bifolia, and laid them on his worktable. "Not only did Zephaniah draw and color the versals, he painted most of the inhabitants and histories inside them. Many of the miniatures in the borders are his as well. His visual perspective is fairly primitive, though, and his human figures are stilted, quite typical of the early fifteenth century. That would be consistent with the initial conclusions of the scholars in 1972. But look at the lines of the versals. They're long and confident."

Inaki was completely absorbed. "Who else?"

Alphaios went back to the cabinets and withdrew another piece of parchment. "Obadiah. He's a master of the visual eye, the seeing eye, and he's one of the reasons this book is so stunning." He pointed to the flowers in the margins. "Definitely Obadiah's work. The brushwork is exceptionally fine. The petals are delicately veined, and his use of shadow makes them seem to float above the page. The vines connecting them are intricate and seem random rather than patterned. His colors mirror the natural world, but are just slightly more vivid—bright but not artificial or forced. He also did the two full-page paintings that aren't Jeremiah's. His work suffers, though, when dealing with larger subjects."

The archivist stood back on his heels, appraising Alphaios. "That's all of them? No others?"

"Just the four."

"Have you seen any of their work before?"

"Certainly none of Jeremiah's. But Zephaniah and Zechariah, I can't say. They were fine artists for their time, but not extraordinary. The calendar is beautifully designed and exceptionally lavish, but its content and artistic techniques are fairly typical. Still, I don't believe I've ever seen their content duplicated anywhere else. The subject matter, of course. I mean the specific sketches and color patterns."

"What about Obadiah?"

"If the date of the book is truly early fifteenth century, Obadiah was decades ahead of his time. The only other work I've seen that matches his technique in flora comes much later."

Inaki stood quietly for a moment. "So, how does all of this help us with the ruined pages?"

"It's time we select one and try to put it all together. Whatever we do, it'll have to pass muster with the commission. I can tell you've put some thought into it. Do you have one you'd like to start with?"

"I'll look at the quires. It makes sense to work it out on one where the rest of the quire is largely intact."

"Good. Anything from the Vatican?"

Inaki nodded. "Seems the book of hours was logged into the Vatican Library in 1555, after it was already in the papal chapel. That's very unusual. There's no record of how it got there, or where Cervini might have acquired it. No provenance was found—no receipts, and no mention on acquisition logs or the Vatican catalogue."

"Odd."

"It also appears that Cervini undertook a pilgrimage to Santiago de Compostela in 1552 at the behest of Pope Julius. There are a number of pilgrimage roads to Compostela, and they're trying to find the one he took."

"He'd spent some time in Trent," Alphaios said, "so he must have had some acquaintances there. Perhaps he covered some old ground. Or went by boat—Rome and Barcelona are nearly at the same latitude. Either way, it's likely he would have traveled through northern Spain. Any word from your other library friends?"

"Nothing yet. So we wait."

"Yes. Wait and work."

Inaki began to put the bifolia away, and Alphaios turned to the scribes' recent work. Today's pages survived his eye, and he slid them back into their drawers to await his brushes. From a separate cabinet, he withdrew a bifolium on which the text had been completed and which already reflected some of the vibrant colors of his craft. He painted cerise into the intricate checkerboard margin. He didn't finish the page as he'd planned, but the conversation with Inaki had been encouraging.

After capping his paint and cleaning his brushes, he opened another drawer and slid out a leaf that would be a major undertaking. He hungered for it, but would study it many more times before laying paint to parchment. He took it under the big south windows and stood looking at it. Today, again, its beauty took his breath away.

This page alone was priceless.

It bore no text. It was a face-page for a prayer to St. Anne, mother of the Virgin Mary. Despite the damage, it was rich with color, and in appearance and content, one of the most striking pages in the book.

Laid against a background of lavender decorated with small gold St. Julian's crosses were three framed pictures. They had been painted by an artist of surpassing talent. It was Jeremiah's work.

The background of the central and largest picture was a distinctly European town with a crenellated castle, a cathedral church, and many large houses. In the forefront sat the Virgin Mary as a young woman, cradling in her arms the adult, cruci-fied body of Jesus. Behind Mary stood St. Anne, one hand on Mary's shoulder, the other reaching an open palm to touch the face of her grandson. Mary's eyes were on the face of Jesus. The eyes of St. Anne were cast upward to the open sky. Far to the left stood a withering dogwood tree.

Most of the bottom third of this portrait was lost to damage. Mary's feet, Jesus' feet, and the one dangling hand of the lifeless Jesus were missing. Those features Alphaios could repair, using Jeremiah's eye and technique. But some details could not be known with certainty. For instance, had wounds to Jesus' feet been depicted? If so, where? How? Were Mary's feet bare, or in sandals? Did the foreground contain some object or theme of significance?

The second picture was up and to the left, a small portion of it covered by the first. Here, in an unusual portrait, St. Anne held the infant Jesus. The Virgin Mary sat at her feet. Behind them was a choppy sea with distant fishing boats drawing up their nets ahead of a storm. Where the land met the sea, mid-distance, was a man in a crimson robe and cardinal's hat. With such a prominent placement, the cardinal was a contemporary whom the book's patron wished to honor or impress.

The central figure in the third picture, which was at the upper right and also slightly behind the first, was also St. Anne. Rays of white heavenly light enveloped both her and Mary, who was depicted here as a young girl, not yet a woman. They were walking in a golden field dotted with shocks of harvested grain. Behind them were a substantial farmhouse and stable with several domestic animals. In one hand Mary held a clutch of wheat, and in the other a goblet. This, too, was a family portrait, with the body and blood of Christ a prominent part of the genealogy that was to come.

The dedication of this whole page to St. Anne clearly indicated that the person who commissioned the book placed great value on her.

St. Anne had been honored by early Christians not only because they believed God had selected her to bear Mary, but because through Anne, Mary was born free of all sin. By divine intervention, Mary alone was free of the original sin that has burdened every other man and woman since Adam and Eve fell from grace. This, not virgin birth, was Mary's own immaculate conception.

The names of Anne and her husband Joachim, father of Mary, were not mentioned in the scriptures; they were found only in later church texts. Nonetheless, interest in her had grown from the second century forward, and Alphaios knew there were some who believed that Anne, as well as Mary, had given virgin birth. This point of view was not evident in this particular book of hours, but wasn't uncommon at the time. It wasn't until 1677 that the Vatican would declare that Anne had conceived Mary through mortal means.

The hour was late, and Alphaios returned the parchment to its place. When a few minutes later he left the library, he turned and walked directly to the monastery. His mind was full of music and images.

It was not unusual for him to be preoccupied during supper and evening prayers. He used this time to reflect on the wondrous, disorderly spirit he found beyond the walls of the monastery. He did not want conversation, so was glad that such quiet was not only welcomed by his brothers but expected. Truth be known, he was now far more attentive to his theological life in the mornings, before his excursions into the city, than after he returned. But yet, he admitted to himself, still not completely so.

Tonight he reflected that for every idea or detail written in a book or painted on some clean white surface, there were important ideas or details left out. Did George Gershwin know his audience for *Rhapsody in Blue* would want just one more bar of his music, and then another, and then just one more?

Had Jeremiah shown the wounds of driven nails on Jesus' feet? Could the question be resolved?

Joachim had bounced his grandson Jesus on his knee and Grandmother Anne had dipped a cloth into goat's milk to let him suckle. What about Joseph? How much of Jesus was formed by the love and guidance of his mortal, even if not biological, father?

Alphaios fell asleep to a remembered clarinet glissando.

 CHAPTER 12

H E OPENED THE OVERSIZED wooden door and
stepped into the noise of the city. At first, his movements were cautious and measured, his eyes downcast.

But just as every day now but Sunday, Alphaios was in the
street only moments before his head lifted. His eyes brightened
and began to dart from face to movement, from flash of color
to blare of horn, to the slice of gray or brilliance of sun between
the buildings high above him. His stride quickened and
lengthened with the energy surrounding him. Harried men
and women rushed to appointments or back to after-lunch
offices. Taxis and private cars stuttered forward, straining for
any advantage in the heavy traffic. He could feel as well as
hear the constant pounding of streets being repaired.

And just as it did every day but Sunday, he felt a small,
private grin appear.

When he reached the unmarked brownstone, he paused for a moment, reluctant to leave the street. Then he went up the stairs, entered the code and was let in. It was quiet inside, even more so than the cloister.

Today, Alphaios planned to finish the upper left corner of a page, in and around a boxed and flourished F first painted by Zephaniah. He would lay luminous gold leaf onto gesso and burnish it, and then brush on paints he had colored with azurite for blue and mercuric sulfide for vermilion.

Two nearly silent hours later, he stood back from the worktable and stretched his neck. Tomorrow he could move to the flourishes at the top right and a tiny picture of a figure sitting in a tree. A challenging St. Stephen preaching to a crowd awaited him further down the page.

His heart began to beat rapidly, not from any strenuous activity, but from a decision he'd made on his way here, one he intended to carry out this very afternoon. He wiped his brushes and quills clean, capped the pots of inks and paints, and laid them all in their felt-lined drawers. He did not bid goodbye to XM, who had been in the room the whole time; Alphaios himself would not countenance such a casual inter-ruption when doing delicate work. Besides, over Alphaios's objections, XM constantly listened to loud, discordant music through headphones, and probably wouldn't hear him anyway. His work had turned out to be remarkably good, however, and Alphaios had conceded the matter.

He retrieved the little brass key from its drawer and gathered up the leftover gold leaf to return to the mixing room. When he was done there, he let himself out the front door and onto the street. But instead of turning right as usual, he stopped at the bottom of the stairs, looked cautiously around, and went to the left. He had almost two hours before he might be considered late at the monastery.

The afternoon had cooled somewhat, but the patio was still in sunlight. Nervous, he entered and chose a table in an architectural nook near the door.

He reddened when he spoke to Nico and placed the five-dollar bill on the table. It was only a moment before the waiter brought out the small espresso. He'd have to settle for the little paper envelopes of sweetener lying on his saucer. He stirred their contents into the tiny cup and brought it to his nose. He breathed in the scent slowly and deeply, and then took a sip. The liquid bit into his senses, strong and sweet and bitter and utterly welcome.

He savored the sensation, then set the coffee down. This was a cup to revel in, not one to be hurried.

Here in this spot he could watch life—life far away from physical walls and solemn regimentation. The contrast could not be greater: near-silence inside the cloister, browns and grays and shadows, catechism and constraint; organized chaos outside, noise, color, variety, incitement of the senses.

Nearby, lovers clasped hands across a small table, friends drank coffee and shared a dessert, and students argued passionate art and social theory over their textbooks. Two old men played chess and talked little. A young couple looked through a movie schedule. One man sat alone, absorbed in some electronic device.

Farther out, on the sidewalk, businessmen in suits hurried by. He could tell the most important ones, or at least the most self-important ones—it was their companions, not they, who lugged heavy document cases. When the cold weather came again, these men would wear white silk scarves carefully tucked under the lapels of long wool coats.

He was pleased to spot the tall and slender woman—perhaps Nigerian—whom he'd seen on the street before. Today she wore a lime-green top, a floor-length orange, green and black skirt, a matching headpiece and white tennis shoes. She carried her infant close against her chest in a sling that let her long bare arms swing free. He again noted that she held her head high and looked straight ahead, absent the slight forward stoop of many tall American women. She was stylish and self-assured. Today a man walked at her side.

Four young black men wearing expensive gold baubles passed the cafe, all with the same practiced, careless swagger. They talked as they walked, but their words and body language were directed outward rather than to each other. They did not so much talk among themselves as make pronouncements to or about whomever might be in sight.

A group of orthodox Jews with black hats and long side curls gaggled by on the street, perhaps returning from yeshiva. They were in animated conversation among themselves, all facing inward as if in some great Talmudic scrum, and entirely indifferent to all others around them.

Two Rastafarians, dreadlocks tight and clothes loose, drifted by from some origin beyond Alphaios's ken to some destination beyond his guessing.

A gray-haired homeless woman moved slowly across his field of vision. She wore a quilted blue coat with its insulation tufting out white at the seams, and pushed a bicycle trailed by a makeshift cart. This bicycle was no longer meant for riding, but for trucking her cardboard household from one heated street grate to another.

Alphaios watched laughing men and boys, purposeful men and boys, drifting men and boys, despairing men and boys, and men and boys using wile to lure the attentions of women and girls. In turn, women and girls demonstrated their own happiness, purpose, drift or despair, and responded, rejected or ignored the come-ons.

And he saw allure. Cleavage, bare midriffs and other pulchritude did not titillate Alphaios, but neither did it offend him. It was one more rich, fascinating thread in the fabric of the city.

No one at the monastery could know of these worldly side trips. Were he to find out, the prior would demand the book of hours be brought back to the monastery or even that another illuminator be found. He'd be angry at Alphaios for his mendacity, and fear far more for his soul than for any complaints of poor light or working conditions. He'd add even more censure were he to see the sizeable place this exotic sensory garden had come to occupy in Alphaios's heart.

He'd not expected to drift from the strict rules of the order. But the life of the city wore the very hues he used in revitalizing the book of hours. He found its colors—for he had taken to thinking of the whole experience of the city in terms of colors— were illuminating him, providing light within his soul. So he would come again to this café to drink in all his illicit pleasures: sounds and sights and scents, and the pungent, delicious coffee of his youth.

Coffee gone and time waning, Alphaios remembered Inaki's advice and left his change on the table. He turned toward a commercial street which would provide a direct route back to the monastery. Not far ahead of him was the familiar green and orange of the tall Nigerian woman. He watched her long, confident strides.

They had walked just a block when it happened. Very near to him, he heard a sudden scream of tearing metal and the roar of a large motor. He jumped back and turned his head to see a yellow delivery truck careen out of control and jump the curb onto the sidewalk in front of him. His breath was torn away as he watched it slam into someone and fling them against the wall of a building. A body crumpled to the sidewalk and lay underneath the front of the still-roaring truck. His own legs collapsed, and he too fell to the ground.

The world seemed to stop in place, except for the roaring. For a moment, he was not certain if it was the truck or the rush of his own blood.

Then, in just an instant, the tableau returned to life—all movement and noise and chaos. He could hear screaming. It was drowned out in volume by the motor, but not in pitch. He could not see the woman.

Someone turned off the motor. Screaming and shouting was what was left.

Alphaios scrambled to his feet and drew closer to the truck. Under it was a vast amount of blood, a red, spreading pool of it.

Cloistered life had not prepared him for such an event or sight as he now encountered, and it was others who took command. Somehow they managed to move the truck a few feet back from the wall and the body under it. It was a man.

From the other side of the truck, the tall woman in orange and green rushed into the space and fell to her knees in the red glaze. She was crying uncontrollably, yelling at the man, pulling at him. It looked almost as if she were hitting him.

It took him a moment to realize the baby was not in its sling.

Some men from the street tried to pull the woman away so they could tend to the man, but she fought back violently, refusing to be moved. They relented for a moment to discuss what to do. Clearly they did not understand what Alphaios now dreaded.

He crept close to the woman and knelt down in the blood, the body of the injured man between them. He looked for a moment into her wild eyes, trying to convey that he understood, and then gently raised the man's shoulder and chest from the ground. There, to his despair, lay the infant, quite clearly dead. He motioned to one of the men to lift the downed man a bit further, and as carefully as he could, removed the baby and placed it in the mother's arms.

She knew instantly her baby was gone. She held it fiercely to her breast and began keening loudly. Alphaios retreated a bit and sat, stunned, with his back against a wall. The other men surrounded the fallen man, but quickly seemed to conclude that he was dead as well.

The woman did not move from her place. She wept uncontrollably. The driver of the yellow truck sat bent over on the curb some thirty feet away, shoulders heaving. Some people knelt, talking to him and trying to give comfort. A second damaged truck, dark green with white, gold-bordered lettering, blocked the street. Its driver paced back and forth in high agitation, smoking and talking incessantly to no one.

The ambulance arrived, howling and flashing, followed by police cars and fire trucks doing the same. This is the way, in vivid color, that Alphaios would remember this day in the city.

A medic from the ambulance persuaded the woman to move a few feet away, and to give him her baby long enough to examine it. After talking over his radio for a moment or two, he wound up giving it back to her. A couple of others worked on the man but soon gave up after they, too, consulted someone by radio.

Another medic came to check on Alphaios, but he shook his head and waved the man away.

While police officers were getting names of witnesses and talking to the truck driver on the curb, one of the firemen approached him. "Are you a priest?"

Alphaios was trembling. "I'm a monk. Who's the man? Do you know?"

"It's the lady's husband. And her baby. She wants you to give them last rites."

"I can't. I'm a monk, not a priest."

"The lady says she's seen you before, and she's asking you to do it."

"I . . . I'm a monk. I don't have vestments, oils—"

"Help her, man!" And then quietly, strained: "Help her."

When he worked his way to his feet, he realized his habit was soaked with blood from his knees down, and his hands were red with it. He could feel wetness on his face where they had flown to help his mind comprehend the scene in front of him.

The woman sat erect on the sidewalk beside the body of her husband, her infant back in its sling, her arms pressing it against her. Her eyes fixed on him as he approached, pleading in them. Her handsome face was jagged now. She, too, was covered with blood. Her keening was still constant, but quieter.

Alphaios knelt by the small family and bowed his head. He was silent for a moment in personal prayer. Then he asked the woman to give him the baby and asked its name. "Magdalena," she gasped.

"I'll do what I can." He held the child gently in one arm, cradling its head in his palm. With the thumb of the other, he made the sign of the cross on the tiny forehead and gently stroked the head with his fingers, as if anointing it. Loud enough that only the woman could hear, he began. "Through this holy anointing may the Lord in his love and mercy . . ." He paused for a moment, and began again, for this life was pure, innocent; there was no need for forgiveness. "Through this holy anointing may the Lord in his love imbue you with the grace of the holy spirit. Amen." His voice faltered. "Through this holy anointing may the Lord in his love and mercy help your mother, with whom you are forever one, with the grace of the Holy Spirit. Amen. May the Lord who frees her from sin save her and raise her up. Amen."

He returned the tiny body to its mother's arms and repeated the "anointing" and the sacramental prayer over the woman's husband, this time without alteration.

The mother thanked him with her eyes and a momentary stillness.

She wept again as the paramedics removed the body of her husband and then carefully extracted the baby from her arms. Exhausted and in near shock, she herself was placed in an ambulance and taken away.

The police were not done yet, and asked Alphaios to stay close and give a report of what had happened. The yellow truck was towed away, showing little damage for all the horror it had wrought. Left behind were the stain of now-dark blood and the flashing of police cars and fire trucks. It was the firemen who would wash away the blood, who would remove the last physical evidence of this tragedy.

Long before he finished giving his witness statement, Alphaios was exhausted. When he was finally free to leave, he stood for a long minute, not knowing quite what to do. When he did move, it was back to the steps of the library. There he sank down in a stupor. He knew he must look horrific, but didn't have the energy to respond to the stares of people passing by.

It was there that Prior Bartholomew found him several hours later, and uttered, "God have mercy." He managed to hail a taxi, then raised Alphaios to his feet, bundled him into the car, and took him home.

It was the next day before Alphaios was able to speak of the tragedy. He asked to see Prior Bartholomew and Father Michael. When they were together, he described the accident. In halting speech, he told of deceiving the woman and the two departed souls. He confessed pretending to give last rites when the sacrament was not his to give, and after it could properly be bestowed. He confessed the pretense of anointment, and to deviating from the language of the sacrament. He prayed God would punish him for his deceits, not the souls against whom they had been committed.

He did not tell them of his trip to the café. He did not admit his love affair with the city and its people and its colors.

Both prior and priest listened quietly, and when he was done, there was a long moment of silence.

Finally, Father Michael asked, "Brother, why did you deceive this woman?"

"To give her comfort."

After a time, penance was ordered. Alphaios was to pray for the souls of the dead infant and man each day for a year. He would do this anyway, as well as for the woman, for whose immortal soul he did not fear but for whose mortal spirit he did.

Prior Bartholomew then surprised him, asking if he wished to study for the priesthood, to take higher vows. The order would sponsor him.

Alphaios closed his eyes. After years of spiritual training, his heart had only recently come alive. He'd come to thrive on his daily excursions, and to find deeper joy in the city—and now greater pain—than in cloisters. He could not let himself lose this new exposure to life.

After a few moments of deep anxiety, he opened his eyes and declined the offer with thanks, saying that his work was to create and restore the beauty of manuscripts. His life was to be that of a humble monk.

Two days later, he again opened the oversized door and emerged into the noise of the city. At first, his movements were cautious, measured, his eyes downcast. He was in the street only moments, however, before his head lifted and his pace quickened and lengthened.

But it would be long weeks before the small, private grin would reappear.

CHAPTER 13

ALPHAIOS WAS ONLY VAGUELY aware of the commotion caused by his blood-soaked habit and the questions
it raised. Violence of any kind was virtually unknown in the
cloister, and the last serious accident at St. Ambrose had been
years ago.

He retreated into silence, speaking only as necessary even
to Brother John and Inaki. He noticed the looks from his
brothers, but avoided even the most inviting and sympathetic
of them. He sought to ease his mind in the rituals of the daily
offices and found sustenance in the singing of the antiphonal
prayers. But more than solace or succor, he sought return to
centeredness, to stability in his spiritual core. He ached to let
the mantle of the cloister settle softly over him. In Rome or
Florence it would have been effortless. Here, it was an uneasy
fit.

The city had shown him one of its natural colors. It had revealed to him the random cruelty of life in its streets. This would not have, could not have happened in cloisters.

But didn't "cruelty" imply intent, or at least some form of thought, before or during the event? Perhaps cruelty was the wrong word, for that would anthropomorphize the city, assign it human characteristics. But if not the city, who or what was responsible for these deaths? Could they really have been just senseless, especially the infant's, whose only guilt could have been the burden of original sin? Just causeless, serendipitous occurrences of no special note? Was there not more order, more benevolence on this mortal coil than that?

Alphaios felt a kinship with the woman. He had no reason to, other than she had become a familiar and welcome sight to him. But her keening, the twist of her handsome face into agony, would not leave him.

It crossed his mind that in some perverse way the woman and her family had been punished for his flouting the rules of the order—it would not have happened had he not sinned by going to the café. It even occurred to him that if he were not traveling outside the monastery to do his work, somehow the cosmic flutter would have led to some different outcome. He was too rational a being to ascribe such causations, however, and let these thoughts pass.

He didn't know what series of earthly events had preceded the accident, which truck driver had done what or when, but they held no interest for him. He wanted to blame God, but in the end couldn't even do that. He, like all before him, could only believe God's goodness would somehow compensate, no, encompass or incorporate the little family.

That he had deceived the souls of the departed with his contrived sacrament did not continue to bother him. That weight had been lifted from his mind. But though he had comforted her with his actions, his deception of the woman still living continued to gnaw at him. Perhaps it was because she must continue to live, always in mortal anguish over her loss.

The weekly chapter meeting was held four days later. Alphaios made a show of normality by attending, but he was physically exhausted and emotionally numb. He had no doubt that Brother Simon or Levi would make some kind of complaint. They would use the accident, or rather his involvement in it, to question the propriety of his working outside the monastery. He didn't feel up to defending himself, but knew it might come to that.

Prior Bartholomew began by leading the usual prayer. He then paused and indicated that this morning he would take the floor himself.

"My brothers, I have noticed loud whispers among us over the last several days. Quite uncommonly, they have centered on a habit that required special laundering." He looked directly at the launderer, who shifted uncomfortably in his seat. "A habit worn by Brother Alphaios and soaked in blood."

The room became still, the monks completely attentive. "Brother Alphaios need not tell you his story. I'll do it for him. A few days ago, he was a witness to an awful accident in which an infant and its father were killed by an errant truck.

He helped the mother free the baby from under its father's body. The child was already dead. In the process, he and his habit became stained with blood. He provided comfort to the mother as best he could under such terrible circumstances. He was asked to remain where he was by the police and answer questions about what he'd seen. When he was done, he returned to the steps of the scriptorium, which is where I found him. As you have seen, witnessing such an event has troubled him deeply."

The room remained silent as the monks took in these details.

"God in heaven." It was Brother John, softly. He looked over at Alphaios, his eyes compassionate. Alphaios heard several other mutterings around the room, monks sharing John's sentiment.

"He should not have been outside the monastery to see such a thing." It was Brother Philemon.

This was the reaction Alphaios had been expecting. It must be a legitimate point.

"And what difference would that have made, Brother?" asked John. "The man and child would still be dead."

"And we would have no knowledge of it, and thus our pursuit of salvation would not be disturbed."

"This is what you have to say to our brother at such a time?"

Philemon had provided the means, so Brother Simon chose this moment to step in and assert himself. "Our brother is quite right, John. Now, knowing of this accident, we will pray for the souls of the infant and its father. But we've chosen to live apart from the world. We do not make the matters of the world our own."

"The mother," Alphaios forced out, his eyes on the floor. The monks turned toward him. "And the mother."

"The mother?" asked Simon. "Was she also killed?"

"No, but I pray for her soul as well."

Simon nodded solemnly. "Of course you do, Brother. So shall we all." After a brief pause, he continued. "But as Philemon has pointed out, and as you must agree, to the extent we burden ourselves with worldly matters, mortal matters, we endanger our own search for salvation. This is the very reason some of our brothers have long had concerns about your work outside our walls."

Alphaios knew Simon was correct, and had begun to wonder if he was right: the Order of St. Ambrose was a contemplative one in which prayer and spiritual pursuit were the essential vocations. Prayers for all humankind were of course offered, but in most cases these were prayers for safety from natural and manmade cataclysms and for the forgiveness of the inherent sinfulness of mankind. All else was conducted simply to feed the body and provide it shelter. Whatever anybody else thought of it, these men had deliberately removed themselves from the vagaries of the world for this singular purpose. For him, it might have been different—it had been the price of an education, and he'd never before thought to regret it.

But now, how did he reconcile the intense pull he felt from this city? How could he endure the pain that consumed him each time the jagged face of the woman came to mind—as it did every other waking moment—or the tiny lifeless body he had held so easily in one hand? The colorful and vibrant city he had reveled in just days ago had now caused his heart to seize. Joy and wonder had been replaced by awful grief. Was his experience in the city indeed a price to shrink from rather than a prize to be won?

Prior Bartholomew spoke up. "We discussed this matter fully before Brother Alphaios arrived here. It was by consensus we agreed to host him here at Cardinal Ricci's request."

"Indeed we did, Prior," Simon said. "With the understanding our way of life would remain undisturbed. Clearly that's not the case."

"How is that?"

"What should we consider a blood-soaked habit if not an intrusion? A blessing?"

"Certainly not a blessing." All in the room turned to Brother Timothy. It was rare to hear him speak in chapter. "Instead, a hardship for a brother who warrants our under-standing and love."

"Ah, Timothy. But of course it is, and we give it freely."

"I'd be hard-pressed to describe just how, Simon." Timothy's voice was tight, controlled. "Let me ask you, were a brother to suffer an accident or some great emotional distress within these walls, would it still first be an intrusion into our prayers? Or would we reach out and provide comfort?"

Brother Levi flared. "But it didn't occur within our walls, Timothy. That's precisely the point." Levi had not left his animus behind. Mad Old George, it seemed, was still in the room.

Today, so was Brother Timothy. "Our brother suffers within these walls, does he not?"

"We all suffer within these walls! That is what we do. Suffer ourselves and each other, and pray for the salvation of our souls."

"And lose our love for our fellow man in the process?"

"Precisely, Brother."

Simon reached out and placed a calming hand on Levi's arm. He wouldn't believe it wise to deal in such extremes. For him, subtlety would be a slower but more certain course; some might see his moderating hand as a sign of deft leadership.

No wonder Brother Timothy chose to speak so rarely. But the old monk was not yet finished. "My brother, where is it written that our souls await our deaths to be judged? Our souls are within us today, here and now. Our eternity, should it be granted, has already begun. What we do with our souls here, however great our piety, does not go unseen."

Levi gathered himself to offer a retort, but Brother Samuel spoke first. "This intrusion wouldn't have happened were Brother Alphaios not permitted to work in the city. We should reconsider our agreement." All heads turned toward him except for Alphaios's. He remained still, his face impassive.

"Does my brother recall the accident that occurred in the manufactory," asked John, "that took Brother Christopher's arm and his life with it?"

Samuel looked annoyed. "I was here only a short time, but yes, I remember Brother Christopher. God rest his soul."

"Did we pray with him, and then for him, when God called him home?"

"Of course, Brother."

"Have we stopped making shoes?"

"No, John. What are you getting at?"

"Let's say, heaven forbid, that one of us chokes during a meal, and we're unable to dislodge the offending piece of food. Does that mean we all stop eating? Does it mean I should stay out of the kitchen and stop cooking?"

"Of course not. What point are you trying to make?"

"Tragic intrusions into our lives can happen. It's a part of mortal life. Just because Brother Alphaios encountered a tragedy outside these walls does not mean he must stop making shoes, so to speak. Simply because he sought to provide solace and became bloody in the process is not reason to force him to starve. In such instances we grieve, we offer each other such comfort as we are able, and we continue our vocation having incorporated those events into ourselves."

John's words apparently hit a chord. For the moment, the room was silent.

Brother Timothy stood up from his bench, an action nearly unheard of in chapter. He raised his frail body to its full bent height. He was trembling, and when he spoke, his voice was high with emotion.

"We have strayed far from our purposes, my brothers, to come to this uncharitable moment. Here we sit and take liberties not only with our founder's charter, but even with our Christianity. It's one thing to remove ourselves from worldly distractions so as to seek salvation. It's quite another to deliberately withhold compassion from one of God's children who is in distress. Or for some of us to pretend such love while truly penurious of heart. Show me this proscription against love, my brothers. Bring out this charter from which we stray so much! Let us examine it."

Timothy was visibly tiring, and his voice dropped. "We are weary of this life, my brothers, and our hearts have become small and hard. But we make our own load heavier by withholding our love from God's children. Compassion lifted Jesus's burden; it was indifference and hate, not compassion that made his burden too much to carry." Unsteady, he reached a hand back to guide himself back down to his seat.

Timothy's intensity raised Alphaios from his lassitude, and he looked around the room. In the immediate silence, he heard several murmurs of agreement. Some monks had eyebrows raised, wondering what drama might come next. Levi sat stone-faced, seemingly unmoved.

Simon affected boredom with the issue, his manner and tone dismissive of his brother's passion. "We've had this discussion before, Timothy. Now, Samuel suggested that our agreement with Cardinal Ricci be reconsidered in light of this incident. I recommend we—"

Prior Bartholomew held up a hand. "I appreciate your concern, Simon, and that of all our brothers. I believe where this event happened is unimportant. Brother Alphaios deserves our compassion. He witnessed a tragic accident, one of God's mysteries that occurred without apparent reason—at least no reason we can comprehend. None of us is immune. But that, my brothers, is not the central point. Had Alphaios not acted in the manner of the biblical Good Samaritan, his habit would not have been bloody, and we would not be discussing this matter now. Which of us would choose to turn aside when faced with a tragedy such as this? Which of us mistakenly recalls that Christ rebuked the Good Samaritan for his deeds?"

He let the questions hang in the air. They met silence.

"Which of you wishes to re-examine our charter in light of this discussion, as Brother Timothy has proposed?"

A half-dozen hands rose slowly to shoulder height. Brother Timothy appeared exhausted and did not raise his.

"And now, my brothers, which of you wishes to revisit our agreement with the cardinal, and then tell him why?"

Not a hand was raised.

Simon's face was red, and Levi was shifting in frustration at this turn in momentum. Brother Samuel busied himself looking at the floor.

When chapter was over, Alphaios remained seated, eyes closed, heart beating hard in pain for the woman, in deep confusion for himself. Slowly, he became aware he was not alone. When he opened his eyes, Brother John was sitting to his right, Prior Bartholomew to his left. Another eight or ten monks remained in their places. Brother Maynard was there. Brother Haman sat beside Timothy, helping the older monk support his weight. Together they found and engaged in a comforting, simple silence.

CHAPTER 14

ALPHAIOS OPENED THE OLD black umbrella with
a whump and stepped out of the monastery into the
flow of pedestrians. Because it was raining, neither sunlight
nor variety of clothes would provide him with color today;
it would be umbrellas with bold tints and intricate designs
floating randomly through a greater sea of black. He imagined
the swirls and eddies of their movement as they might be
seen from above.

Neon signs in store windows announcing ales, photos and
pharmacies, usually lost in the kaleidoscope of sunny days,
today proclaimed their messages in vivid reds, blues and
golds. Raindrops on shop windows reflected tiny flares of
color around the lettering, prisms which turned the window
glass into fleeting impressionist art.

The rain was persistent but not heavy. Gusts of wind buffeted
the umbrella, and Brother Alphaios was chilled by the time

he mounted the steps to the library. He hung up his coat and left his umbrella splayed on the checkered tile floor.

Kenny was in the scriptorium, at work under the electric lights. As the natural light was inadequate for his own work, Alphaios decided to study the next page to be decorated. He wouldn't actually work on it for at least two more weeks, but understanding the spatial arrangements of the original painting, the pigments and inks used, and the techniques with which they had been applied were essential to making a faithful copy.

When two hours had gone by, Alphaios slid the cream-colored bifolium back into its flat drawer. He nodded to the scribe and, as was his custom, left the room without having spoken.

He put on his old coat, pungent with the smell of wet wool, and retrieved the umbrella. He stood in the little lobby a bit longer than necessary, looking through the window at the rain. He opened the door, descended the steps to the street, and seeing no familiar faces, turned toward the café. The espresso would be particularly welcome today.

Because of the inclement weather, the tables and big Cinzano umbrellas were chained together in the small nook where Alphaios liked to sit. He ducked into the café and found a booth midway back. He drew few looks from the other patrons, for he'd become a familiar presence.

Nico brought him what was now his customary drink—an extra-hot espresso and three sugars—took the five-dollar bill and left the monk to himself.

The café wasn't busy, and Alphaios missed hearing the waves of languages as conversations rose and fell. Feeling unsatisfied, he finished his coffee, shrugged again into the wet wool, and left. His shoulders lifted again in response to the cold, but notwithstanding the chill, he decided to explore a circuitous route back to the monastery.

Some distance ahead, he noticed a figure whose movements stood out from the rest. It was a smallish man in an expensive-looking, full-length coat and old-fashioned fedora. He was walking upright but uncertainly, tight against the wall of a building, one hand touching it for support. He appeared to be putting one foot carefully in front of the other. Alphaios, with his quick pace, was coming up on him rapidly when the man stumbled and fell hard onto his hands and knees. The hat flew off, rolled in the wind to the curbside, and came to rest in a puddle.

The people closest to the fallen man walked on as if nothing had happened. He was still down when Alphaios approached.

During his many expeditions through the city, Alphaios had himself become inured to homeless people wandering the sidewalks or sleeping on the warm ventilation grates, not to mention the many who were drunk or drugged. *Inured* was perhaps too firm a word; he was awkwardly, uncomfortably accustomed to their condition. But this man's stature and dress were different, and Alphaios hesitated only briefly before going to him.

"Are you all right, sir?"

"Leave me alone," the man gasped, his head down, his face dripping rain.

"Are you hurt? Can you get up?"

"Go away."

"I'll get your hat." Alphaios retrieved it, shook the water from it, and would have handed it to the man had he not still been down. He seemed unable or unwilling to move. "I'll get someone to call an ambulance."

"No. Don't."

"I can't just leave you here. At least let me help you up."

"Leave me alone. Who are you, anyway?"

"I'm Brother Alphaios, from the monastery over on Broad Street."

The man turned his head to peer at Alphaios for a moment, then laughed weakly. "A monk. Of course you are."

"Sir, long ago I took vows of poverty and chastity. I didn't pledge to stay cold and wet when there are alternatives. Right now I'm both. Can you stand up?"

The man slowly raised his hands from the concrete and propped one against the wall. He permitted Alphaios to grasp the other, and rose unsteadily to his feet. He stood, not letting go. Alphaios could feel him quiver, his weight shifting precariously. He was old and frail.

"You're going to fall again. Where can I take you?"

"To the corner grocery, if you must. Just down the block." The man's voice trembled. "Help me get there, and I'll be all right."

Alphaios placed the man's wet fedora on his head and they started forward. He slid his arm under the other man's and supported much of his weight. Holding the umbrella in his other hand, he tried without much success to keep the blowing rain off their faces. A hundred feet farther, they came to a tiny neighborhood grocery. Alphaios opened the door, helped the man take the one step up to the threshold, and they went inside.

The man started to free himself, but began to crumple almost immediately. Alphaios held him upright and asked the clerk behind the counter if there was a place his companion could sit down for a moment. At first ready to say no, the clerk looked a second time at the small man, then produced an old metal folding chair from behind the counter. He set it at the end of a narrow aisle between displays of beef jerky and packaged doughnuts. Alphaios backed the old man into the chair. He was sick or exhausted or both.

"Is there something wrong with you? Are you ill?"

"I'll be fine in a minute. Just go and leave me alone."

"Is there somebody to come get you?"

"No. Go away, monk! Let me sit."

"Who are you?" the clerk asked Alphaios. "What happened to him?"

"I saw him fall down on the sidewalk, and this is where he wanted to come. Do you know him?"

"He's a customer. A regular." The grocer motioned Alphaios to the back of the small store, where he spoke quietly. "Comes in every three or four days. Always buys a little food, not much."

"Do you know his name, where he lives?" asked Alphaios.

"No. He doesn't say much. He always pays with change, maybe a small bill or two, so I don't think he has much money. But he must live somewhere in the neighborhood."

"Do you have something hot I can give him?"

The grocer shrugged. "There's a hot chocolate machine, there's soup for the microwave, some chili con carne. SpaghettiOs. We have muffins."

"Some soup. Can you heat it up and bring it? And some milk?" Alphaios walked the few steps back to the man, retrieved his umbrella from the aisle, and closed it.

A minute or so later he heard a small bell, and the grocer brought forward a plastic container of chicken noodle soup and a tiny bottle of milk. He went through a door in the back of the store and a moment later returned with a battered but clean teaspoon.

Alphaios knelt in front of the man on the chair and held the bowl close to his mouth. "Eat some of this."

The man grasped the spoon and bowl and, with Alphaios's hand under his, began to sip at the soup. When he finished, Alphaios opened the milk and offered it to him. He took it in both hands and drank it quickly.

Alphaios had no money to pay for the food, and apologized. He opened his coat to show the grocer his vocation. The grocer's eyebrows gathered and he scowled. His eyes asked the obvious question, and Alphaios answered it.

He suggested a second cup of soup and the grocer grudgingly complied. This time, the man was able to hold it himself. He ate silently.

When he was done, the small man slowly unbuttoned his overcoat and reached into a pocket. He brought out a change purse and pulled out some coins with shaking hands. "Take it. If you'll just let me sit for a while, I'll be on my way."

The grocer shrugged. "Most times when you come in, you get milk, a baguette, some kippered herring. Couple of oranges. If that's what you want, that's what I'll let you pay for."

The man nodded slowly. He fished more coins out of the purse, and the grocer started to collect the food. When he had it together on the counter, he rang it up and counted out the coins the man proffered. Alphaios took the quart of milk back to the cooler and replaced it with a larger container. The grocer nodded his grudging assent and placed it into a plastic sack with the rest of the items.

A few customers later, the man stood up carefully and announced he was leaving. He took a couple of stumbling steps toward the counter. Before the man could do so, Alphaios picked up the sack of groceries, then his umbrella. "I'll walk with you." It was not a question. The older man glared but said nothing, and they stepped out into the rain.

Within just a few steps, the man slowed appreciably and allowed Alphaios to put a hand under his elbow. By the time he turned them toward the steps of a building in the second block, he was unable to navigate them by himself. Alphaios lifted him from step to step.

It was not nearly the tallest building in the neighborhood, but it was impressive. A doorman in a maroon uniform and cap met them under a long, fern-green canopy. "Mr. Eastman! Are you all right? Did something happen to you? Who's this man?"

Mr. Eastman—as Alphaios had just learned—pulled himself as tall as he could. "I'm fine, Wilson." He wheezed out a sardonic laugh. "He's a monk. Brother something or other."

The building had enormous double doors made of thick glass enclosed in bright decorative metalwork—long fronds of palmetto woven through a field of interlocking but incomplete circles of many sizes. Equally impressive, on both sides of the doors were bas-relief carvings, perhaps twenty feet tall. High on each was the face of a woman looking straight out. From each head, hair cascaded downward in long symmetrical waves to the portico floor.

Wilson held the big door open and they entered a large, brightly lit lobby. Its floor was constructed of inlaid marble. Long angular streaks of color shot across it, and through this pattern, the outline of a giant gear wheel swung asymmetrically all the way across the large room. High above them was a barrel ceiling on which a stylized silver airplane with a single propeller soared against a backdrop of blue sky and mountainous white clouds.

He would have liked to sit down and just look, but Mr. Eastman led them toward the doors of an elevator. These, too, were elaborate, complementing in brass the décor of the front entrance. The doorman got there first and held the doors open. He relieved Alphaios of his umbrella, saying he would take good care of it, inserted and turned a key for 5P, and wished Mr. Eastman a "good evening, sir."

Only moments after they closed, the doors opened again, this time into a large oval foyer. It was quite dark, but its warmth was welcome.

The room was ornately constructed. A patterned, inlaid marble floor reflected the shape of the room. The ceiling was very high but seemed to be missing a chandelier. Doors and their frames were made of exotic wood, perhaps rosewood, highlighted by thin, patterned strips of inset chrome and lacquered to a high gloss.

It was devoid of furniture. Nor was there anything on the walls or set in the alcoves clearly meant for displaying fine art. And so it was in the wide hallway down which Mr. Eastman slowly led him, and in a spacious dining room with a massive table with one single chair pulled up to it. This was their destination.

Still supporting Mr. Eastman, Alphaios let his eyes roam. It was the largest residence he'd ever seen. It appeared to take up the entire floor of the building. But wherever he looked, there was no other furniture. Elegant walls were bare except for darker rectangles where paintings or mirrors once hung. There were no drapes or curtains. Above the dining table, where once a chandelier must have hung from the high ceiling rosette, dangled a bare light bulb.

He lowered Mr. Eastman into the chair. The man crossed his arms on the table and lowered his head onto them. He was clearly exhausted, and said nothing.

Through a doorway was the kitchen. Mindful of the milk he carried, he went to find the refrigerator. The room was enormous—large enough to accommodate not just a chef but a full staff. Its cupboards and counters and tables all reflected a handsome early-twentieth-century design. The appliances had obviously been expensive, but now were many decades out of date.

Alphaios opened the huge refrigerator. It was empty, completely empty. He put the milk on a wide shelf and shut the
door. He checked a nearby cupboard. It was empty. He crossed
the room and opened another. Empty. He looked in all the
other cupboards and drawers. In all the vast kitchen, there
were no pots and no pans. He found three plates, a couple of
water glasses and a few utensils. But most astonishing, there
was no food whatsoever but what he had just carried in.

He went back to check on Mr. Eastman and found him still
slumped on the table. Feeling almost surreptitious, he began
to explore the flat. He went through room after room. It was
immense, but lit only by the wan light of the rainy afternoon.
Nonetheless, he was able to see it had been, still was, luxurious.

In every room, save what were perhaps servants' quarters,
the floor was inlaid marble, its colors and patterns varying
with size of room and purpose. Wall coverings and paints
were mostly in soft hues: ivory, cream, wheat, rose, pale blues
and greens. In addition to the beautifully patterned floors,
every room had highlights of more intense color inlaid into
the woodwork. There was cobalt, magenta, cardinal, coal,
sulphur, jade, malachite, copper and chrome. The wood itself
was exotic: ebony and cherry and more rosewood, and some
of the metals were so fine they appeared to be filigree. The
high ceilings of the public rooms were all in brighter colors
than the walls, and most boasted strong, angular designs or
murals in styles similar to the building's main lobby.

In a room that ran the full depth of the building—a ballroom?
—Alphaios was astonished to see a brilliantly colored mural

painted in the fractious style of cubism. It seemed to be a portrait. The painting did not run quite the entire length of the interior wall, but as if the wall's twenty-foot height were not enough, it angled onto the ceiling and well over the room. He stood there for several minutes, admiring its boldness and color.

The immense size and opulence of the flat reminded him of the palazzos of Florence, or at least how he imagined them. It differed, of course, in the materials used and its distinctly American brashness.

He found no light fixtures in any of the rooms; where there once had been ceiling fittings and wall sconces, there remained only holes with stubbed wires. And aside from the dining room table and chair, the only other piece of furniture he found was one narrow bed. In that room was also a closet with two worn black suits hung side by side, and one pair of worn but polished black shoes squared on a shelf.

He found his way back to the dining room. This time, Mr. Eastman raised his head and watched him approach. "Seen enough yet, monk?"

"My name is Alphaios. Brother Alphaios, Mr. Eastman. What's yours?"

"Bernard, if you think you should know. You can go now."

"Do you live here alone?"

"Did you see anybody else? Please, go."

"But you aren't well. You don't have any food."

"I am where I choose to be! You fed me at the store, and I have as much food here now as I've had for weeks. That's quite enough. Now leave me!" He sneered and looked Alphaios up and down. "And thank you for your great and virtuous kindness, Brother Monk."

Though he was concerned for the man and curious, Alphaios could not think of a reason to stay longer. He excused himself and returned through the hallway to the elevator.

Back in the lobby, he retrieved his umbrella from the doorman and took the opportunity to ask him about Mr. Eastman. Wilson said he shouldn't comment; he could lose his job if he talked about the tenants. In turn, he asked if Alphaios really were a monk.

Alphaios introduced himself. "I'm worried. I just met Mr. Eastman today, but he seems unwell. Does he have any family or visitors?"

The doorman paused. "Well, it's all right, I suppose. I've been here fourteen years, but I've never seen anybody come in and ask for him, except when he's selling something. That doesn't happen anymore. He gave up his domestic staff years ago. I heard someone say once that he used to own the whole building, but that might be just people talking."

"How does he eat?"

"He goes out some days and brings back little sacks of groceries. He sure doesn't look very well lately. This afternoon's the worst I've seen him, though."

"I'll be back in a couple of days. I'd appreciate it if you'd let me in again."

"I'll think about it. Good night, sir."

The hour was late for Alphaios to be away. He hurried back to the monastery, his mind on Bernard Eastman.

On Monday, he broke the pattern he'd grown to love and did not go to the little café. Instead, hoping it would be enough, he took two of the precious five-dollar bills and went to the little corner grocery. He chose a few inexpensive food items and took them to the counter. When the grocer asked, he told him he'd managed to get Mr. Eastman home and was now on his way to see him again.

Although it was still cold, the sun was shining. As he approached the building, Alphaios noted it was twelve or thirteen stories high and architecturally superb. He stopped for a moment to study it.

It had strong vertical lines. Five stories up it narrowed, and its white granite base gave way to white piers with spandrels separated by patterned brown and white brick. This treatment gave the impression of open mesh, and thus a sense of lightness. It notched in once more as it climbed toward the sky. The carvings he had seen on Saturday were complemented by a sunburst carved into the stone above the front entrance, a third woman's face at its origin. Its spray of sunbeams drove the eye upward to the building's narrow but decorous crown.

It was an impressive building in an expensive neighborhood. Why was a man starving to death on the fifth floor?

When he climbed the stairs to the entrance, Wilson was there to open the door. Without waiting to be asked, the doorman greeted him and said, "He's in, Brother, as far as I know."

Alphaios made a request of Wilson that earned him a strange look. But when he got into the elevator and Wilson turned the key, Alphaios carried not only the sack of groceries but also the small chair from behind the doorman's desk.

He got off the elevator and called down the hallway, "Hello, Mr. Eastman. It's Brother Alphaios." He imagined he heard an echo.

After a moment came the reply he expected. "Go away. Leave me alone." But it didn't have much steam.

"I can't do that, Mr. Eastman." Alphaios started down the hall. "I've brought you some food."

"Who asked you to do that?" Mr. Eastman shouted hoarsely. "Mind your own business, monk!"

"But I made a special trip." Alphaios entered the dining room. Today, the sun lit the outer rooms brilliantly. "And brought a chair to sit on." Mr. Eastman was at his table, fully dressed in one of his suits, his skin sallow against the dense black fabric. Alphaios set down Wilson's chair across the table from the still-protesting man and walked into the kitchen. He found a can opener and used it on a tin of kippered herring and some maple-sweetened baked beans. He poured a glass of milk, found a fork, and took the meal to the dining table.

"The grocer told me you sometimes get baked beans." He went around the table and sat down. "Frankly, I couldn't tell you a thing about them. But then, they aren't served in the refectory."

Mr. Eastman appeared to relax a bit, though he would not give up his irritation easily. He raised his eyes to the heavens. "So now I have a guardian monk? You couldn't send me an angel?"

"When I saw you fall, I was on my way back to the monastery from work. Every day I go out, Mr. Eastman, I steal something."

The man gave a tired, mocking laugh. "Do you see anything here to steal?"

"Not things. I steal time. Time away from prayer. I watch people pass by and listen in on their lives. And at night, when I should be praying, I think about them. If they knew, my brothers would call it disobedience. Why don't you go ahead and take a bite? Ah, herring. It was once a favorite of mine too."

Notwithstanding the fact that he was eating directly from cans, Mr. Eastman was fastidious. He took each bit of food carefully to his mouth and chewed it slowly, examined the fork and licked it clean. He sipped at his milk as if to make it last longer.

"I'm here to learn how a man lives in a remarkable place like this, yet has nothing to eat."

There was silence for a long while. Alphaios used it to look around himself. In the streaming sunlight, it occurred to him that the apartment was remarkably clean. There were no layers of dust, no cobwebs, no stray piles of newspapers or books or old paper sacks.

The man's anger seemed to wane. He finished his meal and rose slowly. He took the cans and milk glass to the sink in the kitchen, where he methodically washed them and dried them with a towel. He placed the glass back into a cupboard and the spoon into a drawer, then opened a closet and put the cans away. When he was done, the kitchen was as empty as Alphaios had found it upon entering.

Mr. Eastman returned slowly to the table, sat down and sighed. "OK, monk. If I must." He appeared to be gathering his thoughts. "My father commissioned this building in 1935, when he was still a young man. It was finished in 1939. I've always been told it's the finest example of art deco in the city. His great legacy." He paused and looked down at his hands. "There won't be another like it."

"You've lived here a long time."

"I grew up at this very table. My parents sent me to the best possible prep school. I didn't do well, but went to Columbia anyway—what they call a legacy admission, an heir's privilege. After all, I was son and grandson of wealthy alumni."

He raised his head and looked at Alphaios with a kind of worn-out defiance. "I finished at the bottom of my class. Last." He waited for a reaction, but went on when no response was forthcoming. "It wasn't that I didn't try. I wasn't wild or irresponsible. I didn't have some pitiful handicap. I just wasn't smart enough. They said I didn't have the *requisite intelligence*." He said the phrase as if it had been a weapon used against him.

He let out some air and weariness replaced defiance. "Graduation was given to me. Can't say I earned it. It avoided embarrassment for the school and for my parents. By the time it finally came around, it was something to be endured, not celebrated." He stared out the window for so long Alphaios had to prompt him to go on.

"I had no aptitude for business or architecture or any other profession. Despite his efforts, my father wasn't able to find me a position appropriate to his hopes. That rankled him, but finally he put me to work as a clerk in one of his own companies. The fable was made that I'd learn the business from the bottom up. It wasn't true and I knew it. I stayed in that same job for eleven years with no expectation of promotion. I was at best average in a world that required phrases like *exceptional intellect* and *extraordinary aptitude*. Other employees climbed to positions of influence while I sat at my clerk's desk. My father's ownership of the company bought me a kind of formal kindness from the others. And I wasn't bored."

He shifted in his seat. "My mother was already gone when my father died one day. It was sudden—he was in his office at work. I was the only child, so I inherited this building." He looked down again and swallowed hard.

After a moment he lifted his head but seemed to be looking beyond Alphaios. "There was enough money to live very well for the rest of my life. But in this home, growth of the family fortune was scripture and verse. I'm sure you know, monk, the story of the wealthy man who gave coins to his servants to care for. I didn't want to be the lone servant who didn't venture out, who hid his coin so it wouldn't be lost."

"Yes, I know it."

Eastman caught Alphaios's eye momentarily, then looked back into space. "Anyway, I knew I couldn't run a business by myself. So I was careful. At Columbia I had a roommate,

David Robert McCray." He spit out the name slowly, derisively. "He was smarter than me and helped me through a couple of tough spots. We got along OK, were even friends of a sort. Sometime after my father died, we ran into each other. Or maybe he found me. He had his own company by then, commercial real estate. Warehouses and such. He had an office just across the river. The lobby had pictures of properties he'd acquired, and he gave me a tour of the company's books. It was impressive, but he needed more capital.

"We made a deal. My money, his business sense. I was a silent partner. Things went well for a couple of years. The company required more of my money, but he was reporting gains. Then one day, right out of the blue, I got a notice of receivership. Delivered right here, right to my door. It said that I had debts of millions of dollars, and that I no longer owned this building." He looked down and swallowed hard.

Alphaios wanted to say something, but didn't know what. Instead, he looked away.

"I went right over to David's office. It was locked up, empty. The bank accounts were gone. They'd been liquidated just days before. The pictures on the wall . . . I never saw or heard from him again. Oh, but I heard from lawyers. Battalions of lawyers. Documents were produced that I'd never seen before, let alone signed. Hundreds of them. I was accused of fraud. It was in the papers for months."

He took a deep, trembling breath, and his voice became so low that Alphaios had to strain to hear it. "I lost my father's building." It was as if he could barely say the words aloud.

"I no longer had any income. The best deal my lawyer could make was to let me live here for as long as I wish, rent-free. I wouldn't own the apartment, and if I were ever to move out, the agreement would end. He did manage to let me retain control of the contents. But then, he had his own self-interest in doing that." He pointed to a wall at the end of the room. "He took the Chagall that hung right there, took it for his fee. *Self-Portrait with Seven Fingers.*" He shrugged. "It always made me feel uncomfortable, anyway. Too stern."

Mr. Eastman slowly rose from the table and went to the kitchen. He took a glass from the cupboard, filled it at the sink and drank slowly but deeply. When he was done, he wiped the glass carefully with a small towel and returned it to its shelf. He came back to the dining room and stood, his hands grasping the edge of the table.

"I still had no particular aptitude, of course, and now had fresh evidence of it." He looked at Alphaios with self-mocking scorn. "I just didn't have the money to make it tolerable any-more. I couldn't find a job, not one I could bring myself to do."

He worked his way to the far end of the room and touched a radiator. "Twenty-six years, and they haven't turned off the heat. It's central heating, so it doesn't cost them anything to speak of. But they won't fix anything. If I tell the building super something needs to be repaired, he just ignores me. Doesn't tell me no, he just doesn't show up. Follow me if you want a tour."

Alphaios rose from his chair and followed Eastman into what might have been a sitting room. His host stood in front of a broad wall. "A Magritte hung here. You know René Magritte?"

He shook his head.

"*The Human Condition*, 1939. Red floor and blue sea and black bowling ball. It appealed to me. It wasn't the first thing I sold, but the money I got for it kept me in food and servants for a couple of years. I didn't get much for the furniture, not what it was worth. Except for the Persian rugs. Come."

Alphaios followed him into a smaller, darker room in the interior of the apartment. "This was my father's study. Most of the books brought in nothing, but he had some first editions I sold at Sotheby's. Some Paul Manship bronzes were particularly good to me, too."

They went to the dim oval foyer. Eastman pointed up. "There was a cut-glass chandelier, six feet wide. Impressive entrance, don't you think? Huge, fresh-cut floral bouquets every day. Good first impressions were important. Over there on a stand was a Tiffany vase, and right here on this wall was my favorite, a Miró. *People in the Night*. From 1949. I kept it for a long time."

They went into an adjoining area, perhaps a library. "The furniture and lamps were very high quality, but didn't bring near what they were worth. The paintings by minor artists I had to let go cheaply. Forty-three of them, all told. All twentieth-century American modernists. They'd be worth a lot more today."

They walked through other empty rooms in silence. Eastman had either lost interest, or was keeping his thoughts to himself.

Alphaios wanted to know more. "What about the big mural?"

Eastman turned and wound through several rooms until they came to the great room with the painting. The sun was streaming through high windows and French doors onto the marble floor. Across a wide veranda he hadn't seen in Saturday's dim light was an impressive view of the heart of the city. The blues, reds, browns and golds of the mural were vibrant, and today they seemed to color the whole room.

"My father loved Diego Rivera's painting *The Architect*. He tried to buy it, but it wouldn't come available. So he tried to get Rivera to do a private commission here in this room, with him as the subject. But after the debacle in the lobby of the RCA building, Rivera didn't spend much time in the United States. Besides, he was done with his cubist period and had moved on. He wouldn't do it.

"Father found a talented young painter who had experimented with cubism, and told him what he wanted. His name was Paul Jacobs. Jacobs wasn't afraid to copy Rivera's style, but it was his idea to angle the painting up and onto the ceiling. *The Architect* became my father at work.

"Jacobs didn't survive the war. World War II. This mural is considered to be his only significant work, and my father was very proud of it. But what I think he enjoyed most was the fact that he wound up looking down at everybody in the room. I'd have sold it if I could."

When the two men returned to the dining room, Eastman was moving so slowly that Alphaios was tempted to take his arm. He made it without assistance, though, and eased himself down to his chair.

"After the art and furniture, it was accessories—the rest of the lamps and some vases. Then the drapes and curtains went, hardware and all. Then dishes and the kitchen utensils. The furniture from the servants' quarters. That's when Mrs. Dickens left. She was the last of the staff. Said she'd had enough, wouldn't sleep on the floor. The light fixtures and wall sconces and some stained glass screens went to a restoration company. Ironic, isn't it? Here I was dismantling my father's masterpiece and selling its parts so that lesser buildings could be restored. Now there's nothing left but the paint on the walls and the marble in the floors. I can't pry it loose."

"Wouldn't your leaving be worth something to the owners? Enough to live on somewhere else?"

Mr. Eastman smirked. "So, the big city's taught the innocent monk a nasty fact of life. Truth is, their most recent offer was well over a million. Not a chance. They can wait me out."

He looked at Alphaios, then down at his hands, limp now. "OK, monk, the parable's over. You satisfied now? Go. Please, let me be."

Alphaios sat for a long moment. Then he nodded soberly and stood.

"And take that chair back downstairs to Wilson. If you don't, I'm likely to sell it tomorrow."

"Good day, Bernard Eastman." He put the chair under his arm and let himself out.

Alphaios was late getting back to the monastery that afternoon. He slipped through the door and went directly to his cell. To the extent he could tell, no one had seen him arrive.

He sighed in relief, moved his chair closer to the window though there was only wan light, and sat down to await vespers.

Three days later, Alphaios went to see Mr. Eastman again, but Wilson wouldn't let him on the elevator. He said Eastman had left instructions not to admit the monk ever again. Alphaios gave Wilson the sack of groceries he was carrying, and asked him to deliver it.

Another week passed before he went by the art deco building again. It was late afternoon on an already dark day. When he looked up at the fifth floor, bright lights were shining from every room. Workmen in painters' whites moved up and down ladders, applying new colors to the old walls.

The fifth floor had a new tenant.

CHAPTER 15

I T WAS A VEXING PROBLEM.

Alphaios stood at his worktable, a six-hundred-year-old bifolium in front of him. It was odd seeing one completely ruined page right next to one that was completely intact. But because of the way quires were constructed, the right and left sides of the bifolium did not actually face each other.

Across the top gutter-corner of the page on the left was an indigo border surrounding rich malachite and lush fuchsia. The rest of the page was left in smears.

It was Jeremiah's work. Jeremiah had not only been the most talented artist to work on the book, but the most adventuresome, the one most likely to take chances, to stretch religious convention or, with a stroke of his brush, snub some character or Church dictum. He was the most unpredictable, audacious illuminator Alphaios had ever encountered.

This complicated an already difficult problem. Somehow, this page needed to be recreated with historical accuracy. Fortunately, the text in the rest of the quire was known. It was from Psalm 44 in the Hours of the Virgin.

Given the size and spacing of script throughout the rest of the psalm, he and Inaki had been able to determine that there was considerably more room on the three contiguous damaged pages than would be necessary for the missing portion of text. So the question had arisen as to whether there had been text on all three pages with significant illumination on each, or text on only two, leaving the entire third page for a painting or paintings. If the latter were the case, the devotion of a whole page to one illumination meant its subject would have had particular importance to the patron. What was it?

As if determining the subject of the page weren't difficult enough, Alphaios wondered how Jeremiah would have treated it. He already knew it would be different from anything found in any book of hours before or after.

It wasn't the first difficult hurdle they'd faced, and wouldn't be the last, but these three pages had thus far stumped him, Inaki, and the entire membership of the commission of experts. Three months ago, Inaki had sent out a worldwide call to libraries and medieval scholars asking for any period reference to a book of hours such as they had before them. They had very nearly given up hope of assistance. Then, just yesterday, Inaki had left word that one possibly relevant response had been received. Alphaios was waiting for him now.

Some thirty minutes later, the archivist hurried into the scriptorium, his face and eyes alight. He was carrying a thin file folder and a rolled document of some kind.

"Got something that might help," he said. "A letter and photograph from a music professor on sabbatical. He's in a town called Uncastillo. Northern Spain. He's conducting research for a book on medieval songs and minstrels. Says my query tickled his memory. He went back through some manuscripts and finally came up with this." He pulled out a photograph. "It's a picture of a page from a journal. The professor says the last dated entry in the manuscript was 1448. He sent it in electronic format, so last night I had it blown up." With that, he unrolled a poster-sized version of the same photograph.

Alphaios placed the damaged bifolium back in its drawer, then spread out the large photograph on his worktable and placed small blocks of wood on its corners.

It was a good photo, taken in natural light. There was no glare, and a ruler had been placed next to the book to identify its dimensions; the professor had known what he was doing. There were indications of cracking on the edges of the page, and though the ink had faded somewhat, it was easily readable. It was in Latin.

The writing had a spontaneous rather than formal or edited feel, consistent with a journal. In it, the writer made reference to a very large, lavish book of hours he had recently encountered; he didn't say where. He was critical of the extravagant show of wealth the book represented, but that was not what had wound him up into a holy screed. The subject of his wrath was one extraordinary illumination, one that covered an entire page. He reported that a person in a royal retinue had one eye closed—winking, he howled—just as the king, queen and other members of a royal court bowed low before a pope and his cardinals. The writer, whose position was abundantly clear that sovereignty belonged to the pope alone, believed the wink to be forthright evidence that the obeisance was contrived. The book's unnamed patron drew the writer's ire for this heresy.

Indignation had apparently not affected his appetite, however, for at the end of the entry was the following note: "Supped on an excellent meat soup under the sign of a horned ibex."

Alphaios leaned back from the table, intrigued. Jeremiah was not beyond playing such a game, but there was not yet enough information.

"The painting described would be unusual for this text," Inaki said, "but it's not beyond the realm of possibility. Perhaps they did choose what's known as the royal psalm to make a point about fealty to the Church—or the lack of it."

Alphaios felt a prickle of electricity. On more than one page, he'd seen Jeremiah indulge in a twist of, or a poke at, some code or precept. Why not a wink? But he needed to know more. "First, do we know of any other manuscript with such a depiction? Any other reference to a wink?"

"I don't," Inaki said. "I'll put the question to the commission. If such a painting were known at the time, it might well have been combustive."

That was true. The question of whether ultimate sovereignty rested with the head of state or with the Church had been more than philosophical. It had been the cause of outright war between kings and popes, let alone the subject of long diplomacy. Alphaios frowned. "Which royal family could it have been? If we knew that, it would not only provide an important clue as to the origin of the book, but could put further light on the consequences of such a picture—perhaps even a reason for keeping it hidden."

Inaki studied the blowup again. "Let's say the scholars were right, and the book was created in the first decade of the 1400s. How many possibilities are there? If the royalty were French, it could have been Charles VI—he was known as Charles the Mad—or any number of major or minor nobles. If it were Spanish, maybe Charles III of Navarre or Martin I of Aragon or others. But if you open the time window beyond just that one decade . . ." He shook his head. "The problem grows even greater. Too bad we don't have a coat of arms or other details."

Alphaios gave him a small smile. "You know your kings."

Inaki shrugged. "They were all adventurous, and they all touched Basque history some way or another."

"And they all had their own quarrels with the Church," Alphaios said. "Don't forget the Church was feuding within it-self. This is right in the middle of the Western Schism. There were Roman popes and Avignon popes and even ones chosen by a council in Pisa, all claiming the Throne of Peter. Arguments about legitimacy were heated and personal, not to mention competition for tithes and taxes. Fealty must have been a very difficult challenge for people of faith. Tenuous, and dangerous."

"All good points. Unfortunately, they don't make our job any easier."

Alphaios thought for a moment. "If this painting really were in our book of hours, could it have had anything to do with Cervini's acquiring it and then taking it for his own private chapel? Was this something more for him than just a particularly beautiful book? If there really were a wink in such a scene, could that have been significant to him?"

"And could it tell us anything about why or how the book disappeared when he died?"

The men looked at each other. The mystery was deepening before their very eyes.

"We're getting ahead of ourselves," the archivist said. "First, we need to go back out to the academic world with this information. If such a painting is known to exist elsewhere, the entry is probably not about our book."

"What's a horned ibex?"

"A kind of goat, I think. I'll have to find out."

"Are there other references in the journal that could be helpful?"

"The professor says not."

"His field's music, Inaki. We need to send someone else to examine the journal, and any other documents that might be there. Perhaps you. Even if there isn't any more about this particular page, the account of his travels might provide more information. Where is this Uncastillo?"

"Near Pamplona, in northern Spain. On the edge of what we consider the Basque country." Inaki rolled up the photograph and prepared to leave. "I'll call Cardinal Ricci's office and propose a trip. Meanwhile, let's continue work on what we know."

Just before the archivist left the room, Alphaios called after him, "Inaki, Jeremiah is capable of this."

Inaki nodded thoughtfully, then closed the door behind him.

Alphaios withdrew the ruined page from its drawer and gazed at it again. With a penknife, he took small scrapings of the smeared paint and placed them in glassine envelopes for analysis, labeling each one with its place on the page. Knowing the minerals and plants used to form the original paint would help him decide what colors, hues and densities to mix. He could see a very rich palette.

He would not wait for confirmation. He knew in his heart this page could only be Jeremiah's work. In his mind, he began to sketch the painting so briefly described by an itinerant critic some five and a half centuries earlier.

CHAPTER 16

ALPHAIOS LEFT THE MONASTERY unsettled. Following lunch, he'd overheard Simon make an aside to another monk, wondering aloud what late hour he would choose to return today. It was at the least ungracious of Simon, and were Alphaios not of a generous nature, he might have called it snide. As troubling as the remark, though, was who had made it.

It was apparent that several other monks also disliked the petty nature of Simon's complaints at chapter, all of which were veiled in piety. Alphaios wished to stay out of the fray, and had not forgotten his encounters with Simon and Levi over Mad Old George and then the accident.

Usually the prior succeeded in deflecting Simon's grievances, but where there was a kernel of truth he couldn't ignore, he might find it necessary to allow discussion of some constraint on Alphaios, or even censure. He would have to be more careful.

The thought of restrictions on his work or exploration of the city and its inhabitants turned his stomach over.

Though it was a warm and sunlit Saturday, he was still troubled when he climbed the steps to the private library and let himself in. He went straight to the scriptorium.

He saw it instantly. A new scribe that Kenny was assigned to train had left a bifolium on his writing table, uncovered and exposed. Worse, the corner of a magazine lay across it. This was an egregious breach of protocol. When not being worked upon, the vellum was to be kept in the flat drawers provided for that purpose. And nothing, nothing but writing utensils and ink was to be near the desk when parchment was on it. Accidents could occur too easily, pages spoiled. He'd seen it happen more than once.

XM was in the workroom, absorbed in a page of text, headphones on. Alphaios spoke his name, but to get his attention had to touch his shoulder. He asked him to put the offending bifolium away. A moment later, XM called him over. The magazine, its cover apparently damp, had leached a triangle of pale blue into the parchment. It had ruined a nearly completed bifolium.

Alphaios was furious. "Has Inaki been in today?"

"Haven't seen him, man. Could be upstairs."

Brother Alphaios strode to his own worktable and returned. He took his largest brush and slashed a great curve of black paint up and across the vellum. "Leave it where it is."

It was rare for Alphaios to be so distracted that he couldn't work, but today he knew his attention would not be complete.

He did not want to make a costly error himself. Instead of returning to his own table, he went to his mixing room, sat down on the floor and leaned his back against the wall. Never since the project started had he been so upset. Perhaps by breathing in the air surrounding the tools of his trade he could regain his equanimity.

Sometime later, he lifted himself up and returned to the scriptorium. The new scribe sat on his stool, his elbows on the table and his face in his hands. Alphaios went to him, his anger spent but not his purpose. He stood beside the man, who did not look up.

Alphaios leaned down and spoke into his ear. "Your name is Christopher?"

"Chris." It came out reluctantly, a whisper.

"Christopher. This book requires your respect. Even your love. This will be the most important work you will do in your lifetime. Do not believe you can treat it lightly. Give me the bifolium."

His eyes red, Christopher watched him take the parchment and feed it to the dragon. He turned back to his worktable and hid his face once again.

Alphaios left the library. He went down the stairs and turned toward home, his mood dark. There would be no espresso today. He would be home early, and for today at least, Brother Simon would win their silent struggle.

He walked only a few blocks before the city recaptured him.

As he came alongside a restaurant called the Green River Bar and Grill, a woman was climbing up a ladder and out of a deep trench in the street. He'd seen her several times before on the sidewalk but never talked to her. Today she had a shovel in hand and was laughing with the men around her. When she was out of the hole, she took off a yellow hardhat that said "Herb" and tossed it to a burly man standing nearby. Her arms and hands were covered with dirt, but she gave no sign she minded in the least.

She wore a washed-out plaid shirt, sleeves torn off at the shoulders, showing muscle and sinew. The tattoo on her shoulder was an old one, faded. The shirt was buttoned over breasts that were generous but neither bound nor proud. She wore scuffed cowboy boots and a belt on her jeans with an oversized silver buckle. He couldn't tell if she knew the street crew personally, but she fit in with them comfortably; she seemed to know their moves, their rhythms, their language.

He was startled to hear himself addressed. "Well, hell, what's with the dress, bro?" It came from one of the men along with a gruff laugh—Bud, according to his hat.

"Barber scare you away?" the man called Herb said.

A third man said, "'Cha use that rope for, man? You like it bein' tied up?"

It was not unusual for Alphaios to be the butt of such remarks, but monastic life had never taught him how to respond. Blushing with discomfort not at what had been said but his inability to counter it, he walked on.

"Sorry 'bout that." It was the woman, striding up behind him. "C'mon, I'll buy you a cup of coffee. Seen you around, and kind of wondered about you myself." She was as tall as him, five-nine. Her dishwater blonde hair was tied into a short, unruly ponytail. The bloom of her youth was gone, though the lines at her eyes and mouth looked like they came not from age but exposure to the elements. She carried herself with an easy confidence.

Alphaios had not had a good day. He was about to decline her offer when he remembered the alternative—getting back to the monastery early and raising Brother Simon's sense of influence among the other monks.

"Coffee sounds good." He followed her into the Green River Bar and Grill.

She showed him to a table at the front window. From here, she said, she could talk and still watch the street crew. It was quiet in the room after the curious sound of a slide guitar slid away, bringing the song on the speakers to an end. She went behind to the bar and wiped her hands and arms with a towel. "Business'll pick up in an hour or so. This is my time." She smiled at his quizzical look. "This is my place. Got it when I came back from Wyoming."

She turned to the man behind the bar. "Put it on, Jack, and bring us some coffee." A moment later a rich operatic baritone came through speakers, followed by a tenor and baritone in duet. Puccini, he guessed, but didn't say so.

She settled in across from him. "Bizet. So, what about it?"

"What about what?"

"What's with the dress?"

He blushed again, but her gaze was friendly.

"I'm a monk. My name is Brother Alphaios."

"I'm Jess. Howdy. So where're you from, Al?"

"St. Ambrose Monastery, over on Broad Street."

"OK, but originally."

"Greece."

She was quiet for a moment. "Keeps the jockey box cool, huh?"

"What?"

"The dress. Keeps it cool."

"We call it a habit."

"I thought nuns wore habits."

"Monks too. Some priests call theirs cassocks, but theirs are black. Only kids and men in hardhats call it a dress. Still, there is the occasional chill."

She laughed.

The man from behind the bar set two coffees on the table. Thick, white ceramic mugs. No frills. It wasn't espresso, but it was strong and hot. He sweetened it.

"It's fresh, most every day this time," she said. "Why?"

She'd lost him. It didn't help that when she picked up her cup, he could see the last three fingers of her right hand were missing.

"Oh, the habit. We take a vow to avoid material distractions that would interfere with our spiritual life. We've avoided modern styles for some eight hundred years now."

She grinned at him, so he went on. "And tradition. We're bound by it. Tradition is hewn into our food, the schedule of our days, how we dress, the way we say our prayers. It's sewn into our very souls. We expect it. No, we depend on it. God save the monk who seeks to change our ways." He was enjoying himself now. "Fifty, sixty years ago, fountain pens were in common use. One of the most contentious debates ever in a chapter meeting, I'm told, was whether ballpoint pens should be allowed."

Jess shook her head in disbelief.

"It's true. Seems there were those who thought ballpoint pens akin to heresy. They represented the easy life, convenience in a mortal world where discomfort is saintly. Now ask me if we have computers."

She laughed again. "You wouldn't in Wyoming."

"Sorry, wouldn't what?"

"Wear that dress. Too windy. Coldest place on God's green earth, far as I'm concerned. Give you hypothermia."

Alphaios felt redness creeping up his face again, but this time succumbed to a laugh. They were silent for a moment or two. While Jess watched the workers in the street, Alphaios looked around the room. No urban chic here. The café was furnished for comfort and conversation. There were round, dark wooden tables and chairs, good light, pressed-tin ceiling, wooden plank floor, ceiling fans turning lazily and a wooden screen door at the entrance. A number of large paintings, all handsomely framed, dressed the walls.

He took the opportunity to get up and look at them more closely: representations of vast plains and rough, barren landscapes without definite horizons. Earth and sky. Weather was distant, or mid-distant, or upon you. A winter blizzard, the snow driving sideways and piling up against a half-dozen bony, huddled cattle. Rugged, snow-topped mountains, but far away. Few signs of human habitation. One exception depicted a broken-down, faded pink camping trailer in the foreground, incongruous yet insignificant against an endless brown hardscrabble and a deep blue, cumulus-loaded sky.

The paintings represented an impressive array of talent and had been thoughtfully collected. They were not of conventional beauty, but there was undeniable attraction in them. Present in them as well was a sense of danger, or hazard, or warning. These were not peaceful pictures.

Above the bar was a large, old-fashioned picture of a reclining nude. The figure in it was clearly past her prime. Somebody had pinned up a handwritten sign under the painting. It said, "Hey, Sally!"

The music ended, and was replaced by a rich contralto. He returned to his seat. "Bizet?"

"Puccini." He heard amusement in her voice.

"So what were you doing down in the trench?"

"Needed a workout. Those guys were nice enough to let me get down there and throw some dirt around. Oil."

He wasn't keeping up with her. "Oil?"

"Oil. Oil fields. That's what I did in Wyoming."

Alphaios didn't know much about the geography of the United States but took a guess. "Green River. The Green River is in Wyoming?"

"Green River the river, and Green River the town. And a lot of nowhere."

"What kind of work?"

"Rigging. Steel work, anything but altitude."

"I don't understand."

"I didn't do high steel anymore."

"Oh. Are you from Wyoming?"

She shook her head and pointed her thumb back over her shoulder. The strange outline of her hand again caught Alphaios's attention. "Across the river. That's where I grew up. Blue collar. Dad was a pipe fitter. Must have gotten to know every steam pipe in the city before he was killed. Got my love of opera from him. Mom was a dress-store clerk till the store went bust."

"What happened to your father? Was it recent?"

She shook her head. "Long time ago. I was twenty, twenty-one. Crane cable slipped, dropped a pipe. Hurt him bad. He lived awhile. Shouldn't have, they couldn't stop the pain. Mom remarried. OK guy, has a pension."

"What did you do?"

"Joined the ironworkers' union." She tapped her belt buckle with her damaged hand. "I wanted to do high steel. Skyscrapers. I wanted the adrenaline and I wanted the bragging rights. I got my wish." This last was said with a bite—disgust, maybe, or anger.

"Twelve years doing high steel. Like every other steel jockey, I could take you around town and say, I did this building, I built that one." She took a drink of coffee. "One day I was up with a new guy. He screwed up with a thirty-foot beam. Let it swing around and clip me on the side of the head. Knocked me flat out. Caught my foot in an angle, and woke up hangin' upside down in my harness, forty-three stories up. My leg was killing me. The guy'd panicked, left me there. Wind was blowin' me around. Took twenty minutes for my foreman to get to me. What's with the hole in your hair?"

She grinned at his confusion. "The shaved part."

Alphaios reached up and rubbed the shaved circle of scalp surrounded by his curly brown hair. "It's a tonsure. It's not required anymore, but I wear it to keep myself humble. Lord knows I need the reminder." He also knew if he were to let his hair grow out after all these years, he would have to face some questions from his fellow monks he was not ready to confront.

"Reminder of what? What's it mean?"

"It's a holdover from early times. I told you we're slow to change. They say that for Romans and Greeks, a shaved head was a sign of slavery. So some priests and monks began shaving their heads to show their subservience to God. It became a rite before they could receive holy orders. I can tell you what I'd have to do in Wyoming."

"What's that?"

"There was a time when a tonsure had to be at least the size of a priest's host— the size of the bread he used during mass. You know the little white skull cap you see the pope wear?"

"I guess so . . ."

"Cardinals wear them, too. Red ones. They're called *zuchetti*. You'll see them on bishops, too. At first they were made to keep their shaved heads warm in drafty churches.

They've stayed around even though they don't do tonsures anymore. Anyway, in your Wyoming, it sounds like a *zuchetti* would be a good idea."

She laughed. "A skull cap. A fur skull cap."

"What happened up there?"

It was her turn to show confusion for a second. "Oh. Broke my leg, but the worst of it was it ruined me for working high. Couldn't face going up again. That wasn't all. The guy that screwed up was the son of a union boss. I tried to get his card pulled, but nobody listened. But I heard he never went up again, either. Got a job at union headquarters instead."

She glanced out the window, upwards. "When you're up there, high, there's just you and the other guys. You got their backs, they got yours. Except he didn't, he left me hanging. Twelve years of dues, meetings and singin' the songs. Turned out the union didn't have my back, either."

"What did you do?"

"Drove cabs for a while. Then decided to do something different, see the world. Heard there were jobs out west. Hooked up with a drilling outfit in Wyoming."

"How did you get back here?"

"Ten years of lovin' hard and leavin' easy." She paused to let her words sink in, then grinned widely at Alphaios's consternation. "Nah, not that. Ten years of workin' hard and livin' skimpy. That and this." She held up her partial hand. "On-the-job injury. Couldn't do steel anymore. Got me a settlement and came home."

"What happened?"

"It was wintertime. Night. Cold, maybe 40 below, wind howling like a banshee through the rigging. The derrick started to tip. Would've lost 600 feet of pipe and drill bit if it went over. Got a D-6—that's a Cat, a tractor—in place to anchor it. Lost a glove, but still had to hogtie a frozen cable." She held up her hand. "The derrick got saved, but it cost me some fingers. Frostbite. Here I am."

"Tell me about the paintings."

Jess leaned back in her chair, serious. "Been collecting them for years. Wyoming is space. Land and sky. Plains and wind. Friendly, yet inhospitable. Seductive but dangerous. Bitter cold and blankets of spring wildflowers. Antelopes and wolves. Cattle starving because ranchers can't get through the snow to feed them. There's an edge to life out there, and it's closer than it looks. The artists who painted these pictures, they saw it, too."

She took a drink of coffee. "Wyoming's big oil. And kids living in forty-year-old trailers without plumbing sixty miles from the nearest school, their dads trying to figure out how to cash in. They won't." She paused to take a breath. "Now these paintings are my high steel."

Alphaios was quiet for a moment, letting her comment settle in.

The front door opened and a group of men filed into the room. The wooden screen door slapped closed behind them, and Jess stood up. "Business calls."

"It's time for me to go, too. Thanks for the coffee."

Jess said a friendly goodbye and picked up the cups to take back to the bar. Alphaios let himself out the door. He was a few yards down the sidewalk when she called after him. "Hey, Al, what's it with that rope?"

He waved a hand in the air, grinned, and headed back to the monastery.

CHAPTER 17

H IS ASSIGNMENT as the kitchen assistant had become quite satisfactory for both Brother John and Alphaios. It was not an adventurous kitchen, for it was bound by a tradition as colorless as the stained glass in the church. They had quickly reached a place of easy comfort, but did not speak much beyond what was necessary to get the work done. It was the rule of simple silence.

It had not taken long, either, for Alphaios's coffee to become a kind of pact between them, a Sunday-morning understanding. No one else came into the kitchen between meals, and they kept the rich aroma far from the doorway. It was not that they wouldn't be happy to share their enjoyment, but if anybody were to find it out, this small pleasure would be unceremoniously terminated.

On this Thursday morning Alphaios felt unusually alive, as happens on certain days when winter turns to spring and summer turns to fall. John seemed to feel it too, for he had been singing to himself. It was after the morning angelus, and Alphaios was kneading dough for bread when an idea occurred to him. "John, did you notice the brothers seem a bit more cheerful this morning?"

"Seems like we all do. Why?"

"How would you like a small adventure?"

John turned suspicious. "What do you mean?"

"You know how it is when the air is fresh, like it is today? Even the food tastes better?"

"Well, yes, I guess so."

"What if we were to help it along a bit?"

"Just what do you have in mind, Brother?"

"Let's say we add some olive oil and rosemary to the bread. Just enough for a hint of flavor."

John drew back, discomfited. "Where'd you learn that?"

"In Italy. Where bread is a gift from God and consumed with the whole spirit."

"I don't think so. This isn't Italy, and it'd cause trouble. The brothers don't like surprises. You got your own taste of that at chapter, didn't you?"

"We'll be subtle. They won't quite know what's different. They'll just think it's the new spring day."

John looked intently at Alphaios, then slowly nodded. "Let's give it a try. But just enough for the noon meal."

Alphaios haggled contentedly with John over small measures of the seasonings, he lobbying for more, the kitchener for less. When finally they agreed, Alphaios added them to the noon bread and let the dough rise. When it went into the big ovens, a delicious fragrance wafted through the kitchen. It captivated John, but alarmed him as well; he fidgeted all the way through the meal service.

Several monks looked at the bread wonderingly, but the rule of silence prevented them from commenting. Tradition also prevented requests for second helpings.

It was hard for Alphaios to decide whether John was more relieved or more disappointed at the lack of response. In fact, there were no comments at all until chapter meeting the next morning, when Philemon spoke up. "Brother John, I don't want to seem unkind, but the bread at supper last night, and again this morning, was unusually bland. Have you run out of some essential ingredient?" Several monks nodded and mumbled their agreement, Brother Simon among them.

John sat a bit taller than usual. "No, my brother, no missing ingredients. But perhaps I can take greater care in the future."

In the face of this criticism, for reasons opaque to all his brothers but one, Brother John grinned throughout the rest of the meeting. Alphaios relaxed and savored the moment, happy for his friend and wondering what they could do next.

CHAPTER 18

THE NEWSSTAND SAT stolidly on the sidewalk, seemingly as permanent as the steel and glass high-rises around it. As Alphaios approached, a small dark man in a rough blue pea coat and featureless gray cap burst from it, banging back a door made invisible by hanging magazines. Muttering aloud, he marched up behind a man in a long dress coat and scarf and yanked a newspaper from under his arm. The second man turned suddenly in protest, but made none when he saw the little man stalk back to the stand and slap the newspaper back on its stack. The vendor gave a disgusted upward wave of his arm and disappeared behind the hidden door.

The moment of action over, the newsstand returned to its inert state. Alphaios paused by a lamppost to observe. He hugged his arms to his chest; it was cold enough to see the transitory clouds both of acrid automobile exhaust and his own breath. It was a busy corner, and added to the usual roar of engines and screech of worn brakes were jackhammers tearing at concrete.

In a moment, the gray cap appeared in the small window at the center of what must be a simple shed. An avalanche of primary colors, beautiful faces and headlines barking sex and diets and atrocities overtook the little window, rendering it tiny and dark. Looking at the man inside was like sighting backward through a camera's viewfinder.

Did the man hear the constant noise? Did he immerse himself in racing forms? Or, with all the newspapers surrounding him, was he conversant with world events, history, science? How could he maintain vigilance over his domain from inside a tiny shed smaller than a monk's cell? How did he live his life?

The man started waving his arms and yelling in anger. It took Alphaios a moment to realize the ire was directed at him, that the man wanted him to move on, to go away. He waved in submission and brought his old coat closer around him against the wind. He continued toward the library, thought of Jess and spent a moment in the sin of envy toward ordinary men who wear pants in cold weather.

When he climbed the steps to the private library and opened the door, he welcomed its encompassing warmth.

Today's page was relatively plain, at least from an illuminator's point of view. It had a few blue diamonds spaced among the words, but no figures and only one decorated versal. This was a long and flourished P with a tail that ran all the way down the left margin in ruby, indigo and yellow—pigment, not gold leaf. At the bottom of the page, it swept under the last line of text. Otherwise, the letter was unadorned: it was neither inhabited in its open space by some portrait nor historiated with a picture telling some story.

Zephaniah had decorated this page, Zephaniah of the steady hand and long clean lines. Alphaios would complete copying it today and was confident it would survive Inaki's critical eye. He prepared his paints, selected a fine red sable brush and bent over the parchment.

While he was still at work, Inaki came into the scriptorium, slipped a note onto the edge of his worktable and left. It asked Alphaios to come upstairs to his office when he could.

When he finished the illumination, Alphaios slid the parchment into its slender drawer and climbed the stairs to the archivist's office. As always, every available surface was occupied by books and papers. He lifted an awkward pile of documents from a chair, found one of the shorter, less precarious stacks to place it on, and sat down. Tacked to the wall above Inaki was the large photo of the journal entry they had received from Uncastillo. The royal wink.

Inaki waited for him to get situated. "Well, my friend, we have some news from the Vatican. Turns out Marcello Cervini did make a journey along the Way of St. James. In 1552. But from the number of books he took back to Rome with him, it may have been as much a business trip as a pilgrimage."

What kind of journey was Alphaios himself on? He had a discomforting sense that his original purpose for coming to this city—though it was at Cardinal Ricci's instruction—had become something greater and far more personal.

He turned his attention back to the archivist. "So there's news of our book?"

"None whatsoever." Inaki paused to let his answer sink in. "But that's what makes this so interesting. Among the forty-five manuscripts he brought back, there's no record of any book like ours."

Alphaios frowned. "How's that helpful? It sounds quite the opposite."

"His route to Compostela was known then as the el Camino Aragonés—the Aragón Road. Still is. It comes south from France through the Pyrenees and then turns west at a town called Jaca. From there, it's not a singular road—there are many side trips, even parallel routes, depending on which churches or shrines pilgrims wish to visit. For instance, there was, still is, a north and a south route through the Ebro River Valley.

He lifted an open atlas from the top of his desk, then set it down again. "It's a long pilgrimage, almost six hundred miles just from the French border to Santiago. Coming from Rome, or even from some intermediate starting point in northern Italy, say Trent, Cervini would have traveled weeks even before entering Spain. He was carrying either large sums of money or the considerable credit and goodwill of the Church. Probably both. He acquired the forty-five books before his return to Vatican City. That's nearly a tenth of all the books he collected in his entire six years as Librarian."

Inaki paused to see if his audience was still with him. Alphaios rewarded him with his head tipped to one side and a frown of confusion.

"According to our friends at the Vatican, there are receipts for forty-four of the books. The forty-fifth had no documentation at all—nothing about what was paid for it or to whom or when. Or if it were a gift, from whom. Seems it was only discovered by the library and then catalogued when Marcellus took it to his papal chapel." Inaki let the mystery hang for a moment. "Anyway, one of the more popular pilgrim stations on the north side of the Aragon Road was the Abbey of San Salvador of Leyre. According to the records, no books were purchased there." He paused as if finished.

This last declarative statement seemed to bear special meaning for the archivist. Alphaios raised his eyebrows but said nothing; he could be patient while Inaki spun his tale. He did not have long to wait.

"Bear with me here, Alphaios. This is my homeland, and its history is my area of study. Last night I went back over some old notes. The Abbey of Leyre is one of the oldest in Spain and considered one of the most significant. It was begun in the ninth century under the Order of Cluny, and it's still there. It accumulated huge wealth and influence over the next several centuries, and at its apex controlled seventy-two properties: towns, forests, farms, priories. It became the cultural heart of Navarre, and a number of kings are buried there. Of most interest to us, though, is that it was known for its extensive collection of manuscripts. As numerous as its holdings were, and given its mission to provide religious guidance, it almost certainly had a scriptorium."

Alphaios listened, his eyes on his friend and nodding his head slightly, but waiting for something more substantive.

"You remember Uncastillo, the little town where our traveler's journal was found? There's a small monastery there, used to be one of the abbey's properties. It's not far from Leyre, a walk of a couple of days. They're both in the lower foothills of the Pyrenees. Now, about the ibex, the journal entry. It's a type of wild goat with long horns that rise from its head, then sweep back almost horizontally. It's extinct now, at least the Pyrenean strain. But it would have been common throughout the region in the fifteenth century."

Inaki turned sideways and rested an elbow on a book. "Oh, I should mention that in the 1200s there was a struggle for control of the abbey between Cluniac Benedictines and the Cistercians—it went on for seventy years before the Cistercians finally won." He paused. "It seems there was no peace anywhere, not even in cloister."

Alphaios nodded. "So it would seem."

"At the beginning of the fifteenth century, the king of Navarre's court was in Olite. That's just thirty miles from the abbey at Leyre, and about twenty-five from Uncastillo. All within easy travel distance."

Alphaios held up his hands. "Where's this going, Inaki? I'm lost."

The archivist lifted a bottle of water from his desk. As he took a drink, he raised his eyebrows. "You were talking about the Western Schism, so I checked. I've learned King Charles III of Navarre was a strong supporter of the Avignon popes. His neighboring king in Aragon, though, supported the Roman popes. If Charles or someone from Navarre were the patron, then it would seem likely—"

"That our book would be of the 'use of Paris,'" Alphaios said, "as in fact it is, rather than the 'use of Rome.' But, my friend, there's more than one fault with your reasoning. Just because kings took sides doesn't mean that monastic orders like the Cistercians would simply follow suit. In fact, they'd have exercised far more independence from both Rome and Avignon than either of the papal camps would have liked. In any case, either use would have been acceptable to them. And if our book were commissioned, it's most likely that the wishes of the patron, not the scriptorium, would dictate it."

"Even if the king of Navarre had a personal interest?"

"Even then. Perhaps especially then. Rome itself is more tractable to outside influences than monastic orders are. It's in their charters, it's in their blood." He smiled wryly at his colleague. "I can tell you with some authority that imperviousness to the outside world is a trait that continues even today."

"All right," Inaki said, "we can agree there was a wealthy patron for our book, probably a secular one. We've concluded this based on its enormous cost. And we've agreed that because its illuminators are otherwise unknown, it was very likely created in a monastery."

Alphaios nodded. "And your new information lends support to the premise of a secular patron—if indeed it turns out the book was made at Leyre. Had the abbey remained Benedictine through the fourteenth century and into the fifteenth, I'd have to argue it was made by the monks for their own use. But the Cistercians lived a far more austere life. It's very unlikely they'd spend such sums for their own glorification. If the book were created at a Cistercian abbey at Leyre as you are trying to reason, it would support the theory that an outside patron was involved. If they had a scriptorium, such a rich commission would have been welcome, but only for the support of their mission."

He shifted in his chair and caught in midair a sheaf of papers he'd dislodged from the table. "But let's go back for a minute, Inaki. All of this is based on a record that indicates Cervini did not buy our book—or any books at all—at Leyre. Yet you argue that it must therefore be from Leyre."

"You got it." Inaki waggled a thumb toward the wall behind him. "That, and the wink in the journal."

"Ah, and an inn with the sign of an ibex that served meat soup. There must have been scores of them along the Pyrenees." Alphaios sat quietly for a moment. It was his turn to think out loud. "You know, don't you, there was already an illuminated book of hours purchased by Charles III? In 1405. It's known as *The Hours of Charles the Noble*."

Inaki visibly deflated. "But the patron wouldn't have had to be Charles, just someone quite wealthy."

"I've had the chance to study photographs of it," Alphaios said. "It's beautiful, and justifiably famous. It's earned its place in history."

Inaki nodded. "I could make a pretty strong case that Charles III was a pre-Renaissance man. He was a bright light for his people, my people, and highly accomplished. He built canals, set about making the rivers around Pamplona navigable, and began to rebuild the Cathedral of Pamplona after it collapsed in 1391. He even removed taxation on poor Jews so they could survive and contribute their skills to society—one of the few royals in Spain to do so. He admired French royalty for their interest in the arts, and became something of a patron in his own right. He rebuilt an old fortification in Olite to serve as his palace, and filled it with gardens and music. He's still well-regarded in the Basque country today."

Alphaios rubbed his forehead. "So then, let's turn our reasoning around a bit. Notwithstanding its fame today, would such a king think his purchase of a small book of hours in Paris, though notable, was adequate to his ambitions? A great achievement, as he might think of it? As beautiful as it is, his *Hours* was assembled for him by a bookseller. Its text was subcontracted out to numerous scribes, and its illuminations to trade painters— six of them, if I'm not mistaken. They did include, notably, the Master of Brussels' initials. It was an expensive book, to be sure, and Charles had his family crest pictured throughout it."

Inaki raised a finger. "But . . ."

"Exactly. It's nowhere near as remarkable as our book of hours. Its size is rather common, some five by eight inches, more for personal use—small and portable. By contrast, our book's place is on a lectern, clearly designed to be shown to the world." He paused and reflected. "But the world never got a chance to see it."

"Apparently it was hidden or lost from its very birth," Inaki said. "But if you're going where I think you are, there isn't any heraldry in it at all."

"*Très Riches Heures du Duc de Berry.*" It came from Alphaios's mind quietly, wonderingly.

It was the archivist's turn to be puzzled. "The famous book of hours that was never finished? Its calendar of the saints is exquisite. The blues are so deep I became lost in them. But why's it relevant here?"

"Lapis lazuli. Inaki, you said Charles admired the enlightened princes of France. Could he have known Jean de Berry—Duke de Berry—who commissioned *Très Riches Heures*?"

"Well, the term 'enlightened' probably carries too much freight for the time. 'Art collectors' would be better. But I suppose he could have. Why not? When he became king, Charles also inherited a French title, albeit a minor one, Count d'Evreux. It'd be likely he'd travel to Paris."

"Charles purchased his book of hours in 1405. Let's suppose for a moment that he knew Jean de Berry, perhaps even visited him. What would he have found there?"

Inaki shrugged. "Lots of fine books and manuscripts, as well as a great deal of other conspicuous wealth."

"And perhaps the Limbourg brothers, who, if memory serves, entered Jean de Berry's service in 1408. They did a number of other pieces for him before starting *Très Riches Heures* in 1412. After visiting Paris and the duke, might Charles have aspired higher? Would he conceive his own great book? He might have, Inaki, he might indeed."

Inaki looked at Alphaios with astonishment.

Alphaios stopped short and threw his hands wide. "But obviously we don't have enough information."

After a long quiet between them, wondering what was possible, he met the archivist's eyes. "So, when do you leave for Uncastillo?"

Inaki grinned. "Tuesday. I'll be gone for a month."

"Find out all you can about this monarch when you're there. And this abbey of yours at Leyre."

He left the stack of documents where he'd set it and went down the stairs. He let himself out of the library, looked over the street, and turned toward the café. The afternoon had been rich and full, and he still had time to immerse himself in colors and voices before returning to his cell.

CHAPTER 19

MANY DAYS LATER, Alphaios settled happily at his favorite table to watch the city and its inhabitants. Just after his coffee arrived, a man at the next table began blaring into a cell phone; it was one end of some kind of business transaction. He had no interest in it whatsoever, but it imposed itself, unwelcome and unavoidable. He drank his coffee quickly and got up to leave. Nico raised his open palms and shrugged helplessly.

After wandering a bit, he arrived at a small leafy park. The day was warm, the park full of people sunning themselves, reading, or absorbed in games of chess. A pair of lovers lay under a tree, no doubt wishing they were alone and pretending to be. A group of old men played a languid game of bocce. After taking a turn around the park, he found a place on one of the dark green metal benches that circled it. He had half an hour or so before he needed to start back to the monastery.

At the other end of his bench sat a man, perhaps forty years old. A dark suit-jacket was folded over the back of the bench, and his collar and red and white-striped tie had been loosened for comfort. Several black and white pictures on backing boards were arrayed on the ground in front of him, and some lay on the bench to his side. More were stacked on his lap. He leafed through them and then looked outward, as if studying something particular. Alphaios could see they were photographs of buildings and cityscapes. They showed signs of wear; several of them were bent at the corners, and some of the photos were coming loose. There were also several rough sketches of very tall buildings.

After a bit, the man gave a heavy sigh and slumped back against the bench. He let his head roll back and turned his face toward the sky, eyes closed. He sat like that for a few moments, then returned his attention to the picture boards. He didn't seem to be finding what he was looking for.

"Forgive my curiosity, sir, but what are you working on?"

At first the man seemed annoyed, then looked over and took in Alphaios's appearance. He considered for a moment before speaking. "Can you see up that street?" He raised his arm and pointed. "Straight up there, eight blocks. What do you see?"

Alphaios was puzzled, because he couldn't see anything of note. There were some high-rise buildings in the general area, but nothing notable straight ahead. "Nothing. All I see is sky."

"You're right," the man said. "What I'm looking for is the shape of the skyscraper that's going to be built there. Some old warehouses will be torn down, and a building, sixty-five stories tall, give or take, will be built in their place. What'll it look like? That's what I want to know."

"I don't understand. Don't the people building it know what it's going to look like? Doesn't the architect know?"

"They haven't selected one yet. There's a competition for the commission. I want to be that architect." He eyed Alphaios's clothes. "So what are *you* working on?"

Alphaios gave a small smile. "My soul is my primary vocation, and the Lord knows I need to keep practicing at it. I'm a monk. There's a monastery over on Broad where I live. What brings you here? It's a long way from the building site."

"A search for inspiration," the architect said. "But it's really not very far at all. A skyscraper fills a cylinder of space that stretches from under the ground to a place much higher in the sky than it actually occupies. From here, it'll look huge, it'll dominate the skyline."

"These sketches are what you plan to submit?"

The man's mood turned sour. "I hope to God not. Eight months of work and all I can come up with is tired, or has been tried, or is laughably bizarre. I'm worse than a first-year student who walked into the wrong class. Four months to go, and I'm dead in the water. There won't be another competition like this for years."

"Do you know what you're looking for?"

The architect nodded ruefully. "I've got the function down, but not the form. I can tell you what I think I'm looking for: Planes, multiple geometric planes that treat the eye from any vantage point. Visual interest, not only from the viewing deck of the next skyscraper over, or just in the photo taken from across the river. I want the people who walk into it every day, or who dine in the neighborhood that will grow up around it, or who just drive by, to be aware of its presence. I want their eyes to be drawn to it from different places and different approaches, consciously or not. I want it to have a place in their imagination."

"That's a high aspiration."

"This particular competition welcomes innovation. That's rare. Investors are notoriously conservative, scared to death of any design that diverges from already successful structures— which means fully leased out. It would be a disaster if potential occupants didn't like it. But this sponsor wants to open things up, to test architectural vision for the future. That's great. You'll hear every architect you meet argue for greater freedom in design." He raised his index finger into the air, as if speaking to others. "But the greater the freedom, the harder the job. That's because when we enter the competition, we're being challenged to prove our vision, where before we could just boast about it."

The man grabbed his tie and threw it over his shoulder as if were an impediment to his efforts. "I can build conventional, but I'm tired of conventional. A novice can do conventional. But can I build the unconventional? Right now, I can't even see it, let alone sketch it."

"I know I'm keeping you from your work," Alphaios said, "but do you mind if I ask a question?" He went ahead without waiting for consent. "If you look around this city, most of the large buildings are monochromatic. There are various shades of white through grays or browns to black, lots of aluminum and steel, and vast monoliths covered with glass of the same blue or green tints. You don't see brighter colors except on a few domes or entryways or other small design elements, like awnings. I can understand it in poor countries, or where building materials are scarce, or where education is limited. But why aren't more colors, brighter colors, used in architecture here? Humans have used and experimented with color for eons—robes, dresses, ties like yours, makeup, art, rugs, interior design. Why not exterior design? I've seen pictures of buildings that have more color at night than they do during the day. Red or green neon lights, but that seems more like an afterthought. That's marketing, not architecture."

The man looked at Alphaios more closely. "Well, that's not just an idle question. Where'd you get such an interest in architecture?"

"Besides being a monk, I'm a book illuminator. A painter of the art you see in old handmade books. I work with colors nearly every day. I study them, mix them, use them."

"Where could I see some of your work?"

Alphaios smiled. "You might find it if you were to go to the right monasteries and libraries in Italy, but even then they likely wouldn't let you look. And I don't get to sign my name to any of it. You might say I have a very select and somewhat jealous employer. The work I'm doing here won't see the light of day for at least another year. And then it will have a primary audience of one."

"I hope to have—I *have* to have—a much bigger audience than that. I didn't get your name."

"Brother Alphaios. And yours?"

"Robert Peaches." He gave Alphaios a rueful look. "Architect-in-Quandary. OK, color. You'll find it used on some pretty good-sized buildings in Mexico City and other places in Latin and South America. Even some in Europe and the Middle East. They use mostly paint and colored tiles. As for most European and American cities, I suppose it's partly that colored materials haven't proven to stand up to a hundred years or more of exposure to the elements. The sun and weather and smog damage and discolor surfaces over time. So far, the tougher construction materials are in grays, browns and blacks. Ecological damage can occur very quickly when inferior surfaces are used."

Peaches looked around at the nearby buildings. "I suppose it's partly fashion, too. Colors come in and out of style within just a few years. Using them risks obsolescence. Visually, I mean. With very large, very expensive buildings, investors can't afford the risk."

"I understand about the materials," Alphaios said. "Though it seems to me that in the last fifty years or so, alloys, plastics, and other materials I know nothing about must have come a long way. Perhaps it's a case where they'd be more advanced if they were more in demand. As to the vicissitudes of taste, some colors remain compelling throughout generations, even centuries. Colors of the sun and moon, the earth and sky. Water. Fire. Verdant growth. Ruby and malachite . . ."

Alphaios looked up; it was late. "I'm sorry, Mr. Peaches. Though I've just opened the subject, I must go. My brothers will be expecting me. Thanks for tolerating my curiosity." He rose from the bench.

The picture boards on the architect's lap nearly fell to the ground as he abruptly stood up to shake Alphaios's hand. "OK, then. Yes."

Alphaios returned to the monastery, mildly interested in his exchange with the architect. It was pleasant, but not one that would live on in his imagination or distract him during the evening's prayers.

A week later, upon his afternoon return to the monastery, Prior Bartholomew asked to see him. Alphaios had not been returning unusually late from his work at the library—or his exploration of the city—and so was not particularly worried by the request.

"You've had a visitor. A man came to the door today, asking for you."

Alphaios frowned. "I'm sorry, Prior, but I don't know who it could be, or why."

"He gave his name as Peaches. Robert Peaches. Said he was an architect. He left a card."

Alphaios was nonplussed. Guilty evidence of his surreptitious adventures in the city had come knocking on his very door. It was a terrible moment.

He gathered himself. "Peaches? He's a man I met just the other day. What does he want with me?"

"He didn't say. This has something to do with your work?"

"I'm sorry, Prior. I didn't expect to be the cause of such an inconvenience. We were discussing colors. I had no idea he would come here."

"Colors?"

"I met him by chance on the way home the other day, and we engaged in a brief conversation regarding colors—his use of them in architecture, my use of them in books. It was quite . . . educational. But I never expected to see him again. What did you tell him?"

"That we don't accept visitors here." The prior frowned. "How did this conversation come about, Brother?"

"He had some sketches of skyscrapers. I told him I'm drawn to color as a matter of occupation. I wondered aloud why they aren't used more often in the construction of buildings."

"Why did he come here?"

"I have no idea. I didn't expect ever to see him again."

"And how did he know where to come?"

"He noticed my manner of dress, asked my vocation. I told him I live here."

"Is that all, Brother?"

"Yes, that's all."

"You know better, Alphaios, than to let the outside intrude on our life here, our devotions. Your work outside the monastery affects not only you. After the accident, you must be painfully aware just how easily something can upset our equilibrium. Some among us wonder about you rather than focus on their own work. Don't become too much of a distraction, my brother."

"I'll try to avoid it. Thank you."

Some of the monks, most notably Brothers Simon and Levi and a few allies, had shown themselves more than once to chafe at his relative freedom, or at least wanted others to think they did. They would not be unhappy if his "privileges" were curtailed. But Alphaios did not believe it was his freedom his brothers envied, for they didn't want freedom at all; indeed, they all had made a lifelong vow of separation from the temptations and distractions that the larger world offered. What they wanted was for him not to be different from them.

In its own way, the monastery must not be much different than any fraternal organization. Failure to conform generates dislike and distrust, and their quest for holiness in eternal time did not entirely remove his brothers from the petty jealousies of mortal life. This was virtually set in stone here, given centuries of tradition and conformity. It was even possible that the order's strict adherence to prayer times, meal times and work times protected some of the monks from themselves.

On the other hand, if one thought more generously, it was only small things, just the details, over which the monks had any influence at all.

That being said, why did the architect come here? How could he stop him from doing so again? Alphaios could not find answers during vespers or compline, nor in all the restless night. On this night, he would even have happily endured three a.m. matins.

The next morning, Alphaios endured a sideways glance or two from Brother Simon, but nothing else was said about the unwelcome visitor. When it was time for him to leave for the scriptorium, he still did not have an answer but was as eager to go as usual. His stride was long when he stepped out the front door.

It was not a minute before his pace faltered, however, for on the sidewalk across the street was Robert Peaches.

For once, he was happy there were no windows in the monastery's wall. He did not want more questions from the prior, especially ones whose answers would raise yet further questions. He didn't have any more to give.

"I need to talk to you," the architect said even before Alphaios stepped up onto the curb. He was wearing a white linen suit and yellow summer tie over a starched pale blue shirt. He looked excited.

"Mr. Peaches. Hello. I'm afraid you've caught me at a poor time. I'm on my way to work."

"I need to talk to you. I have a sketch to show you."

"I don't understand how I could possibly help you, Mr. Peaches. You design enormous buildings. I'm a poor monk who does tiny paintings that few will ever see." He started walking toward the scriptorium.

The architect caught up with him and matched his pace. "Color. You were talking about color. Let me drive you to work. We can talk on the way."

Alphaios kept on walking. "That's not possible, Mr. Peaches. I'm afraid I must go. And please don't look for me at the monastery, it's an imposition on my brothers, an unwelcome one."

"All right, but please meet with me somewhere. Anywhere. Our conversation the other day gave me an insight. I've been wrestling with this for more than half a year, and until we met the other day, I hadn't had one decent idea."

"It's beyond my calling to involve myself in your business."

"Look, I'm surrounded by experts of all kinds—architects, structural engineers, interior designers—but I need your point of view. Your perspective is completely different."

Partly to disengage himself, and partly because he was now intrigued, Alphaios agreed to meet the architect after work. It wouldn't be appropriate to use the private library, so he suggested the Green River Bar and Grill. It offered more space and less noise than the little patio café, the only other place he could think of. And, he admitted to himself, he would enjoy seeing Jess again.

He worked his two hours in the scriptorium, and to assuage just a bit of guilt, an additional twenty minutes. Then he left the library and walked toward Jess's place. He was worried this happenstance acquaintance could turn into a problem, but the architect had piqued his curiosity.

Like Alphaios, Robert Peaches had been drawn to the paintings on the restaurant walls; he was standing in front of one windswept landscape when Alphaios entered, the screen door clattering shut behind him. Jess and Jack were behind the bar, but the café was otherwise empty. A familiar aria in a rich soprano flowed from the sound system. Today he did not try to guess the composer.

The architect came over and shook Alphaios's hand. "This is quite a place. The paintings are remarkable. I'll have to come back here and look around." He quickly shifted gears.

"Look, I know your time is short, and you must think I'm a pest, but I need your help."

Before he could say more, Jess came up to them, a broad smile on her face. She was again dressed as if for outside work—sleeveless, faded black work shirt, worn blue jeans and honest cowboy boots. She slapped him on the back. "Al, good of you to come by again. Can I get you and your friend some coffee?" Alphaios accepted, the architect demurred, and they settled at one of the round wooden tables.

"You were asking about structures and the lack of color," the architect said. "You're right when it comes to serious architecture. You'll see color used in some smaller commercial structures, fifty- or sixty-year buildings, but hardly ever in a hundred-year project. I think I gave you the reasons why."

Jess brought over the coffee. As before, it was strong and hot. "Jess, let me introduce you. Robert Peaches, architect, this is Jess, the owner." He was about to go on when Jess broke into a guffaw. It startled both of them.

"What? What did I say?"

"Peaches!" Jess laughed out loud. "Perfect."

The architect seemed taken aback. Despite, or perhaps because of the ribbing the name had undoubtedly cost him during his youth, he didn't look at all amused. Even Alphaios, who had already experienced Jess's brand of humor, wasn't sure how to respond.

Jess seemed to sense the architect's discomfort, for she choked back her laughter and sat down on the edge of a chair. She leaned into the table, her forearms against its edge. "The painting over the bar? The nude?" Both men looked, then nodded. Alphaios felt uneasy. "Men talk to her sometimes. They call her Sally. Me? I've always called her Peaches." She laughed again. "It's just that I've never run into—" She sobered herself up. "An architect, hmm? Well, any friend of Al's is a friend of mine. Here, let me bring you a cup. It's on me." She got up and went to get another coffee.

The architect seemed vexed, but started again. "You got me to thinking when you talked about timeless color. Why can't the color palette be used more? I'm not talking about sea foam and mango here. You were talking about defining colors, archetypal colors. And then I began to think about changing colors, and began to wonder if the path of the sun and the brightness of the day could be used to change shades of color, or perhaps change colors altogether. I wondered if I were to somehow integrate color, not as an accessory but into the structure of the building itself, what colors would serve across time."

Peaches leaned further into the table. "I got some structural and chemical engineers together, and they've been reviewing glass and ceramics, composites, alloys, paints, stains, anything that will stand the rigors of time in large applications. As of now, there's a ceramic product that looks promising."

He paused a moment as if assessing Alphaios's mood. "This is where you come in. I've made a sketch. Although the core of the building, its internal engineering, would be conventional, its shape is different than anything that's been built before. With the right colors and materials, it could command the eye for generations. Without color, though, it would lose some of its esthetic."

Peaches opened an artist's case and laid a large drawing flat on the table. In it, a tall, oddly serpentine building rose into the sky. It had both flat planes and curved ones that combined to give it a sense of upward movement. It definitely caught the eye.

Alphaios stood up and backed away from the table to get a better view, then suggested the architect prop it up on the next table. Once it was there, he studied it in silence.

Jess brought over the cup of coffee and set it in front of the architect. She had another cup in her hand as well, and stood to one side, sipping at it and taking in the sketch. He suddenly remembered the awful accident she'd described, forty-three stories up; perhaps he should not have brought the architect here. But if she were uncomfortable, she was keeping it inside. She made no comments.

As Peaches had said, it would dominate the landscape. One side was dramatically higher than the opposing side, creating a sharp angle at the top, perhaps fifty degrees. On the higher side, two long scoops cut through the otherwise flat face of the building, one very high, one low. The scoops were more dramatic in height than depth, like a knife's shallow, curved cut through butter. Each scoop swept upward across fifteen, maybe twenty stories. They did not meet—between them were ten or twelve stories of flat, vertical wall.

On the other side of the building was just one scoop, of apparently equal size. This one was almost but not quite centered between the opposing two, midway up. Then, at the base of the building, as if it were continuing underground, was the very top of another such scoop.

The first side of the building was thus dominated by curves, the other side more by flat surfaces. The combination of the sharp angle at the top of the building and the high scoop that nearly reached it created an angular terminus. It was reminiscent of a spire, but was asymmetrical and sharply off vertical.

If he focused on its skin, the building was angular. But if his eyes followed the midline upward, it was comprised of gentle S curves. It was a curious, bold design.

"How will the building be oriented?"

"The high side with the two shallow cuts, due east. What I envision is that the concave areas will catch and refract light as the sun rises and sets, the colors in them changing in tone and intensity as the angle of the sun changes. How they appear to the viewer might well vary from different vantage points."

"How widely can the colors differ in a single scoop?"

"That's determined by the physics and method of construction of the ceramic. We need to decide what we want. Ultimately, we'll have to meet with the manufacturer and develop the specs."

Having said his piece, the architect seemed content to let Alphaios ruminate. The room was quiet now, the music over.

"In the single scoop on the west face," Alphaios said, "deep gold when the sun is high, transitioning through its hues into a deep cranberry red as the sun begins to set. Glory. Richness. Fire, warmth, family, love. Home."

Peaches remained silent. Jess was looking at Alphaios with new interest. She must have been wondering why he was being consulted at all by this architect—in their one previous conversation, the subject of his vocation had not come up. In fact, as a former steel worker, she undoubtedly knew a lot more about architecture than he did. But here the subject was color, not structure.

"On the east face, the upper scoop: pure yellow when the sun is rising, to silver as it reaches midday. Optimism, openness. New day, clean slate. Opportunity."

It was a while before he spoke again. "The lower scoop: cobalt to malachite. Deep blue at sunup: sky and space combined, limitless, infinite. Green when the sun is reaching towards its zenith: spring, growth, earth, life. Aspiration."

There was silence again, coffee cups forgotten. Peaches reached into a pocket for a pencil and began to make some notes.

"The mind finds it hard to draw the eye away from pure colors," Alphaios said, "which is one reason why they last through time. Take a look at stained glass, for instance. Hundreds of years of examples: deep blues, reds, purples, gold in abundance are characteristic of the most famous, most cherished windows, regardless of subject matter. In my work, the most prized pages of an illuminated book, generally, are those richest in color. Consider the history of fabrics for clothes, and thread for rugs as well: the more saturated the shade, the more treasured. Regardless of culture."

The architect gave him a puzzled frown. "You didn't ask what material or tint the skin of the building will be. How can you know what these colors should be if you don't know that?"

"Some colors bypass our intellect and speak to us viscerally. To our souls. It's like the lower ranges of the cello, or the rhythm of deep drums." He paused. "These are the colors that will make the building. Choose the materials for the rest of it to serve these colors, not vice versa."

After a moment, the architect nodded his understanding.

It was but a few minutes later that Peaches placed the sketch back into its case and said goodbye. He was effusive in his thanks, embarrassingly so. Jess invited him, warmly, to come by again. Jess and Alphaios both smiled when the architect could not resist looking up at his namesake on his way to the door.

Jess brought them both a fresh cup of coffee. "Dvorak," she said. "'Song to the Moon.'"

Alphaios grinned. "Thanks. I didn't know."

"Seems you're more than just a pretty face in a dress, Al. You didn't tell me you're an artist. You a scholar or painter of some kind?" Jess raised her eyebrows, then swept her damaged hand around the room, at the landscapes on the walls. "What would you paint, of empty spaces and the dangers in them to the unwary?"

Alphaios could not suppress the thought of life in the monastery without his work, without his daily forays into the mortal, flawed, yet spiritual vitality of this city and its people. He did not answer Jess's question.

CHAPTER 20

HE LAY ON HIS BACK in the little graveyard behind the refectory, near Timothy's reluctant garden. It was a little after three in the morning and as dark and quiet as the city would ever get. Most of the lights in the high-rises towering above him were off, and the garbage trucks had not yet started their hydraulic howls and rude hammering of metal against metal. This is how peacefulness would be measured in this city, at least for those who did not live high above the din.

He had come to feel that life in this monastery with its futile walls and surrounding buildings was like being at the bottom of a high-sided box, one like those offering kittens on the street. The only view, the only space, was either upward or inward. Tonight, both were infinite yet confining.

He remembered what Robert Peaches had said in the little park about a building's occupying not only its own physical space but also a cylinder that continues both below and above its material structure. He imagined the city block the monastery occupied and, using the skyscrapers around him as a sighting instrument, tried to project it into the heavens. But though the night was clear, he was unable to discern among the stars where this little cylinder might go, or where it might arrive.

He was no more successful in terms of his inner space. For the first time in his life as a monk, uncertainty had come to cloud his peace and keep him awake. The rhythm of monastic life, the mantra of ritual prayer, the balm of the chant no longer calmed his soul.

It occurred to him that some atonement might help him regain his focus. Flagellation had long ago been abandoned, but perhaps some other form of self-mortification would do. It was chilly, and a sharp rock or stick pressed painfully against his shoulder blade. He told himself to lie motionless and not to move at all, even when it became unbearable. He would remain there, unmoving, until it was time to help Brother John with breakfast.

He should not have been surprised that it was Jess who had driven a needle to the very center of his conscience. No, not his conscience. His consciousness, his being. She was, after all, direct and incisive and unpredictable.

Deep down, Alphaios had been half-expecting the question to be raised by Prior Bartholomew upon discovery of some exploit, or stumbled upon during some blunt gambit by Brother Simon or Levi. But in one probing moment, it was Jess who had brought it all to the surface.

He did not concede to the growing discomfort of the rock, at least not on purpose. His thoughts began to drift through the city and its people, and he simply forgot his intention. It was not long before he raised himself up, absently rubbed his shoulder and returned to his cell.

Later, after lunch, he walked directly to the library. The day was clear and bright—just as the night had been—and he would be able to start work on the intricate little painting that waited for the right combination of light and energy. Not only that, Inaki would be returning from his research trip to northern Spain, a full week later than planned.

He was eager to learn what Inaki had found. Whatever it was, it must have been important to keep him there an extra week. Meanwhile, he would focus his attention on the task at hand.

The bifolium in front of him had somehow escaped water damage. Neither, remarkably, had the passage of some six hundred years dimmed its beauty. One of its pages was an early fifteenth-century masterpiece equal to any period painting he'd ever seen in Florence or Rome. He attributed it to Obadiah: it had a very serious mien and was traditional in both interpretation and artistry. Though he was more predictable and doctrinal than Jeremiah, Alphaios still counted Obadiah among the best illuminators of his time.

On the outward, right-side margin was a narrow, vertical painting of three virgin martyrs in full figure. They overlapped downward from right to left and back to right, and were entwined together in gold leaf filigree in the form of ivy. The figures were unconstrained by a formal frame. It was exquisite in detail and color, with very fine brush and pen work.

XM had done beautiful work copying the text. Alphaios had already illuminated the grandly flourished initial capital letters on the page—unmistakably Zephaniah's work—and had penned in the small purple budded crosses that were interspersed among the text. He had laid the gesso for the gold leaf. Now his task was to copy the exquisite painting with absolute faithfulness. The first step would be laying and burnishing the breath-thin gold leaf into the threads of ivy. This had to be done before the painting, because gold leaf would not adhere to a painted surface.

At the top right was St. Catherine of Alexandria. She was in a gown of wine red with gold thread embroidered across the bodice. Here the gold would be crushed and bound together with gum arabic. Instead of the sheen of gold leaf, this gold would sparkle in the light. Over St. Catherine's shoulders was a long, luxurious cloak in a rich bronze with golden highlights. In her right hand she carried a book. Parts of a broken wheel rested at her feet.

Legend had it—for with every saint, it was often legend rather than historical fact which underlay their veneration— that as an unusually learned young woman she confronted the Roman emperor in his court for worshipping pagan gods and persecuting Christians. She was imprisoned for her audacity, and the emperor's scholars were employed to use reason to get her to recant her faith. Instead, she persuaded many of them to become Christians, including the emperor's own wife and his most-trusted general. All of her converts were martyred by the emperor, and Catherine was condemned to a torturous death on the wheel. At her first touch, however, the wheel collapsed. The emperor ordered her beheaded. Angels were said to have carried her body to Mount Sinai, where a church and monastery were later built in her honor. Among many other groups, Catherine became the patron saint of wheelwrights, mechanics, philosophers and the dying.

Below her and to her left, in a simple lilac garment that became purple in its folds and shadows, stood Margaret of Antioch. In one hand she held a silver chain with which she tethered a scaled, ungainly green beast at her feet. Part of a boiling cauldron stood off to one side.

St. Margaret's story was brutal. She was said to have been born to a pagan priest. As an infant, when her mother died, she was put under the care of a distant shepherdess. Under that woman's influence, she became a Christian. When she was a young woman, a Roman official attempted to force his attentions on her, but she refused. Angry, irritated, or just because he could, he denounced her in public and she was put on trial. Faced with a painful death unless she renounced her faith, she chose the former. Death by fire was attempted, but in the face of her prayers, the flames did not burn her. Boiling water failed to cook her alive. Finally, she was beheaded. After her death, many apocryphal acts were attributed to her, among them being swallowed by Satan in the form of a dragon. She escaped, legend said, when the points of her cross irritated the dragon's throat. St. Margaret became the patron saint of pregnant women and childbirth.

The last figure, further down and to the right, was St. Barbara, golden-haired and wearing a finely woven gown of pure white. A sky-blue cloak draped around her back and over both arms. In her right hand she held a gold chalice from which a holy light emanated. In her left was a palm frond, a sign of martyrdom. Behind her was part of a stone structure showing light from three small windows.

Her story was even worse. As a young woman, said the hagiographers, she was secluded in a tower by a domineering father, a pagan, to protect her from the outside world. Through her own prayer and study, and perhaps through surreptitious teaching by a local priest, Barbara secretly converted to Christianity and was baptized. When her father had a bathhouse constructed for her, she had an extra, third window put in to symbolize the Trinity. Upon learning she'd become a Christian, her father denounced her before the civil authorities, offered her up for torture and beheading, and subsequently took up the axe himself to complete the task. His fate? To be killed by lightning on his way home from her execution.

Perhaps because of the lightning and the thunder that must have accompanied her departure, Barbara became the patron saint of artillerymen and miners. She also came to be sought out by the faithful for assurance that they would receive the gift of last rites before dying—a last opportunity for penance and the Eucharist.

Each woman had a delicate gold halo above her head.

Alphaios noted that these were the only three women in the group of saints called the fourteen holy helpers. The helpers were considered by many to be the most accommodating intercessors for the prayerful. It wasn't unusual that only the women were depicted, for individual variations were a hall-mark of such books of hours.

Much of Alphaios's religious education had included recita-tions of the saints, and the daily formal prayers of his order still called upon many of them for their help in gaining heaven's final favor. As far as he could tell, his brothers in the monastery still believed in their literal power. Suffrages to the saints and entreaties for their assistance continued to be a fervent part of their daily prayers.

He couldn't quite remember when he'd begun to doubt, but it had been long ago, and now Alphaios viewed saints mostly as good people—although there could be some who were not—who had lived their faith or died their faith. Yet even in this context, *goodness* had different meanings. It could mean zeal more than charity, even the relentlessly rooting out of heretics and others who gave any challenge at all to Church doctrine.

The legends that had grown up around saints, he had come to believe, were used by priests and popes primarily to reach the faithless and to keep the faithful. Lay people them-selves had pressed for the sainthood of many beloved figures, perhaps as a way of buttressing their own beliefs, making a personal connection to their faith, or bending the Church to their will.

For Alphaios, sanctity was not to be found in bombast but in whispers; not in heroic deeds but in humble service; not in self-mortification or other hardships for imagined sins, small sins, or sins never committed. If saintliness were to be achieved inside a cloistered order, it would not be because of prayer in seclusion, but because of service to the others who lived behind those closed doors.

These thoughts did not prevent him from applying his craft, and before he knew it, he'd reached his two-hour limit. He was inspecting the bifolium and his worktable for stray slips of gold leaf when Inaki came through the door of the scriptorium. He clapped Alphaios on the back.

"I stopped by an hour ago, but you were so deep into your work I decided to come back."

"You kept me waiting for news of your trip?"

"News? What makes you think there's news?"

Alphaios took his friend's hand and shook it warmly. "I can see it in your face. Welcome back. Besides, you didn't stay an extra week just to sun yourself in San Sebastian."

"I was tempted." Inaki looked at the worktable. "Ah, you've started the ladies. I hoped you would."

"Let me put them away. Then tell me about your trip."

When the sheet of parchment had been stowed and Alphaios's tools were in their places, they went to the scribes' work area. Each found a high stool and sat down. They were surrounded by angled worktables and cabinets. Not a single pencil or piece of vellum was out of place.

"The professor was right," Inaki said. "The journal didn't have any more references to anything like a royal family kneeling before a pope—wink or no wink. Just the one page he sent us."

"What about other writings by the same author?"

Inaki shook his head. "None in Uncastillo. Not in the monastery, not in the town's archives. Nothing."

Alphaios was disappointed. He knew in his heart the lost painting with the wink was the work of Jeremiah. But he was as eager as Inaki to find a better description of it than the professor had found. And any further clue to the painting might also provide information regarding the book's birthplace.

"But . . ." Inaki drummed his fingers on the worktable next to him, then grinned broadly. "I did find some sixteenth-century codices that hadn't been known before. Think of it— previously unknown manuscripts!   And they center on Basque life and history. That's what kept me there. They were stuffed into a broken-down cupboard in an old stone barn. It'd been shoved back against a wall behind some old lumber and farm tools. I found an early Bible in Euskara. I don't have a date on it yet, but the first known translation was in 1571. This one was printed on a mechanical press and could date as early as only fifty years later. Not even the monastery had a record of them!"

Alphaios was happy for his friend. For an archivist, unearthing such ancient documents about his own ancestral lands would be the find of a lifetime. But they had no bearing on the book of hours.

"Let me show you," Inaki said. "I brought a couple of documents back. I nearly had to turn over the deed to the library to get them, but I persuaded them to check my credentials.

So here we are. Let's go upstairs." He stood up and headed for the door, waving Alphaios along.

Inaki was so enthusiastic that Alphaios held back further questions of his own—he would have ample time later. Not reluctantly, but not sharing his friend's exuberance either, he followed the archivist out of the scriptorium and up the stairs.

Spread out on Inaki's desk was a dark piece of felt. The archivist lifted it, and before him lay an illumination on old parchment. He approached it, and when he got close, his heart began to race. "Jeremiah," he whispered.

There was no reaction from Inaki. The building was silent.

The page was small, from a book probably meant for an important man's library, perhaps a bishop or a noble. It was well scribed, but it was the miniature painting that stood out.

"Jeremiah," Alphaios said again, aloud this time.

"Are you certain?"

Alphaios nodded and pointed to the small painting. It was of a bishop dining with a small group at a table. "Look at the position of this hand. It's typical of him: a more natural position, more physiologically correct than most illuminators of his time. And the bishop's forehead, here? The blemish. Maybe a birthmark or a boil? Jeremiah frequently shows some physical flaw in such figures. He used it as a covert way to under-score their mortality and bring them down a peg or two. I can show you examples."

He stood for long moments more. "Remarkable. Where did you find it?"

"There in Uncastillo, at the monastery. It was in a book that had lost its binding. The miniature looked familiar to me. I couldn't say for sure, or even why. I found the traveler's journal, but there weren't any other references to the wink in it. No clues at all about where he might have seen the book. I looked through the other manuscripts they had, books that traced back to the fifteenth and sixteenth centuries. They had twenty-seven of them. Remarkable, really, but disappointing for us. I passed by this illumination while I was looking for written references, but then something about it nagged at me. I couldn't have told you why, but the more I looked at it the more I thought you should see it."

"Is there any other work like it in the book? Or the others?" He meant Zechariah, Zephaniah, and Obadiah. "Did you get the opportunity to study it?"

"Tomorrow, Alphaios, tomorrow. I must go home to my wife." He smiled broadly. "She has missed me too, you know."

Alphaios felt his face warming. "Of course, Inaki. Go home. We'll talk more tomorrow."

Half an hour later, he was at the little café, speaking with Nico. He sat near the fence, for his favorite table was occupied. The day had been good—sunshine, Jeremiah's art, the collegial pursuit of knowledge—and now an espresso invited his appreciation.

He was watching a nearby sketch artist at work when the tall Nigerian woman appeared on the other side of the street. She was smooth in her gait, and today wore a striking long dress and matching cap in a modern pattern of dusty light blue and tan that contrasted handsomely with her ebony skin. She was alone.

He had seen glimpses of her a number of times since the awful day of the accident. He hadn't spoken to her, though, and realized he still harbored deep pain for her and guilt at his deception.

As he watched, the woman's head turned his way, and for a brief moment their eyes met. She changed direction and walked directly toward him.

Alphaios stood up as she approached. For the second time that day, he was aware of his heart pounding in his chest. He observed again that she was considerably taller than him. There was deep sadness in her dark, direct eyes. He didn't know how to greet her, what to say.

She reached across the low patio fence and laid her open palm over his heart. "Father," she said fiercely, "I will marry again. I will have children."

He nodded dumbly. He could not think of anything to say, and before he could gather himself, she was gone. It was too late to tell her he was only a monk, but it no longer mattered. Strangely, Robert Peaches's buildings and their cylinders of space came to mind. He had a sense that his own personal one had just grown wider.

CHAPTER 21

ALPHAIOS WAS EAGER to hear the rest of Inaki's report, and as soon as lunch was over he set out on his first and most direct route to the library.

Over an entrance to an escalator that took commuters underground to the subway, he noticed a new billboard. It featured a long-haired, slender woman, naked. She sat forward on a floor, her arms and legs crossed to cover exactly what the advertiser wished his viewers to see. Beside her was a tiny cobalt blue jar with simple gold lettering. The picture did not shock or even surprise him, for he had seen even more explicit advertisements during his few outings in Rome. He wouldn't be able to say the same for his brothers, though.

When he reached the library and let himself in, he hurried up the steps to the archivist's office. Today the scriptorium could wait.

Inaki stood in front of his desk looking down at the new Jeremiah page. Alphaios entered and quietly joined his colleague. There was no doubt—this was Jeremiah's work.

"When you found this, did you get a chance to go back and look again at the rest of the book?"

"No, I'm afraid not." Inaki remained still for a long moment, then reached over and lifted a second dark cloth. Under it were the remains of an ancient book, its spine and cover missing. He grinned. "So I brought it with me."

Alphaios laughed. "How did you manage that?"

"Cardinal Ricci was persuasive."

"I thought you were going to show me the books you found in the barn."

"Set you up, didn't I?"

Alphaios nodded and laughed again.

"That's what kept me there longer than planned. The monastery wouldn't release them, but they let me have a good first look. There's nothing in them for us, and the monks want to find out what they have before they're opened up to academics. Can't blame them for that." He took a breath. "But I'll be the first scholar to have access. If all goes well here, I'll be going back next year."

"Congratulations, my friend. You've earned it."

"Speaking of research, why don't you study the illuminations in this book, and I'll focus some more on the text. Let's see if we can come up with some clues."

"I'll start today. But what about Leyre? What about Charles III and the Duke de Berry?" Alphaios was not about to let Inaki slip away from his questions again. He went to the same chair he'd emptied of its burdens before and sat down.

"All right, Brother, questions and answers. And I'm betting you'll have more questions. I know I do."

Inaki took a notebook from his brown leather bag. "Let's start at the abbey. We already talked about the monastic orders that used it. There's an old monk there, must be eighty-five years old. Brother Joseba. He's been the abbey's historian most of his life, and the library's his own personal fiefdom. He's Basque, hard of hearing and eccentric." Inaki chuckled. "Hair stands out from his head all day long. Fingers are as stiff as rusted hinges and black from battles with his fountain pens. Can't remember yesterday, but seems to know what happened centuries ago. Keeps muttering to himself. In Euskara, of course.

"So anyway, I began asking questions about the first decades of the 1400s. Yes, there was a scriptorium there, large and productive for centuries before the printing press was invented. Then they acquired a press themselves, only the fifth one in all of Spain. Amazing. He showed me some pieces of it in a back room. Felt like I'd stepped all the way back in time to Gutenberg himself. I swear I could hear the rattle of block type being put into the trays."

"Living history." Alphaios had sensed such ghosts more than once. The sensation was profound and startlingly real.

"I asked Brother Joseba if he knew of any book with the size and characteristics of ours. He didn't. I asked him if he were aware of any illuminators of the time who were known to have extraordinary talent, or if he'd ever heard of a book or illumination with a controversial wink. He didn't know of any. I spent ten full days in the stacks at Leyre. It's an impressive collection, more than a thousand old books, very well catalogued. But there are almost none before 1420, and all of those are rather ordinary. It's like the scriptorium didn't exist until then. Or like some catastrophic event occurred.

"Turns out it did. In 1419. There's an account of it in the abbey's records. Lightning struck the scriptorium one night during an especially violent storm. Started a fire. Roof burned and collapsed on a group of monks. They'd run in to save the books."

Alphaios bowed his head, sensing what was coming. "Who would be more likely to try to save books than those who created them?"

"That's my thought, too. Worse yet, there was an especially ascetic faction in control at the time. Seems the abbot saw the angry hand of God in the fire—His disapproval of the library's riches, the wealth accumulated by the Benedictines. So they stood by and let it burn. The books, and their brothers, too. Threw any stray books back into the fire."

A shiver rolled up Alphaios's spine. Inaki paused for a moment, then continued more quietly.

"When it was rebuilt, the scriptorium and library were only for sober books, utilitarian books. Any pre-fire manuscripts there now were either returned to the abbey from its monasteries or were gifts from patrons or other collections."

"They let the monks burn. How did they know they were already dead?"

"They didn't."

The office was silent for a long while.

When Alphaios spoke, he was quiet, sober. "I truly don't know which has the greater potential for catastrophe, the forces of nature or mere men donning the mantle of holiness."

It took a moment for Inaki to respond. "If only in potential, it's nature." He let the sequitur hang unstated in the air.

Alphaios let it sink in. If Jeremiah and Obadiah had been among those killed and their work destroyed, it would explain why he hadn't seen their art before, why nothing was known of them. If they had been its creators, at Leyre, it would date the book sometime before 1419. And it would offer a powerful explanation of why the book of hours would have been hidden away—little is more virulent than religious extremism. Hundreds, perhaps thousands of books and works of art had been burned in Florence during Savonarola's purge of everything secular in the 1490s. The apocalyptic cleric's bonfires had even consumed paintings by the remarkable Botticelli before his own hanged body was touched by the hot lick of flames. It was not the first time, and it pained him greatly that it would not be the last time, that zealots would destroy the works and ideas of others on behalf of some imagined godliness. Or would read into great events some godly portent by which they could further their own causes.

"You said Leyre owned some other monasteries. Did you get a chance to inquire into them?"

"Just their catalogues. They seemed complete and detailed enough, but there could be other troves somewhere like the one I stumbled onto. The inventories include a large number of Bibles, breviaries and books of hours, but I didn't get the chance to trace them all down. Joseba said any books of real historical note or artistic interest had been brought to the abbey long ago. Nonetheless, the abbot has agreed to do a review."

"Given the history of our book, I have to ask. Did you get any sense that Brother Joseba might be misleading you?"

"Good question. I wondered that too. But no, no sense at all. Not from him, not from the abbot, not from anyone else. They seemed open enough, and quite curious themselves. When I showed them the photographs I took along of our book of hours, I saw great wonderment, but no signs of recognition. If there was some mystery at the monastery regarding our book, it's long since been forgotten. On the other hand, someone, somewhere was a master at hiding our book and succeeded for nearly six hundred years. If I were being misled, I might not have known it."

"Nor would I. Any new information from the Vatican?"

"Nothing yet."

"What about Charles III?"

Inaki stood up from his desk and cleared off a chair at the table. He turned it around and straddled it, his forearms resting on the chair's back. While he turned some pages in his notebook, it occurred to Alphaios he'd never seen a chair used in this way; given his long habit, he surely wouldn't be able to do so. He shifted his weight and turned his own chair toward Inaki.

"Some of my old colleagues at the university and the Department of Antiquities are working on it. Haven't received anything definitive one way or the other. He certainly spent more time at home in Navarre than his father did, but he also traveled regularly to Paris. We don't have anything yet that shows he actually visited any of Duke de Berry's homes, but it remains probable that all the nobles knew each other well, and not only at court. They'd hunt, socialize and dine together, and certainly discuss the intrigues of the day."

"Is it fair to presume his family traveled with him?"

Inaki nodded. "Especially to court. Marriages, families, children were all means of diplomacy, not only for securing new lands and titles, but for attaining political stability. In fact, when royal marriages failed, relations between kingdoms often did as well."

"Who was his family?"

"Charles married Eleanor, daughter of the King of Castile, in 1375. They had eight or nine children, depending on which source you use. They had two sons, but both of them died in early childhood. In fact, only their firstborn daughter, Blanca, survived to adulthood. When she was fifteen, she was wed to the King of Sicily, crown prince of Aragón. As I said, diplomacy. And Charles's own sister, Joanna, was Queen of England—the wife of Henry IV. Attending court would have been the pinnacle of royal life. Anyway, When Charles died, Blanca succeeded him as queen regnant. Why do you ask?"

"Just pursuing a thread. Was Charles a freethinker? An intellectual? A religious adventurer?"

"If he was, there's no record of it. He was a pragmatist. He sought peace with his neighbors for the most part, and invested huge sums in Navarre's infrastructure. He became a patron of the arts. Unfortunately, little of it has survived."

The office became quiet as both men sorted out their thoughts.

"Did you know," Alphaios said, "that years of works by the Limbourg brothers were also lost in a fire? Three years after the Duke de Berry retained them in 1408, his chateau burned down, taking their work with it. It was after that they started *Très Riches Heures*. And then, five years after the fire, in 1416, all three of the brothers died from the same illness, just months apart. They weren't even thirty years old. Just imagine what they could have done. Jean de Berry died the very same year, though from a different cause. So *Très Riches Heures* was never finished."

Inaki simply nodded, and once more the room drifted into silence.

After many minutes, Alphaios roused himself and stood up. "Good work, Inaki. You've done well. I'll take the book and see if I can spot any more work by Jeremiah."

Inaki was still sitting at the table musing when Alphaios left the office.

Downstairs at his worktable under the big windows, it did not take Alphaios long to find the answer. Only the one page of the book was Jeremiah's. He did not see the hand of Obadiah at all.

When he was done, he let himself out of the library. Instead of turning to the patio café, he wandered through the city

without particular direction. Today his thoughts were turned
not outward to its visual feast, but inward. Though he was in
a city he had grown to love, though he was in the midst of
work that challenged him like no other, he felt despondent. It
was not until he was back at the monastery and settled into
his cell for the night that he understood. He was grieving.

There would be nothing more found of Jeremiah and
Obadiah. Though they had died nearly six hundred years
ago, he'd only just become acquainted with them. When the
book of hours was completed, he would find no more intimate
conversation, no more intense collaboration with his two
eclectic thinkers, his two master painters.

They would leave him all too soon.

CHAPTER 22

THERE WAS AN ODD alertness among the monks this morning at chapter. Though they all were present, minor finance and housekeeping issues were resolved with unusual dispatch. There had been little discussion even with the report that a new vegetable purveyor would have to be found. Alphaios was pleased. He usually found it difficult to endure these meetings, but today even Brother Richard, who could often quibble over the smallest detail, was silent.

He was expecting to join in the closing prayer when Brother Simon spoke. "My brothers, there's one more matter we must discuss. Recently, our prayerful life was disturbed by a knock at our door. A worldly man, a man from the city who identified himself as an architect, was seeking Brother Alphaios. While our brother has extraordinary dispensation to forgo the solemn rigors of our life, perhaps we should ask him to explain this intrusion."

Alphaios groaned inwardly. It had been more than two weeks since Robert Peaches's knock at the monastery door. He'd relaxed, thinking that Prior Bartholomew's mild rebuke and Peaches's agreement to stay away had put the issue behind him. It obviously had not, and today he would be tested again.

He had long ago learned that even a minor disturbance such as this could be used as fodder by Simon. He would invariably use criticism or exploit what he saw as a weakness in another. Perhaps it was God's design to test Alphaios's tolerance. If so, He had chosen Simon well.

The prior nodded for Brother Simon to proceed.

"We are happy to host Brother Alphaios here in our humble surroundings, as we prayerfully agreed to do as a favor to Cardinal Ricci. We asked in return that our holy seclusion from the distractions of the world not be disturbed in any way. Assurances were given, yet we've already had more than one such interruption."

Several heads tilted in agreement.

"We're also happy to offer our services to the completion of this book of hours. It is, after all, to be a gift for His Holiness. Yet we've noticed a certain lack of punctuality in Brother Alphaios with regard to our duties, our prayers. He's a member of our order, so we shouldn't call it indifference to our way of life or to his soul. But we must impose upon our good brother to explain two things. What does an architect from the city have to do with this book? And if indeed there is such a role, which is difficult to imagine, why would Brother Alphaios presume to have this architect disrupt our search for salvation?"

Brothers Samuel and Levi nodded energetically. Several others were looking at him expectantly. The prior's head was bowed, but Alphaios could see his eyes watching from beneath his brows. Simon had laid some groundwork for this challenge; this was not spontaneous.

He gathered his thoughts. He would need to be careful today if he were to retain his relative freedom. The only thing now as precious to him as his work on the book of hours was his liberty, albeit limited, to explore the joyous, painful, sweet, rough, raw, beautiful, chaotic life of the city. It was in the city, not here among his brothers, where he now most sensed a spiritual presence. But it was only here, in the quiet of the monastery, that he was able to reflect on his experiences, to draw them into himself.

A rush of feelings came into full bloom and reminded him of Jess's probing questions. Yet this was not the time to speak of such things. There was much at stake for him today, and Simon seemed to know it, even relish it. He must retain his equanimity.

"My brothers are indeed generous, and I regret having been the cause, however small, of any interruption of our holy devotions."

Simon did not let him go on. "I'm sure Brother Alphaios would agree he has misspoken. After all, he was elsewhere when this intrusion occurred."

"Yes, I was, my brothers, carrying out my work, just as you were. I will answer my good brother's second question first: I did not invite Mr. Peaches here. I was as surprised as you at his coming, indeed, at his seeking me out at all. I met him only once. I had no reason to think I'd ever see him again."

"As for intrusions, I ask my brothers how this knock on the door, this inquiry after me, differs from the occasional knock of the curious passerby, or the pilgrim on a tour of religious sites, or even the vendor seeking our business. Surely we're accustomed to such approaches, and brush them from our thoughts as we do a fly when deep in prayer. This knock was no more intrusive than any other, except perhaps to those who choose to swat at the buzzing fly."

He noticed a suppressed smile or two among the group; Prior Bartholomew was not among them. He must be careful— his purpose here was not to incite Brother Simon or to sow discord.

"It's quite different," Simon said, his voice tighter. "This visitor asked for you in person; he had some specific purpose in mind. Has our brother sought an architect's advice regarding our humble monastery buildings?" This also drew smiles, more nervous this time. "Or does this architect have some involvement with the book of hours? If so, our brothers wonder what it might be. And flies are one of God's many gifts to test our piety. Are you suggesting that this architect's visit came from God?"

Alphaios almost never spoke to his brothers about his work on the manuscript. When asked, he'd reply only in the most general of terms. "It's a fair question my brother asks, though who can say architects are not also of God's creation?" He smiled at Simon. "But no, my brothers, I have no desire

246 J. S. ANDERSON

to improve upon these buildings. And my chance encounter with him had no direct connection to the book."

"If not a direct connection, then what?"

"Colors." He was not surprised to see a few raised eyebrows. "I use colors in my work as an illuminator. I paint with colors. I therefore study colors, how they're made, their uses, even their meanings. I had a chance encounter on the street with this man. He was looking at sketches of buildings, skyscrapers. I asked him about the use of color in architecture; more precisely, I asked him about the lack of it. Our conversation lasted only moments, and I thought that was the end of it."

A few monks nodded in understanding. They were ready to accept this explanation and let the chapter meeting come to an end. But Simon was not yet done. His next point came through Brother Levi.

"But what, Brother Alphaios, is the use of further study? It's our understanding that the book of hours is being copied, that you are merely replicating the work of others. The figures you paint, the colors you use, are already there. Why does a simple copyist require continued study, especially study that interrupts the pious life of others? Couldn't it be said, my brothers, that such a study of colors is simply a form of self-aggrandizement, a sin of pride?"

To Alphaios's dismay, a fourth voice joined in. It was Brother Philemon, usually a timid man but always doctrinaire. "Brothers, we're a reclusive order. We shouldn't forget that colors themselves may distract us from our vocation. That's why you don't see adornment in these structures, on these walls."

Brother Samuel went back to the prior point. "Does a cook need to study new food dishes when he is using only recipes that have been handed down for generations?"

Brother John sent a baleful smile Samuel's way. "Well, it might make some of you happier. Me too, I might add. Who likes to make the same thing over and over, year after year? Sometimes it seems an unholy burden. Weren't the taste buds the Lord's creation?" This was an unusual complaint from John; perhaps it came because he was one cook who, through no fault of his own, never received a sincere compliment from his diners.

With a small shake of his head, Simon sought to swing the conversation back in the direction he'd intended. "We're talking about Brother Alphaios and copying paintings, not your food, John."

"I pray daily for forgiveness for many sins, among them pride." Alphaios looked pointedly at Simon. "I fear that as mere mortals seeking salvation, many among us must do the same."

"That doesn't address Brother Levi's question." A couple of monks looked at Simon sharply, evidently disapproving of his tone.

"Perhaps I can explain. I'll start with copying. In order to be an illuminator, one must learn to paint—much as a scribe must learn to write before becoming a calligrapher. Before ever being permitted to alter or retouch a manuscript, I was required to demonstrate mastery of painting. That meant I had to learn to see as an artist, to mix and use colors, and to master the brush and quill. Because illuminated books have originated in different countries and many different monasteries, I had to learn to understand and match the techniques of many different artists. There are even illuminated books written in Arabic. In just this one book of hours, for example, there are four different artists. That means there were four different colorists, four different methods, four different styles."

For the moment, he had the group's attention. Only Simon and Levi were looking away.

"There are two more difficulties. Brother Levi is right; this book of hours is to be a copy, as exact a copy as humanly possible. This book will have a place in history, not only for our own order, but in the history of the popes."

He decided to bring the subject back to earth. "The original book is some six hundred years old. The paints were hand-mixed, probably by the artists themselves. They used lead and other minerals, vegetable matter such as seeds and flowers, even urine. That means paint quality and color varied widely. We can match those colors today, but it takes a trained eye, and at times even a chemical analysis. In this case, color isn't simply a refraction of light that reaches the eye; it's matter, a physical substance, as well."

He paused to consider his next words. "One more thing. The book has been severely damaged. Many pages have suffered insult to the extent that portions of them are unreadable. Some text and illuminations are missing altogether."

Simon saw the opening. "You said this is to be a copy, an exact copy. Perhaps, Brother, you should tell us how one copies something that isn't there."

"That is the true difficulty of it, my brothers. One cannot."

"Well then," Samuel said, "how does one present to His Holiness a copy of something that can't be copied?"

"That's where continuing to study painting and colors comes in," Alphaios said. "Four painters illuminated the original. Let's suppose Brother John here was one of the four. From the pages before and after the ruined pages, we can tell which of the four worked on them—we can deduce with reasonable certainty that Brother John was the painter. Having studied his technique and use of color, we can now duplicate it."

Levi followed Samuel's theme. "So you can paint in the style of Brother John, but you still don't know what he painted on that page."

"True. The chief archivist and I, aided by a commission of scholars, must decide the content and appearance. These are derived from the subject of the text we know is missing from the page, the work of Brother John elsewhere in the book, the known beliefs regarding the subject at the time the book was created, who the patron of the book was, where it was made, and so on. I propose a design, the archivist reviews it, we take it to the commission, which approves it, asks for revisions, or directs us to start over."

"Then Brother Simon's right," Levi said. "It's not a true copy, as we were led to believe."

Prior Bartholomew held up his hands. "Brothers, it's not up to us to decide what's possible or desirable with regard to the book of hours. Brother Alphaios has described a difficult and laborious process. These problems were surely known to Cardinal Ricci and others before this very considerable task was begun. Shouldn't we accept that Brother Alphaios was sent here because of these very difficulties?"

Simon was quick with his next line of argument. "Brothers, each of our honest work is transparent to all others here. We work at our daily tasks, we observe each other's labor, we benefit from the fruits of each other's vocations. Except for Brother Alphaios. We don't see it and we don't benefit from it. Nor does he share rigorously in all our prayerful life."

Though Simon knew full well that Cardinal Ricci provided for his support at the monastery, Alphaios didn't mention it. This was not a debate about money.

"Perhaps we could ask our brother to bring a sample of his work here to show us," Brother Samuel said. "It might enlighten us, assure us that he's carrying an equal burden, that he is indeed a skilled artist—even if still in need of further study in the subject of colors."

"The degree of his skill is not ours to determine." The prior turned toward Alphaios. "But maybe our brothers' concerns might be tempered if you brought some examples." He clearly hoped to bring the matter to a satisfactory end.

"Thank you for the suggestion, Prior, but I'm afraid it's not possible. None of the work is permitted to leave the scriptorium. No eyes beyond those working on it are permitted to see it until it's been presented to His Holiness. It's an inviolable rule, placed upon us by the cardinal himself."

"Then paint us a picture," Brother Richard blurted.

There was a surprised silence, then a buzz of excitement. Brothers began talking among themselves about such a prospect. For as long as anybody could remember, there had been only one painting in the monastery—a large dark painting of St. Ambrose in the refectory, and a small copy of it in each monk's cell.

"What good will that do?" Simon said. "The issue here is whether this knock at our door, this intrusion that has caused all this disruption, had to do with Alphaios's work. And whether this study of colors, as he calls it, is an appropriate pursuit for a guest in our midst, especially for one who has taken vows."

"'That was how you constructed the question at first, Simon," John said. "But you've managed to question not only our brother's skill—for which he was selected not by us but by others—but also his truthfulness and depth of faith. And I must ask my brothers, which is the greater fault, the initial disruption itself, or magnifying it to the point of collusion among brothers and argument amongst us all?"

Simon flushed in anger, but John went on. "Having raised the question of producing some of his work for all brothers to see, then let's see it. Alphaios, can you paint us a painting?"

He thought for a moment. "If that's what my brothers wish."

Simon was seething but remained silent. Samuel again came to his aid. "If we must have this exercise, so be it. But let's set some conditions. If we have to look at a picture, let it be of an appropriate subject. A humble monk seeking the salvation of his soul."

"And only with the colors of this monastery." Levi looked around at the gray walls, the brown habits, the dark wooden furniture. "That shouldn't require further study, should it?"

The prior looked at Alphaios. "Is that acceptable?"

"It is. I request only that I be allowed to bring the tools of my craft to my cell so I can proceed." Then another thought occurred to him. "And that when it is done, my brothers view this painting quietly for five minutes before discussing it."

The prior glanced around the gathering. "Is this arrangement acceptable to all our brothers?" They all nodded except Simon, Levi and Samuel, who looked on sourly.

"Then let us bring this meeting to an end. And let us remember, each of us, that we're here to address salvation in harmony and community."

Father Michael began the prayer. It seemed a hopeless benediction.

Alphaios could paint, of course. That wouldn't be the issue.

It had been several years since he had exercised any artistic freedom on a work of his own, and oddly, he found himself hungry to do so now. The little natural light from the tiny window in his cell was the least of his concerns. But what could he paint that would quiet Brother Simon? He didn't need Simon to go from antagonist to enemy, yet could not set aside his own feelings on the matter.

He did not start the painting for more than a week, but in the end settled on the idea, a visual impression that had come to him right after the chapter meeting. His decision made, his thoughts nearly leaped onto the canvas.

When it was completed, he asked Prior Bartholomew to come alone to his cell. Upon seeing the painting, the prior's eyes widened. He stood before it for a long time before speaking.

"Is this truly what you see here?"

"Yes. It's what I see."

"It will cause trouble."

"I know. Do you wish me to destroy it? If so, on Friday I'll admit failure and we'll move on from there."

"How can I ask you to destroy what your eyes and heart see? How can I ask you to destroy beauty? Pray for goodwill among our brothers, Alphaios, and show your painting. Then it must go. It cannot stay here."

"Yes, Prior."

Three days later, chapter meeting was again held. His covered easel sat in the sunlight under the clerestory windows, pulling taut the attentions of them all. Routine matters were disposed of quickly. When it was time, he asked one of the younger monks to undrape the picture.

In the direct sunlight, the large portrait was a riot of color. In the lower right hand corner, a monk, clad in brown, knelt in prayer in his cell. He was painted in a traditional manner, within gray walls and shadows. But the eye was quickly drawn outward from the monk as the palette expanded as if in rays until the colors became wide, complicated swatches of brilliant greens, blues, reds, yellows. Beyond the monk's cell, the style was reminiscent of cubism. The church's spire was just recognizable among the patterns.

For just a moment there was silence. Then, furor. There were shocked cries of outrage: "Heresy," "Irresponsible," "Hedonistic."

Brother Simon was yelling and red-faced. Consternation filled his brothers' faces. It was as bad as he had feared.

Simon's voice finally achieved ascendancy. "This is apostasy!"

Alphaios sat quietly as the noise buffeted him, hands folded in his lap. When the room finally quieted down, he said, "My brothers, we agreed you would view the painting for a short while before commenting. I have presented the painting asked of me. I beg you to sit quietly and study it."

Some of the monks were not easily settled, and calmer brothers had to encourage them back to their seats. Finally, there was an uneasy quiet. Alphaios could see, however, that there were silent but angry communications among several of them.

After five agitated minutes—which must have seemed longer than evening prayers to some of his brothers—several monks started talking all at once. Prior Bartholomew stepped in and asked them to speak one at a time. He invited Brother Simon to go first.

He was still red. "How, Alphaios, do you have the gall to present this to us? It was to be a portrait of a monk in prayer. There's one there, but he's . . . he's tiny," he sputtered, "compared to all the . . . rest of it. You've demeaned and belittled us!"

Alphaios had expected a strong reaction, but not an outright personal attack. He forced down his anxiety and responded as calmly as he could. "I don't demean you or any brother here. This is my vocation as well. May I ask you, Simon, how large, in all of God's creation, is a humble monk? How large should he be?"

Simon was stopped short for a moment, and Brother Samuel stepped in. "But surely, in a portrait of a monk, the monk could be larger."

"Yes, he could," Alphaios said.

Simon regained his footing. "We proposed, and you agreed, to paint a monk at prayer. It's not the monk you've diminished, Alphaios, it's prayer itself!"

There were muted noises of agreement at this line of argument.

"And how, Brother," Alphaios asked, "do you conclude that the prayer is small, if I tell you the whole painting is an expression of prayer, of faith."

"But the monk is so small . . ."

"I count myself among the smallest of specks on this mortal sphere, yet I have faith my prayers are heard. How much bigger do I need to be?"

"You're twisting my meaning."

"I'm stating my faith, within the teachings of St. Ambrose."

"All the colors!" Levi said. "You've broken your word. You agreed to use only the colors here in the monastery."

"And I have done so, Brother. I found each of these colors here inside these walls."

"Where? I don't believe you. But it's easy enough to prove. Show us your colors."

The prior stepped in to mildly rebuke Levi for his direct language and to ask for civility. Then he turned to Alphaios. "Can you show us where these colors come from?"

"Where would you like to start?"

"The red," Samuel said. "Where is all the red?"

"There are many reds in the painting. There's the red of the wine we drink, and the red of the blood it symbolizes. There's the red of the geranium Brother Timothy tends so carefully, and you've surely noted it's different in the sunshine than in the shade. The red of the cardinal that visited our steeple last year, and the more common flash of the red-winged blackbird. The red of the tomato we eat, and the different red of the tomato soup. There's the red of the clay in our earthenware, the red of the rust on our gutter pipes. I can continue."

"The yellow," another said. "Where's all the yellow?"

"The sun, most obviously, which lights and warms our days. The corn in our meal. The leaves that float over our walls come autumn. Squash. The yolks of the eggs Brother John cooks for us from time to time."

He went on. "The pale orange appears on the parapet above the cloister when the sun is setting on warm, clear days. And carrots, of course. Not to mention the navel oranges Brother Benjamin's sister in Florida sent him at Christmas."

Some of the monks had started to peer around the refectory, perhaps looking for a glimpse of Alphaios's colors. "The pink? Our own Brother Malcolm, you will admit, turns many shades of pink when embarrassed or exerting himself. He's obliging us right now." This brought forth a few smiles.

"Yes, yes, and I suppose the greens are from Timothy's plants," Levi said. "Here in the monastery, the colors you're pointing out are tiny by comparison. Yet they dominate your painting."

"And the tender shoots of the trees in the spring, and their leaves in the summer," Alphaios said. "The weeds that come up between the flagstones despite Brother Timothy's best efforts. And do you notice the black? This isn't the black of the night, but the blue-black of an iridescent beetle."

Alphaios paused again, hoping for silent attention. "My brothers, I study colors every day, everywhere. Then I apply what I learn to my craft. I don't expect you to approve of the style I've chosen to paint, nor of my generous use of colors. I know this painting will not be hung inside these walls. But two questions were presented to me to answer. And I hope you will permit me to answer a third. First, am I a painter or a copyist? The answer to that question is both. Second, is further study necessary for me to accomplish the work I've been called to do? I hope I've demonstrated that studying color is inherent to my craft. I've been trained to seek out, to see color wherever it is. For me, noticing color is like breathing."

He paused again, and the silence held. "Finally, if I may, there is the question of whether or not color is a distraction from our prayers. We all have distractions—hunger, physical urges, anxieties, memories. For some of you, colors may be a distraction. I will not impose them upon you. But as for me, my brothers, I celebrate colors in my prayers. I must say, in fact, that I pray in color."

There was a long silence in the room. The sunlit painting was no longer the center of attention. The monks were thinking of their own spiritual labors.

After a long moment, Prior Bartholomew broke the silence. "And where in the monastery, Brother Alphaios, did you find that remarkable clear blue, that one there, just above the monk?"

"That's easy, Prior. To see the clear blue of the sapphire, I have but to look into Brother Simon's eyes."

CHAPTER 23

ALPHAIOS WAS TROUBLED. Since the day the prior had given it back to him, the portrait had been sitting, still wrapped, behind one of the wooden cabinets in the scriptorium. He didn't know what else to do with it.

As a restorer of the artistry of others, he was accustomed to his work being anonymous and having a limited audience. In fact, there was a certain congruence of his vocations as illuminator and monk. His vows called upon him for near anonymity of self in a relentless search for salvation. That was the life he'd chosen as a youth, though back then he couldn't have had any conception that he'd find himself here today.

His portrait of a monk in prayer would be anonymous as well, but the painting tugged at him. It had been a very long time since he he'd vested as much of himself, tried to convey as much in a single work. He wanted to do something with it, not just hide it away.

Perhaps it was so important to him only because he had so few opportunities to express himself—not in the form of some forebear, but as himself. Maybe if he were to do fifty original paintings instead of just this one, it would have less value to him. Then again, this one had been born of a challenge not just to his skill but to his very view of the world. There was much of him to be discovered in it by the discerning eye. That was why the prior had kept it as long as he had. Given the amount of discord it had caused, he certainly could have directed Alphaios to remove it immediately.

Instead, after the turbulent chapter meeting, Prior Bartholomew had taken the portrait to his cell and kept it there for seven days. On the eighth, he'd wrapped it in the heavy brown paper used for shipping shoes and solemnly given it to Alphaios. "Find it a home."

The feelings expressed in chapter had not entirely gone away, but most of the monks had settled back into a general sense of goodwill. Even if he hadn't won agreement among them, perhaps he had at least earned a measure of respect for his work. That did not extend to Brother Simon, of course, nor to his closest allies. There had been no further incidents, but they stayed watchful of him. If they wished again to ignite their deliberate indignation, they would do so and it would be beyond his control. He would not constrain himself so far as to gain their approval, which would be churlish even if granted.

One Thursday afternoon, rather than going to the patio café, he took up the painting and walked to the Green River

Bar and Grill. The wooden screen door slapped closed behind him when he entered. Oddly, its sound made him feel welcome.

Jess wasn't there, and Jack, the barman, wouldn't speculate as to when she might return. Alphaios chose the window table he remembered so well, and leaned the painting against the wall. For a moment he stood and watched the flow of traffic and smiled at the memory of that first, unpredictable conversation with her. It had been like chasing fireflies, but in the end more substantive than most.

Jack had a crooner on the sound system—opera seemed to be Jess's taste, not his. Alphaios went to the bar and asked for a cup of coffee. His offer to bring payment on the following day was refused, and he returned to the table with the steaming white mug.

He didn't know exactly why, but now that he was here, he found himself relieved that Jess was not. Now she could look at the painting, study it, and like it or not without him there to watch her reaction. Her response was important to him, yet he felt shy about observing her form it.

Jess didn't know he was going to bring the portrait by. She didn't even know he was capable of such a painting. He didn't expect her to hang it in the café—that would be presumptuous, and beyond him. Anyway, it wouldn't fit in among the vast, spare landscapes that rooted the café in the American West. Not this work, its exploding colors its only topography.

He'd thought about hanging it in the scriptorium, but it carried emotions he didn't want to face every day. He could offer it to Inaki, but then faced the possibility the archivist would feel obligated to hang it in his office. It could go to someone on the commission for disposition, but its members were not associated with his personal life at all, and he wanted to keep it that way.

Jess, more than anyone he knew, had a grasp of the emotions around the creation of such a painting. She took herself into the paintings on her walls as if they were life itself. Her high steel, she had called them.

Alphaios sat for half an hour, watching people walk by. Second only to the serendipitous encounters he sometimes had with the citizens of this city, this was his favorite pastime.

Finally he roused himself. He asked Jack for a pen, and wrote "I'll be back" on the paper covering the portrait. He leaned it against the wall, nearly out of sight, and left the café.

For the next several nights, he speculated about what Jess's reaction might be. He wondered what she might suggest as a home for the portrait. And if she even thought it worth the bother.

On the following Tuesday, Alphaios returned. When he arrived, he was brought up short: the portrait, now framed, hung in the café's front window. Its bright colors were intense in the late-afternoon light.

He was stunned. He stood in front of it, bewildered; he didn't know what to do. His intensely private painting was being displayed for anyone and everyone to see.

After several awkward moments, he heard the screen door slap. Jess emerged from the doorway and stood beside him on the sidewalk, also facing the painting. He didn't so much see her as become aware of her presence.

"It was left inside," she said without preamble. "It's not signed. Not too bad, really, for an anonymous painter. It needed a frame, though. Looks a whole lot better now. Don't know why someone would just leave it here. Wrote a note, but didn't say who. Thought if I put it in the window, someone might recognize it."

She was playing with him, but he couldn't come up with a retort. He could barely put a thought together.

"Interesting composition, don't you think? Very fine detail in the guy kneeling, maybe a monk? Looks something like you, by the way, the what-do-you-call-it, tonsure? Extraordinary, really. Reminiscent of the early masters there in the corner. Vermeerish. Is that a word?" She swept her hand through the air. "But then there's this great radiant, modernistic, what? Universe? Is it what he dreams of? Is it his idea of heaven? Or is he hiding from it? What do you think?"

Alphaios still couldn't speak, and kept staring at the painting. He hadn't been ready for such a display, let alone such penetrating questions.

"Captivates you, does it? Me too. Not my style, though. Have to say I thought twice about hanging it, but I wanted whoever left it here to know where it was. Still don't know, nobody's come by for it."

He was drawn to Jess, her straightforwardness and unassuming ways. He'd enjoyed her intelligent playfulness the first time they met, but it was even more disconcerting today. He didn't quite know how to take her. She kept him off balance.

"Cat got your tongue? Come on in and have a cup."

Not knowing what else to do, Alphaios followed her into the café. She got them both a cup of coffee and led him to the table immediately behind the painting. As soon as they sat down, she turned serious.

"So, when did you paint it?"

"About two months ago. It's the first painting of my own I've done in years."

"Why'd you bring it here?"

"I don't have a place for it. It can't stay in the monastery, it disturbs my brothers. I hoped you might have some idea where it could go. I don't mean here. I mean . . . somewhere."

"You left it so I'd discover it. Why?"

Alphaios blushed. "At first I hoped you'd be here, and I could ask you about it. But then you weren't, and I decided I'd rather have you look at it without me. I figured you'd know whose it was, even if Jack didn't tell you. How come you put it in the window?"

Jess grinned widely. "'Cause I knew you wouldn't expect it. 'Cause I figured it'd make you uncomfortable."

"Touché."

"What do you mean it's the first painting of your own in a long time? Last time, you said you paint small pieces. What's that mean?"

"I'm an illuminator. I'm helping make a copy of a very special book that's irreparably damaged. That's what brought me here."

"So . . . , why don't you paint more of your own stuff?"

"I'm a monk. The only reason I did it at all was because some of my brothers questioned my credentials. The only way I could prove my capability, my usefulness to the chapter, it seemed, was to paint a picture. They chose the subject— they wanted a monk at prayer. And I promised them I'd use only the colors I found inside the monastery."

Jess laughed in delight and gestured toward the vivid portrait. "So you gave them this?"

"I kept my promise. But it did cause a commotion."

"You think?" She laughed again.

"The prior asked me to take it away for the sake of calm. I've had it in the scriptorium—my workshop—wrapped up and sitting behind a cabinet ever since."

Jess looked at him closely, as if she could see inside him. But this time she didn't make fun. "A couple of customers have commented on it. And a woman who said she was an art dealer came in yesterday. She insisted I take it down so she could look at the brushwork more closely. Asked me who the artist was. Told her I didn't know. She gave me her card in case he came back in. Here, I'll get it for you." She got up and went to the bar. In a moment she was back. "Want it?"

He was nonplussed. He'd only wanted Jess's idea of what to do with the painting and, if he were honest with himself, her opinion of it. Now it hung facing the street with people of all kinds seeing it, and Jess was pushing him into territory where he didn't want to go.

Alphaios looked at the card. It was from a gallery. "I'm a monk. I can't sell a painting."

"Didn't think so. But she thinks it's good. Real good. So, what are we going to do with it?"

Alphaios took Jess's "we" as a signal she was willing to help. "I don't know. I thought you might give me some ideas."

"I'm not exactly the art agent type."

"I don't want an agent. Just to figure out a good place for it."

"Okay, so you can't have it in the monastery. How about where you work?"

He blushed again. "It's personal. It reveals things about me that I don't want to mix with my colleagues."

Jess snorted. "Of course it reveals things about you. That was obvious as soon as the wrap came off. Why else would you paint?"

Again, he found himself without words.

"What it reveals to me," she said, "isn't the full extent of what you put into it. I'm willing to bet your brothers didn't take from it everything you thought you were revealing."

"Many of them didn't see at all. If they even thought about it, they saw me mocking their beliefs. They didn't see my expression of those same beliefs, albeit shown—" He stopped, suddenly aware he had revealed more than he should.

She looked at him shrewdly. "So, you share the same beliefs as these brothers of yours? Then tell me again why it can't stay in the monastery?"

Alphaios reddened once again. This time he chose not to respond.

"Get over yourself, Al." She was all business now. "You value this painting. You should. But other people won't see into your very soul just because they see it hanging on a wall. They're more likely to see what's in themselves, not what's in you. If they even bother to look. As many paintings as you see in your work, you should know that by now. So hang it where it can be seen. It's good. Exceptional, maybe. If you don't want it in your workshop, there's got to be somewhere else in this library of yours."

"I suppose so . . ." He was still smarting from Jess's insights.

"I'll take it down and wrap it back up. Come by tomorrow on your way to your library, and you can take it with you. The frame's on me. Improves it, don't you think?"

Alphaios stood to leave and, still flustered, thanked Jess for the coffee.

He'd taken just a few steps down the street when Jess called out behind him. "Hey, Al! You oughta paint more often!"

He grinned as he often did in response to Jess, and waved.

The next day, he carried the painting to the private library. After ringing himself in, he went directly into the scriptorium. A few minutes later, he emerged, carrying the unwrapped portrait. He found a hammer and nail in a housekeeping closet, and took it all to a little-traveled place in the first floor corridor that caught the afternoon light. There he hung the portrait of a monk in prayer.

Newly added in tiny brush strokes, in Greek letters, was his signature.

CHAPTER 24

NICO BROUGHT HIS ESPRESSO and Inaki's brewed coffee as soon as they sat down. Both men nodded their thanks and sweetened their drinks to taste. The little supply of five-dollar bills in Alphaios's mixing room never ran out, and when they were here together, as today, Inaki always picked up the bill. Their arrangement remained unstated but was no longer embarrassing to either of them.

It was a glorious day, and they were at a table in the afternoon sun. On the sidewalk, a brown-skinned woman no taller than a child moved slowly toward the corner. She wore a coat of dense black fabric that hung so long it covered her hands and feet. Around her neck looped a delicate and fringed pink scarf. Tied above her round face and over her hair was a headpiece of some kind, black and white. She dragged two shapeless pieces of luggage on the sidewalk behind her; they did not have wheels. She seemed entirely self-contained and sedate, wholly unaware of the world around her.

Behind her, a courier in a red ball cap had upended his bicycle. He bent over it, studying its rear tire intently as he turned it slowly with his hand.

When both men had settled in and Alphaios turned his eyes back to the archivist, Inaki began to speak. "You asked if Charles the Third's family traveled with him to court in Paris. I'm not sure where you're going with that, but after we talked, I called on my friends in San Sebastian and asked them to include members of his family in the scope of their search. They've sent me copies of records they've found, along with a list of leads they're still working. You ready?"

"Ready."

"As sources commonly say, Duke de Berry was the son of one king, brother to a second, and regent-uncle to a third. He was as close to a crown as one could get without actually wearing it. He lived for seventy-five years and was active in affairs of court until his death. That's a long time to influence king and country. Perhaps longer than anyone else, ever. Come to think of it, that would be an interesting course of study . . ."

Alphaios raised an eyebrow. "Some other time, Inaki."

"Okay, okay. Jean de Berry was born in 1340, twenty-one years before Charles. He was forty-seven when Charles assumed the Navarrese throne—Charles was twenty-six at the time. De Berry attended Charles's coronation in Pamplona." He paused for a sip.

"Did Charles ever visit the duke?"

Inaki sucked some air into his mouth to cool the coffee already there. "Be patient, my friend, my colleagues' work deserves a bit of suspense. The duke's chateau burned down, but they managed to track down the visitor register in some obscure museum of the royals outside of Paris—well, obscure to anybody who doesn't have an intense interest in the comings and goings of nobles in the Middle Ages. Anyway, it shows a month-long visit by Charles and Eleanor in 1382. That's five years before he was crowned. He was twenty-one. There was another extended visit two years later."

"Social visits or business, do you think?"

"Both, no doubt. For decades, Charles's father had been a thorn in the side of nearly every country in the neighborhood. For a time, he even swore allegiance to the King of England against his own brother-in-law, the King of France. He was far more trouble than seems warranted by Navarre's size. The only reason he could get away with it, apparently, was that he controlled the main pass through the western Pyrenees between France and Spain. So it wouldn't be surprising if Duke de Berry had an interest in reshaping relations with the successor-to-be. You'll recall Charles II had earned the moniker Charles the Wicked."

"I remember you saying that."

"Charles's visits to the duke's chateau didn't stop there. They resumed after he was crowned, and became annual events when the children arrived. Charles would stay for a few weeks or a month, then go back to Navarre to oversee his projects, sometimes leaving the family behind. There are only the visitor logs to go by, but the pattern is one of a growing personal relationship between the families. I don't know, perhaps Jean de Berry was more of a father figure to Charles than his own. Anyway, the records are there. Daughter Blanca was born in 1387, the same year Charles became king. For her, the duke's chateau must have been an exquisite playground, even a second home."

The sound of breaking china momentarily distracted their attention, and Nico swept in to assure an embarrassed woman that all was okay.

"When he became king, Charles managed to settle some of his father's disagreements with his neighbors. He gave up some disputed lands and traded in the lower title of count for a duchy. One could guess that de Berry had a hand in this. In any case, it moved Charles into the highest echelon of French nobility. His ambitions were to rebuild his kingdom, something his father never had any interest in doing. So, the question is, where did these impulses come from, such a sense of governance? From his own father?"

"Doesn't sound likely," Alphaios said. "How long did the visits go on?"

"Many years. Blanca married in 1402. She was only fifteen, but that was the custom of the time. Her visits continued all through her childhood, then with her husband. When he died young, she went alone. In fact, across some twenty-four years, she spent more time at the de Berry chateau than any other person on the guest register."

Alphaios let this information sink in. "Did her visits extend beyond 1408?"

"Until the chateau burned down in 1411, and then to his other homes. Why this line of questions?"

"Do you remember the year the Limbourg Brothers entered the service of the duke?"

"I believe you said 1408." His eyes opened wide. "You think . . . ?"

"It makes some sense. Her father became a patron of the arts in his own country. That could only have come from an outside influence, and you said he admired such traits among the French royalty. Who was a greater collector of the arts than Jean de Berry? And what form of art is he remembered for most? Illuminated manuscripts. Charles acquired his own book of hours in 1405. Come to think of it, that's about the same time the Limbourg brothers completed *Belles Heures* for the duke—even before they entered his service. It's a much smaller book of hours, and beautiful in its own right. But it pales beside *Très Riches Heures*."

Inaki leaned back and nodded. "Makes sense. Charles's appetite was whetted for something more grand."

Alphaios frowned. "Except we've ruled him out—at least I have—as a likely candidate for patron, because of the unconventional nature of our book. So I've been trying to think of who besides him might have fallen under such an influence. And you've now answered that question. Someone who had the means and knowledge to commission our book of hours, yet perhaps a more . . . irreverent way of looking at things."

Inaki's head started back, his eyes large. "Blanca?" It took him a moment to absorb the thought. "How . . . ? I suppose she could have gotten to know the Limbourgs, watched them at work . . ."

"That's what I think, Inaki. She watched them. And heard them talk among themselves. Even witnessed conversations between the brothers and the duke."

Inaki became cautious. "But it's all conjecture. Sure, the visits are there, but the rest of it?"

"Think of the book, Inaki."

"What about it?"

"What is its strongest theme?"

Inaki shrugged his shoulders. "It's a book of the hours of prayer. Aside from that, what's most noticeable are its size and the beauty of its illuminations."

"One other thing, Inaki. Think of characters in the paintings, and the saints they chose."

Inaki pondered, shook his head, then looked annoyed. "Now you're keeping me in suspense." It's a book of hours, has the hours of the virgin. What else?"

"All along," Alphaios said, "we've been thinking Jeremiah had a unique perspective that amounted to genius. I still think that's true. But if you look at the intimacy of the nativity painting, the importance given to St. Anne and the three holy helpers, just those paintings alone—"

Inaki bolted upright. "The point of view! It's a woman's point of view!"

Alphaios let out his held breath. "Exactly, the strong influence of a woman. Think of the Expulsion of Adam and Eve. What might terrify a woman the most, especially a woman? The absolute unknown."

Inaki sat back in his chair, eyes wide, head nodding. "Blanca knew the scriptorium at Leyre, and if you're right, she would have taken it upon herself to get to know the talents of its scribes and illuminators. It was only a day's carriage ride from the palace in Olite. Plenty close to follow the book's progress and make her wishes known."

Inaki paused, then continued more soberly. "A book of hours with a freethinking woman's point of view may not have been received well in such a reactionary time. It would be something to be hidden away and deliberately forgotten about, especially after the fire at the abbey."

Alphaios nodded. "That's what I think, too. There were plenty of inquisitions during the period, long before they were formalized there in Spain. If you've had such an extraordinary book made at great cost and taken on some of the common beliefs of the time, why take risks with it? If there's a threat, why not hide it away in the royal palace, far from prying eyes? And from the fires. Never speak of it publicly again."

The men sat quietly, absorbed in their own thoughts.

Inaki was the first to break the silence. "All the evidence is circumstantial, but it all fits together. There are those who would dispute it, but it makes sense."

Alphaios nodded, and they settled back into a long quiet.

"Inaki? The royal wink? It's a woman. It's a woman who's winking."

Inaki's eyebrows started upward once again.

CHAPTER 25

SIMON AND HIS ALLIES had not taken kindly to Alphaios's reference to the color of his eyes. Anger was not a Christian virtue, for wrath—one of the seven deadly sins—was closely linked to such sins as pride and envy and stood in the way of charity and forgiveness. Nonetheless, he felt its hard, rough edges each day from Brothers Simon, Levi and Samuel. He was unsettled, but believed that at chapter he had acted not to provoke others but to reveal himself in prayer.

Counter to his intuition, after the chapter meeting he worried less, not more, that his exploration of the city might be discovered and used against him. He had bared his heart and soul to his brothers. Some had accepted it, some had not. Those who had not, would not, for reasons Alphaios could neither understand nor control. He did know that he would not let them squeeze his soul into a tight mold not his own.

He would not let them drain the color from his faith, the joy from his spirit.

Returning from the scriptorium some weeks later, he opened the monastery's big door to the sight of monks running across the courtyard and into the church. Brother Maynard called out, "It's Mad Old George!"

Alphaios's stomach clenched as he recalled the physical eviction of the old man from the church. He was probably mentally ill, and Alphaios's own supposed sin had been not bending to the angry will of Levi.

He joined the rush and ran through the door to the choir and into the nave. The church was quiet for the moment, but not without drama. Mad Old George was lying motionless on the floor. Brother Samuel knelt beside him, and three other monks stood over them, breathing heavily. As before, Mad Old George had removed all his clothes except for a kind of loincloth. A dozen or so regulars had edged up the aisles to get a closer view. Someone thrust open the front door and ran out.

Brother Haman was standing to one side, red-faced and frightened. "He came in while I was helping a woman in the chapel. I heard him yelling, but by the time I got to him he'd already taken off his clothes. He was flailing around, and I couldn't get near him. I begged him to stop, to be quiet, but he wouldn't listen to me. Called me a devil! Philemon heard him, didn't you, Philemon? Philemon?" He paused until the other monk nodded, then went breathlessly on. "Then all of a sudden he fell down. Just collapsed."

"Is he alive?" Brother Maynard asked.

"His eyes are blinking and his chest is moving," Samuel said, "but he isn't responding to anything. It's like he isn't seeing anything, either."

Alphaios heard Brother Levi came up behind him. His voice was ice. "Well, praise God in heaven. Even He has had enough of this madman. Haul him out of here. Maynard. Haman."

Alphaios couldn't permit it to happen again. He turned and spoke quietly. "No, Levi. The man is sick. He needs help."

Levi stared at him. This time his voice was tinged with something sour. "You will defy me again?"

"If you insist on throwing him out again, yes, Brother, I will."

"Alphaios is right, Levi," Maynard said. "Whatever Old George did, it's over. He needs a doctor. Haman, go ask Bartholomew to call for help. If he's not there, call 911 yourself. Tell them we need an ambulance. Quickly."

Haman had made it only halfway to the side door when Levi spit his invective again. "Samuel, you help me! Take his arms, I'll take his legs."

Though Levi stepped forward, Samuel didn't rise. "No, Levi, you can't take the weight. Besides, I agree with Alphaios and Maynard. Leave him here. Let the medics handle it."

Levi's face turned dark, an unhealthy purple. He stared at each of the brothers in turn, then spun around and stalked out of the church. He brushed past Brother Haman as if he weren't there. Haman stopped and looked back, as if uncertain what to do next.

"Now, Haman," Maynard called. "Go!"

Brother Samuel turned back to Mad Old George, and Alphaios's attention was drawn to the men and women huddled at the first pew. Some seemed to be simply curious, but he could see genuine concern on several faces. He crossed the small space. "Do any of you know George?"

A woman nodded. She was of unknowable age and wore a rough, crusted blue scarf over stringy gray hair. "You need to talk to Jimmy."

"Jimmy?"

"You know him, Brother. Jimmy."

Alphaios finally recalled the slight man who had been eager to help him replace the broken tiles. "Oh, Jimmy Belkin."

"Dawg went to get him. He'll come if Dawg can find him."

Alphaios assumed that Dawg was a person. "Thank you. Does anybody else know about George?"

The response was a wave of shaking heads. Several of the group turned away or backed up a step, eyes downward to avoid any suggestion of personal involvement.

"How is he, Brother?" called a voice.

"We don't know. We're calling for help."

A few minutes later, the front door of the church opened and Jimmy entered, trailed by the man who'd gone to find him. Jimmy strode to the front of the nave and worked his way through the clutch of onlookers. His eyes found the man on the floor, then Alphaios.

"What'd they do to 'im?"

"Nothing, Jimmy. He was agitated and screaming. Then he collapsed. I don't think anybody touched him."

Jimmy nodded as if it were expected. "How is he?"

"Breathing but not saying anything. Haman's calling 911."

"It'll be a while 'fore they get here. Can I go to him? He knows me."

Jimmy moved past Alphaios and stood for a moment by Brother Maynard. He sat down on the floor facing George, then took the man's limp hand and held it in his own. He looked at Samuel and then up at the other monks. "Can you give us some room? He's with me now."

Jimmy didn't fuss over Mad Old George. He simply sat there beside him, holding his hand. Alphaios watched George's eyes seek out and find Jimmy's face. Once there, they stayed.

Something in Jimmy's calm suggested this was not the first time something like this had happened. This wandering, homeless soul was far better at comforting a sick man than all the monks around him. Here was the Samaritan among the Christians.

When they arrived, the ambulance crew knew Mad Old George. They spoke to him by name—leaving off the "Mad Old" nomen. They seemed more efficient than kind. They gave him intravenous fluids, and before long had him strapped to a gurney and on his way toward the front door. Jimmy walked beside him. One of the church regulars collected George's clothes and followed them out.

Alphaios approached a medic who was gathering up his gear. "Has this happened before?"

"Let's just say we know George pretty well."

"Does he do this often? I mean in churches?"

The man nodded. "Seems to have a thing about churches. He's pretty much okay until his meds run out. Then we get one of these calls. Seems the only time he can get meds is when we haul him in. Have to say, though, seems a lot worse this time. Gotta go."

Alphaios watched the doors close behind the ungainly little recessional.

The group of parishioners was smaller now, but still huddled near the front pews when he left for his cell. Maynard and Samuel had already gone. Brother Haman was sitting down, looking somewhere between prayerful and dazed. Alphaios knew how he felt.

Tension was palpable when the monks gathered for vespers—George's intrusion and Brother Levi's outburst were known by the whole group. There was no hint of what might come next, but they knew it would be something.

Levi didn't appear at vespers or compline that night, nor did he come to dinner. In the morning he showed up for lauds and resumed his place at the meal table. He was subdued but not spiritually quiet. All was not yet right.

~

BROTHER HAMAN must have been waiting for him, for when Alphaios came back through the great doors the next day, he came immediately into the courtyard and waved Alphaios toward the church.

"Brother! Brother, I must see you."

Alphaios smiled. "Why, Brother Haman, not even a pleas-antry?"

Haman looked confused, then blushed. "Good afternoon, Alphaios. Now, I must see you."

Alphaios didn't want to torment the shy monk. "Of course. What is it?"

"It's Jimmy. He's been in and out all day asking for you. Says it's urgent."

Alphaios would be happy to see Jimmy, but wondered what he could need.

"He says it's about Mad Old George," Haman said. "But that's all he'll say. He's here now."

Alphaios nodded and followed Haman. Inside, Jimmy was pacing the nearside aisle. Ordinarily he would have been in-structed to sit down and let others pray in peace—this was a pleasant fiction, of course, for virtually all of the "parishioners" were there for their physical comfort, not prayer. Still, the rule was generally enforced, and by and large followed without complaint.

Jimmy almost ran to him. Alphaios put a finger to his lips and guided his visitor back down the aisle and out the front door. The steps were not exactly private, but here they could talk. He waited until a delivery truck roared by in low gear. "What is it, Jimmy?"

"It's George, Brother. He's in the hospital."

"I was afraid of that. How bad is it?"

"They won' tell me. They've always lemme in to see him before. This time they won't even lemme on the floor. I think he's dyin.'"

"Have you seen him?"

"I followed a nurse through a locked door. Chased me out, but not before I saw 'im. He's 'tached to a bunch of tubes and wires. I saw a priest come outta his room. Brother, he has to go see 'im 'fore it's too late."

"Who has to?"

"You don't know?" Jimmy flushed, then took a step down the stairs. "Sorry, Brother. Didn' mean to bother you."

"Jimmy, what is it you expect me to know?"

But Jimmy kept moving. When he reached the bottom of the steps he turned to look up at Alphaios. He looked apologetic, but all he said was, "You have a good one, Brother."

Alphaios raised both arms in frustration. "Jimmy! Who has to go see him?"

Jimmy looked up at him strangely. "Well, Brother Levi." He stated it as if it were obvious.

Alphaios was thoroughly confused. "Why in the world . . . ?"

"You don't know?"

"Know what, Jimmy?"

"Levi's George's brother."

Alphaios felt his heart rate shoot up. He grasped the handrail for support. "You mean . . . how?"

"Well, half-brother. Differen' fathers. Told me so hisself. Wouldn't say much, 'cepting that."

George, Levi's brother? He stood there, letting it sink in. "Who knows this? Anyone else?"

Jimmy shrugged his shoulders. "Dunno. Thought all you brothers knew. Why wouldn' you?"

It was a good question.

"Been trouble there for a long time," Jimmy said. "They need t' sort it out while they still can. Can Brother Levi come t' the hospital?"

Alphaios couldn't conceive of Levi going to visit Mad Old George. But there was another problem. "He's taken a vow, Jimmy. He's cloistered here."

"You go out."

"It's different. I was sent here with a requirement to do my work someplace else. But Brother Levi doesn't leave the cloister."

"Even with his own brother dyin'?"

"Even then."

Jimmy shook his head in disbelief. "Seems downright un-christian." He banged the heel of his hand slowly on the iron handrail. "Brother Levi made a choice to be alone. George didn't. It's jus' always been that way, his bein' alone. Who's going to help George now? Who's going t' mourn him, he dies?"

Alphaios wondered what could be behind such a long and lacerating rift between family members. "I don't know that, Jimmy. I don't know."

Jimmy gave his head a slight shake, then turned to walk away.

"Let me know what happens with George."

Jimmy paused for just a moment. Without turning back toward Alphaios, he gave a small nod. Then he stepped into the flow of pedestrians and was gone.

～

AS SEEMED INEVITABLE in a chapter of faults, the subject of Mad Old George was brought up once again. It was not accusation this time, but a query from Brother Richard, who had not witnessed the event. He wanted to address it, he said, because it had broken the peace among them yet again.

It was not Brother Simon who brought up the matter, and Richard had no tone in his voice that indicated anything but sincerity. This was not preplanned by Simon or Levi; perhaps the fact that George had been so unresponsive had softened their feelings.

Alphaios knew none of his brothers had forgotten the last time they had discussed Mad Old George, and noticed their bodies shifting with anxiety. Most of them did not like conflict. He knew he didn't.

Richard turned his question to Brother Levi, inviting him to respond first.

Levi had been silent until this time, seemingly closed to what was going on around him. But when this subject surfaced, his back stiffened and he looked at no one but Richard. He started with a deliberate, forced quiet, but then his voice rose steadily.

"We battle the devil with every breath we breathe. We cast out this blasphemer, yet let him enter God's house again and again. And now, given the opportunity to confront and expel him once more, do we do so? No, we permit Satan, feigning some mortal illness, to remain in the House of the Lord!" He was loud now, disconcertingly so. His voice turned bitter, sarcastic. "We coddle him. We hold his hand. We ask him,

'How may we help you, O great Satan? How may we ease your stay?'" Now, he was shouting. "Are we not men of God? I ask you, Brother, are we not men of God?"

There was a shocked silence in the room. Richard looked shaken—he'd clearly not expected such an outburst.

Simon reached out and rested his hand on the older monk's arm. "Of course we're men of God, my brother. I'm sure those involved can see the error of their ways."

"Not at all, Brother." Maynard was red in the face. "We sought help for a sick man. He posed no threat. He was no longer cursing or defaming anyone. He was ill."

Levi shook away Simon's hand. "Ill? God struck him down for his blasphemies, yet you give him succor? You offer him comfort?"

Maynard started to answer, but was interrupted by another shout. Levi had stood up, and was bent forward with emotion. "Do you not yet know that he's the devil?"

After a moment or two, Levi realized he was standing. Shaking visibly, he sat down.

Simon appeared ready to say something to Levi, but Alphaios spoke first, gently. "Brother Levi, who is George?"

Levi looked at Alphaios, and his eyes widened. He spoke at normal volume, but with ice again in his voice. "The voice of the devil, and you are his protector."

"Brother," Alphaios said, again quietly, "who is George?" He could feel the eyes of Prior Bartholomew and his brothers as they wondered what he was getting at.

Levi's response this time was blustery, but Alphaios could see awareness dawning in his eyes. "He's Mad Old George! He's a curse to our sanctuary!"

"Yes, he's Mad Old George. But who is he?"

Levi's voice was climbing again. "How should I know who he is?" The question hung in the air.

"Is he your brother?"

The room was silent for a long, long moment. The monks Alphaios could see were wide-eyed, some with their mouths open.

"No! He's not my brother! How did you get that—?"

"Half-brother, Levi. Do you share the same mother?"

Levi's bluster was gone. He looked at Alphaios with incredulity. Then he seemed to crumple where he sat.

No one moved. Everyone, including Brother Simon, was looking at Levi with open astonishment. No one spoke as realization began dawning upon them.

What were they to say? Alphaios had had a day to ponder it and still wasn't certain where to go from here. Yet he needed to offer something. With the slightest shake of his head, Prior Bartholomew signaled him to wait.

The silence stretched out again while the prior gathered his thoughts. His voice was gentle, too.

"Levi, it's true? George is your brother?"

"Half-brother," Levi mumbled. "He's my half-brother."

Prior Bartholomew let the silence absorb some of the electricity in the room.

"Brother, none of us knows what awful circumstances or pain or injury might have befallen you. Or what might have caused such alienation between you and your half-brother. Except we can understand it must have been torturous, too painful to bear. We don't need to know what befell you, and will not ask. We offer our understanding and compassion. As you well know, the privacy and blessing of the confessional are available if you wish."

Levi did not respond. His head was hanging low, his shoulders sagging. In contrast, Alphaios's body was buzzing as if all his nerve endings were firing at once. He didn't know where his actions this day might lead, but needed to tell Prior Bartholomew about George's medical condition and Jimmy's wish to have Levi visit him.

CHAPTER 26

IT WAS JUST DAYS LATER and approaching sext, when
Haman—now the churchwarden for both mornings and
afternoons—found him in the kitchen cutting vegetables for
the evening soup. Alphaios nodded at his request, finished
his task, and once more followed his brother into the church.
Jimmy was back and pacing again, but with tears running
down his cheeks. Streaks of dirt showed where he had used
his hand to wipe them away. A group of men and women
drawn by his distress had gathered close by.

"He's gone, Brother. George is dead."

Alphaios crossed himself. "God be with him. When did it
happen?"

"This morning. Just came from there. Saw them take him
outta his room. Will you tell Levi?"

"When I can, yes. What will they do with him?"

A tall, thin black man with a deeply etched face spoke. "They'll send him to a mortuary, probably for cremation. Cheaper'n a casket. Don't know which one. After then, potter's field if there ain't no kin."

"Where is this potter's field?"

"Don't know. No headstones, nothing."

"Jimmy, can you find out where they've sent George?"

"Maybe. What you got in mind?"

Alphaios wasn't ready to share the thought that had tripped across his mind. "I don't know, Jimmy. Maybe if we know where he's going, we could pay our respects."

"That'd be real good, Brother. You and me?"

"Get the name of the mortuary and meet me outside the front doors the day after tomorrow."

Jimmy seemed newly energized. "You got it, Brother."

On Thursday afternoon, Jimmy led Alphaios to the mortuary. They told a clerk what they wanted and were directed to a sitting room. After a long wait, the mortician came out holding a small, plain box. He set it down carefully on a table, then looked at his visitors. His eyes spent considerable time on Alphaios and his habit before they moved on to Jimmy. Monks were likely less frequent among his clientele than homeless men.

"My name is Clay Morton. If you intend to take him, gentlemen, you'll need to pay the cost of his cremation. What relation are you?"

"No relation," Jimmy said. "I'm his friend, but don't got no money."

"Then he'll go to potter's field. We've got him down as George Doe. Do you know his last name?"

Alphaios and Jimmy looked at each other. Both shook their heads. "There'll be a funeral?"

"The city chaplain will say some words over him, here or there. Unless some family member shows up with funds to pay for one."

"We know only of a half-brother," Alphaios said.

"Where is he? Is he going to come forward?"

"He's unable to." Alphaios knew that in his present state of mind, Levi wouldn't come even if he could. "He has no money, either."

"Well, then . . ."

"When'll the chaplain be here?" Jimmy asked.

"Whenever he can fit it in. With all due respect to the remains of . . ."

"George," Jimmy said.

"George. There's a score of such remains he has to deal with every day. Here and other places. So, it's when he gets here."

"Then what?"

"We'll send him over for recording and burial. You can go over there and look for him."

Alphaios thought of the veneration monks gave to their own who died, and the commendation they sent to the Lord in prayer and song on their brother's behalf. Was George simply to be cast aside in death as he had in life, too much trouble for anyone to salve his wounds, to calm his soul? This man who was tormented by demons either human or devilish?

"Release the remains to me." The thought had been building since first hearing about the anonymous burial. Jimmy looked at him, startled.

"Can't do that. He's got to be recorded. I do it, and then they have to do it over there, at potter's field."

"Mr. Morton, George was ill. Not just physically. He had an illness in his mind, and he drove away every person that might help him, except Jimmy here. George's half-brother is a monk, like me, in the Monastery of St. Ambrose. His vocation doesn't allow him to leave the cloister. So here I am."

"You're here on his behalf? Perhaps you have something in writing?"

Alphaios shook his head. "He's chosen to spend his life in seclusion, even with regard to the other monks." Jimmy's eyebrows rose. "No one can speak to him unless and until he decides they can."

"Even regarding the death of a member of his own family?" Jimmy was not the only one curious.

"Even that. A monk's vocation is a compact with God. Births and deaths, though God-given, are fundamentally temporal events. But if you'll release the ashes to me, I'll find a way to honor George."

"I can't do that, not without a court order."

Alphaios found and held the mortician's eyes. "Mr. Morton, you're a compassionate man. You understand that George's remains can go to this field you speak of, where he'll remain anonymous forever, or you can entrust them to me. I will see to his burial among people of faith and family. I believe you can find a way to let this happen."

The mortician was still for a long moment, then reached down into the cabinet and took out a black cloth sack with a drawstring. He put the box into it and gave it to Alphaios. "I see far too many lost souls come through here. Most have no advocates whatsoever. The city doesn't need one more. Take him, but don't tell anyone." He looked intently at each of them until they nodded their concurrence.

When they were once again on the street, Jimmy wanted to know what Alphaios had in mind. "Where'll you bury George, Brother?"

"I truly don't know. I have no idea what I'll do next."

"But I thought . . ."

Alphaios shook his head. "Maybe we can get Levi and George to reconcile someday."

Jimmy gave Alphaios a sideways look, then a tentative grin.

When they returned to the monastery, vespers had already begun. He left Jimmy and went through the cloisters and into the choir, where he laid the little box in a deep shadow and joined his brothers. When the office was completed, he remained as if deep in prayer, and then, when the others had left, picked up the box and took it into the nave. He crossed in front of the altar and knelt before the statue of Mary. He reached behind her right foot and found the small, virtually invisible wooden door that had been fitted neatly into the carved wood. He'd found it while dusting the statue during one of his mornings as churchwarden, when he'd bent to inspect what had looked like a scratch or defect. In the small space behind it he'd found a red glass candleholder like those used in the sanctuary for the offering of prayers. It was shattered, and its shards scattered over a faded photograph of a gaunt, angry-faced woman who looked too old to be the mother of the boy who clung to her on one side and the boy who stood apart on the other. He'd left them undisturbed.

Now he pried the door open and carefully removed each splinter of glass—their purpose, however acute, however consuming, was gone. The picture, however, he left in the little space. He slid the small box in its cloth sack in beside it and replaced the door.

"Wait here, George," he whispered. "Wait here until Levi is ready for you."

~

HE CHOSE TO WAIT until the blessedly uneventful chapter meeting was nearly over and the benediction approaching. When he spoke, it was quietly, reflective. "I've been much troubled, my brothers, over the matters relating to Mad Old George. I've told Prior Bartholomew this news, and he has conveyed it to Brother Levi. When taken from here to the hospital, Mad Old George was extremely ill. He died there just a few days ago. This troubled man will bother us no more."

From their earlier reactions to the deaths of the infant and its father, Alphaios knew this revelation would be received very differently from brother to brother. Not wanting to be subjected to another disturbing debate over George or any other person not their own, he continued. "Sometimes painful conflict can lead us to reflect on the ways of our hearts and souls when they are untethered from love." He paused to let his words sink in. "As contentious as his visits have been for us, I believe that Mad Old George has served to distill each of us down to our essence. Now, upon his death, I am confident that he will remain among us.

"May we have the benediction now, Father?"

Prior Bartholomew raised a puzzled eyebrow as Father Michael began the prayer.

CHAPTER 27

ALPHAIOS EMPTIED his cup, nodded to Nico, and left the café.

The last several days had been cold and dismal. Heavy fog kept the sun away, and the light from the scriptorium's windows was so poor that he had not even put brush to page. Today he'd checked the new stock of vellum for flaws and then fled to the warmth of the café. There he felt guilt, though small and brief, that his monastic brothers would not enjoy such comfort.

When the weather was bad, he would sit inside the café and listen to the music in the voices of others around him. They could be sweet and low, round or flat, light and laughing, harsh, guttural, boisterous or demanding. He also found great interest in the conversations about everyday life. There were friends and lovers, families and co-workers. Sometimes there was the heat of anger, but mostly it was ordinary, routine, the subjects very different from his own life.

But today the traffic counter was there, making rounds of the tables and dominating conversation. The cold air must have driven him inside, for he usually stood at one of the intersections and counted cars as they went by. He carried a clipboard-like platform with eight manual click counters across his arm. He was a compulsive talker. Whenever he could capture a listener, he would stop watching cars to describe the complexities of the task and explain at length that he was researching the number of Russian cars on the streets. He had a theory that Americans wouldn't buy them, so their numbers reflected the presence of unfriendly foreigners. The more such cars, he argued, the weaker the American position in the world. But so far as Alphaios could tell, the most he ever tallied was one or diplomatic limousines a day.

Alphaios had been caught more than once—the traffic counter was insistent and could make it very difficult to pull away. Here in the café, he'd found fertile ground. However much they may have regretted it, most people were too polite to brush him off.

Alphaios was not yet ready to return to the monastery and its chill, its perpetual grayness, but he wanted to move. He gathered his coat around him and set out at a brisk pace for a brightly lit commercial district four blocks away. He was searching for color to serve his soul, and remembered the art galleries on 32nd Street. They would have to do.

Though it was mid-afternoon, few pedestrians were about, and the heavy air quelled the usual street noise. The small neon signs in shop windows blurred colorfully in the moist air as he approached them, but they appeared and disappeared in the fog within moments.

He was nearing 32nd when he heard a muted shout of alarm followed by the clatter of small wheels on rough asphalt. An overstuffed grocery cart burst from an alley directly in front of him, straight-armed by a dirty, bearded man in a lopsided run and wearing a fireman's long yellow coat. His eyes were wild as he passed Alphaios and did not even seem to register his presence. A moment later, a small, round and equally unkempt woman followed. Her head and chin were tipped up as if to draw in more air, and she hurried as fast as her short, inflexible legs would permit. She was wrapped in several layers of clothes, topped by a blackened purple jacket. She carried three or four plastic sacks in the elbow of each arm, each bulging with who knew what. They seemed to make her just as wide as she was tall.

Then they were past him and into the fog. It was quiet again.

The unexpected flurry startled Alphaios, and his heart raced. He was just a half-block from the lights, but here there was only shadowless gloom. He didn't consider himself a brave man, but felt compelled to see if somebody was in trouble. He braced himself and slowly entered the alleyway. The fog was so dense he could see shapes distinctly only when he came close to them.

He was just a few steps into the narrow space when he noticed a pile of garbage bags against the side of a dumpster.

Several were torn open, their sour contents strewn across the greasy pavement. As he drew closer, a small blue and white box at the bottom of the heap drew his attention. It looked new, out of place.

He hesitated a moment, listening. Hearing nothing, he approached the pile. The container was plastic and insulated, like the ones used to carry drinks, ubiquitous among office and construction workers. Looking closer, he could see a label, orange and black, DONATED HUMAN ORGAN— TISSUE FOR TRANSPLANT. Next to it was another label, a pink one, HUMAN HEART. A shiver slid up his back and down through his arms. His breath caught in his throat. He stumbled backward and nearly fell down.

This must have been what terrified the couple. They'd been scavenging for food or treasure and had come across this container. He gathered himself, jumped forward and hurled aside the bags of trash that nearly surrounded the little chest. When it sat alone he could see a disconcerting biohazard label.

The tape around the carrier had not been broken; its seal looked intact.

Without knowing what he would do or where he would go, Alphaios picked up the chest in both hands and began to run. At the mouth of the alley, he turned again toward 32nd Street. Once there, he ran toward the brightest lights he could see. He didn't know his destination, only that he must do something. Someone would need this box and its . . . contents.

Given its momentous cargo, the box was very light. He did not want it to swing as he ran, so he held it in both hands, up near his chest. This made running awkward, and he hoped he wouldn't stumble. He startled a number of people as he ran by in the fog. They looked at him fearfully or strangely and moved away to the edges of the sidewalk; none seemed inclined to help.

At the end of two more blocks, Alphaios's breath was ragged. When he came to a DON'T WALK sign, he stopped and set the little cooler down on the concrete. He looked ahead and from side to side, but found nothing that would help him decide where to go. When the light changed, he picked up the box and ran on. He began to sweat heavily under his coat, and the placement of his feet was becoming uncertain. His breath came in noisy gulps. When he could run no more, he stopped and once more set his load down. He bent over it, his hands on his knees, his chest clutching for air.

He was still leaning over, head down, when he heard the sweep of tires and a brief, sharp splinter of siren. A police car, lights suddenly flashing, turned abruptly and skidded to a stop, angling toward him. He was still straightening up when he heard an officer bark, "Step away from the box!" Breathing harshly, still more visceral than cognitive, Alphaios didn't move. "Move away, sir." The officer now held a gun held in a shooter's stance. A second officer joined the first.

"It's a heart!" Alphaios choked out.

"Move away! Back off!"

"It's a heart, a human heart!" His throat was raw.

"We know what it is. Step back, now! Put your hands behind your head!"

Finally comprehending, Alphaios raised his hands and laced them behind his head. He took a step away from the cooler. His breath was still coming in gasps. He was exhausted and wanted to sit down, but was afraid to do so without the officer's permission.

The second policeman circled around and came up behind him. He told Alphaios to stand still, and ran his hands over his body. "Take off your coat. Slowly."

Alphaios lowered his hands and complied. When he finished, the officers stared at him. He must have looked very strange, sweating heavily in his rough brown habit, rope belt and bulky shoes. For just a moment, the cold air felt good against his hot wet skin, then it chilled him deeply. He wrapped his arms around himself.

"What's your name?"

"Brother Alphaios." He was still breathing heavily.

"Where do you live?"

He gave the name and address of the monastery. The officer nodded in recognition. "What're you doing out here? I thought you monks didn't come out."

"That's right, mostly. But I work outside in the city."

The officer with the gun bent over to inspect the small cooler. "It's the heart, all right. It hasn't been opened. It's a damn shame it's too late."

"Let's get it to the hospital," the second officer said. "Maybe it's still good."

"They called off the search an hour ago."

"Let the docs decide. Let's go. We'll have to take him along. Don't have time to wait for backup."

The officer closest to Alphaios told him to put his arms behind his back. He felt the bite of cold metal on his wrists and groaned, but the officer persisted. He pushed Alphaios toward the patrol car. "You're going for a ride. You'd better hope like hell the heart's still good, or there's a murder charge in it."

The first officer had the container. "Get him in, let's go."

Alphaios was shoved roughly into the back seat, his coat thrown in afterwards. The cooler was placed gently on the floor. The officers leaped into their seats in front, and the car jolted back. Lights and siren on, the driver swerved back across the midline, reversed direction, and raced through traffic as if the fog didn't exist.

At first, he thought only of the moment: He'd never been in a car being driven so fast among so many obstacles. It swung through traffic, narrowly missing other cars twice. The siren wasn't as loud inside the car as he'd imagined. His wrists hurt. Then it occurred to him to ask. "Whose heart is it?"

He got no answer.

Very quickly, only about three minutes later, the patrol car swung into the emergency entrance of Presbyterian Hospital. Both officers bounded out of the car. One reached in and grabbed the cooler by its handle. They ran up a ramp, through sliding glass doors and out of sight. Another police car, unmarked but lights flashing, slammed to a stop just ahead of where he was sitting. Two men emerged and followed the others through the doors. They wore dark suits rather than uniforms.

He seemed to be at the epicenter of a light-storm; red and blue and white lights flew across the walls and ceiling of the covered driveway.

Alone in the car, Alphaios began to collect his thoughts for the first time since finding the chest. He retraced his steps mentally, but couldn't get over the mountainous, throat-catching implications of what he'd stumbled onto: a human heart taken from one newly expired person and meant to save the life of another. A heart abandoned. How had it disappeared? Had he been in time? Why was he sitting here restrained when he wanted, needed, to know the fate of the heart?

After long minutes of anxiety approaching terror, and chilled air turning to chattering cold, he turned to what he knew best: memorized, internal prayer. This discipline was so deeply embedded in him, had been repeated so often, that he could recite prayers while still allowing his mind to wander, to search. In a few moments his mind quieted and he forgot to notice the cold.

Some thirty minutes later, the officer who'd pointed the gun at him came to the car and opened the door. He instructed Alphaios to get out and walked him into the hospital. They went through a large room full of people waiting restlessly for medical attention, and into a white, nondescript meeting room with a SECURITY sign on the door. There, the handcuffs were removed. He was told to sit down at one end of a table, which he did, rubbing life back into his wrists. The little blue and white cooler sat at the other end. The seal was broken; it had been opened.

There were five other people in the room, all of them grim. He recognized the second uniformed officer and the two other men who had run into the hospital. One of them, a black man, had on a stylish ice-blue tie. The second was shorter, rumpled, and wore a brown tie loosened at the neck. There was also a woman in a loose, sage green garment. A cap covered her hair and she wore no makeup or jewelry. He guessed she was a doctor.

Alphaios was the first to speak. "How's the heart?"

The man with the brown tie answered bluntly. "It's no good anymore. All it is now is evidence in a murder investigation."

"Oh, no." He bowed his head, shaken. "God have mercy."

The same man responded with barely controlled anger. "God have mercy? On who? On you?"

"On all of us. On whoever was to get this heart. On whoever gave it to save another. On whoever caused this tragedy."

There was a momentary silence in the room. From somewhere, Alphaios could hear someone yelling in pain.

"I'm Detective Rohn," the man in the blue tie said. "That's Detective Jameson. These officers report they found you running down the street carrying this container. Why?"

"I found it in an alley. It scared me when I saw what it was. It scared me witless. You don't expect to find a human heart on the street. I knew I had to do something fast. I didn't know what. I ran toward the lights. I didn't know where to take it."

"Where did you find it, exactly?"

When Alphaios answered, Detective Jameson pulled a cell phone from a pocket and stepped out of the room. Before the door shut, Detective Rohn said to him, "Bill, while you're out there, find this man a blanket and some hot coffee." He turned back to Alphaios. "When did you find it? How long before the officers saw you?"

"Minutes. Only long enough for me to run a few blocks."

"Why were you in the alley?"

"A couple of street people, a man and a woman, ran out of it as I was passing by. They looked terrified. I thought somebody might be in trouble. I went in to find out."

Rohn looked at him askance. "You know how many people do that in this city?"

Alphaios thought for a moment before speaking again. "I couldn't just turn away and leave." He looked at the little cooler, sitting on the table as innocently as if it were someone's lunch, then down at his hands.

Rohn asked him more questions: Where had he started walking, where was he going, why was he permitted outside of the monastery, where was the private library? What was the name of the little patio café? Why was he walking in a direction other than toward home? What did the street people look like? Had he seen anybody else go into or out of the alley?

Alphaios answered directly and openly, fearing these questions from the detective less than he feared them from his own prior. However virtuous—and however fruitless—his actions were in trying to save the heart, Prior Bartholomew would quickly deduce that he had again stretched his privilege.

Sometime during these questions, he could sense a change in the room from hostility to simple fact-finding. The doctor left the room. She'd made no comment, raised no question.

He was grateful for the blanket and coffee when they arrived. Jameson nodded silently to Detective Rohn.

Alphaios needed to ask. "Who was the heart for?"

The detectives looked at him, and Jameson said, more civil this time, "We can't tell you that, it's private medical information." Rohn confirmed it with a nod.

"What about the donor? Can you tell me about the donor?"

The detectives shook their heads.

He felt desperate. How was he to put this frightening discovery, the death of this heart, into a framework he could understand? "I don't need a name. Was the recipient a man or woman? A child?"

Rohn shook his head again. "Each answer will just breed another question. I'm afraid we can't. Thanks for your cooperation. The officers will drive you home."

"Wait. Can't you at least tell me what happened? How did the heart come to be in that alley?"

The detective sat down on the edge of the table. "I suppose we can let you know that much. A courier was delivering the heart from University Medical to Presbyterian. Thirty minutes by car, max. An easy, routine trip. Some punk kid stole her car out from under her. She's lucky to be alive, the way some of these things go down. We found the car, but the heart was gone. Whoever took the car must have realized what he had and stashed it in the alley. We had an all-points bulletin out, but didn't find it in time."

He paused for a moment. "A donor heart's only good for four hours out of the body. After that the cells deteriorate, and the docs say a graft into a new body won't take. We were about six hours into that timeframe when you found it. The docs checked it out, but the window had closed. The recipient was prepped, but it looks like he won't make it now. The doc in here was the lead surgeon. Damn shame."

Alphaios had his eyes fixed on the tall detective as he listened. When the man finished, Alphaios bowed his head for a moment, absorbing what he'd heard. Then he looked up and nodded his thanks. The detective stood and walked heavily from the room.

The uniformed officers took Alphaios back to their car. The drive was quiet. Nobody spoke, not even when they dropped him off at the monastery's front door.

He stood and leaned against the wall for several minutes. He watched the city go by, quieter than usual because of the fog, but otherwise normal. It was as if nothing had happened in the city, as if there hadn't even been a stitch or stutter in its heartbeat.

He wasn't even particularly late returning home.

Shivering from the sweat still soaking his habit, Alphaios went through the heavy monastery door and walked directly to the communal lavatory to wash up as best he could in the tepid water. Somewhat refreshed if not warmed, he returned to his cell, lit a candle, and sat down on the edge of his narrow bed. After a moment, he stood up, pulled the blanket from the bed and wrapped it around his body and over his head. He sat down again and remained there through vespers, supper and compline.

He wouldn't be able to say when, but sometime during those hours he reverted again to the nearly subconscious rhythm of ritual prayer. Once more it calmed his heart and freed his mind to search for order and meaning in the day's events. He reviewed his own actions, knowing he'd been driven by fear rather than rational thought.

He imagined the theft of the car and the thief's discovery of its immensely precious yet damning cargo. He found a way to look at the physical presence of the heart not as the terrified passerby who stumbled upon it, but from the perspective of the surgeon, the caring but necessarily dispassionate clinical practitioner. He put himself in the shoes of policemen who live their lives being called upon again and again, always urgently, to prevent terrible crimes or to solve them, and who are too often disappointed. Only then, painfully, did he turn to the grief of the donor's family, and then the horror of the recipient's when they learned the heart they had been told was theirs was lost, spoiled beyond use.

He did not emerge from his cell until the next morning, after lauds. When it was over, he found Prior Bartholomew in his office and asked to meet with him. When they were settled, he looked at the prior. "I have thought and prayed all night, but I still don't know how to begin. These are not matters ordinary in cloistered life, so forgive me if I offend or startle. Yet the police may seek me out again."

Prior Bartholomew's eyebrows rose, but he remained silent.

Alphaios told him of the events of the previous day, leaving out only his stop at the café for espresso and his motivation for the unusual route back to the monastery. Perhaps it was forgotten in listening to the remarkable narrative, or perhaps it was the prior's wisdom, but he did not ask Alphaios to explain this detail. Instead, he thanked him for his disclosure and asked after his well-being. Alphaios was grateful he did not get a sermon on the virtues of true monastic life. Instead, as he left the little office, he received a long and searching look.

When he arrived at the library that afternoon, he didn't go directly to the scriptorium. Instead, he climbed the stairs to the archivist's lair. Inaki was in, and upon seeing the monk's face, made room for him to sit. Alphaios once again told the story of the stolen heart. When he was done, he asked his friend to search the obituaries in the local newspapers for clues to its owners.

Both of them.

~

THREE DAYS LATER, having gained the prior's permission, Alphaios sat in a small wooden church several miles and across a bridge from the monastery. Inaki, whose search had been successful, had driven him there and was sitting beside him now. It was midmorning.

A tall spray of white flowers flanked a white casket at the front of the church. A picture of a black woman, Margaret Alfreda Brown, had been placed on a stand nearby. He could not take his eyes off it. Her eyes showed light and the promise of a laugh. His skin prickled. It was this woman's tiny, fallow heart he had carried in his desperate but futile run.

He guessed there were thirty-five or forty people present. A large family huddled in the first two rows, sobbing deeply. All of them had on Sunday dresses and suits except one young man with a red pizza-shop shirt. Alphaios guessed he would have to go to work after the funeral.

A tall man stood holding his face in his hands, his shoulders shaking. A small boy wrapped his arms around one of his legs and wouldn't let go. His eyes were large with fright. Next to the man was a girl, perhaps thirteen or fourteen, standing erect, desperately trying to show strength in the face of despair. Perhaps she was her mother's daughter. An older woman, maybe the girl's grandmother, stood in the middle of the group, rigid, asking for no sympathy and offering none. Her eyes were burning with anger.

The pastor knew the family, and his comments were personal and sympathetic. It was from him Alphaios learned that Margaret Brown had died after being struck by a car, a hit-and-run. She'd been on her way home from her job as a practical nurse when a car came out of the dark and hit her in a crosswalk. It continued on its way, never stopping. Her head injury was devastating, and she never recovered consciousness. A donor card had been found in her purse.

God's purpose is pure and good, said the preacher, however painful and unknowable it seems to us now; all will be revealed in time. To Alphaios it sounded as if the pastor had uttered these words too often yet knew he'd have to use them again.

Perhaps the family's pain could be assuaged, he said, and even some understanding of the tragedy gained, by the woman's offering of her heart, her kidneys and her eyes so others might live and see. He called her strong in life, deep in faith, and generous in death. Amens and hallelujahs came from the small congregation as if gifts back to the preacher.

Alphaios could hardly breathe. Her kidneys and eyes as well? He suddenly was frantic to know if they had reached their destinations safely. Were they now living in men or women who had been hoping against hope for renewal of life or sight? He felt Inaki reach over and place a hand on his arm. He nodded that he was okay. His breath began to return to normal.

For all his sympathetic efforts, the choir seemed to come closer to reaching the family than the pastor did. Some of them joined the soaring voices and clapping hands, the swaying bodies in their green robes and their joyful praise. The older woman did not.

This was Alphaios's first encounter with an evangelical church, and as different as it was from his own life, he too found a sense of relief, of release in this music that was as much celebration as lament, as much joy as sorrow.

He would reflect later on this experience, probably more than once. But right now he felt his whole being consumed by a need for information about the heart he had found, and now this woman's eyes and kidneys.

When the service was over, he and Inaki got up to leave before the family filed out. To his surprise, Detective Rohn was standing at the rear.

The car was silent during the drive back downtown to the second funeral, this one for the heart's intended recipient. Alphaios was thankful that Inaki was absorbed in his own thoughts.

When they approached the cathedral-like structure, they found black limousines lined up in front of it. First Presbyterian, it said. They had to a settle on a parking place four blocks away. When they finally climbed the steps and made their way inside, the pews were full. An usher looked askance at Alphaios's habit, but handed each of them a funeral program and directed them to a small alcove off the nave. They could stand there, he told them.

"Jonas Winston Treadway, In Memoriam," the program said. It showed a picture of a handsome young man at the helm of an impressive sailboat. Alphaios concluded from the man's birth date that he'd been sixty-seven.

This time, the church was filled with black-suited men and expensively dressed women, and Alphaios was too far away to see the family. Multiple candelabra and sprays of flowers dressed the chancel. A pipe organ filled the air with ponderous, carefully measured music.

He looked around. He didn't expect to see anybody he knew, but there again, just inside the main door, was Detective Rohn.

After a couple of scripture readings and a beautifully sung "Laudate Dominum," the minister began to speak. He too referred to the will of God, unfathomable to mortals but to be revealed upon reaching the gates of heaven. The preacher brushed over one of the most pervasive but most unsatis-factorily answered questions in all of religion: Why do the faithful suffer? Why the innocent?

This minister didn't personally know the deceased or his family, or perhaps had only the slightest acquaintance with them. After a brief personal comment, he turned his atten-tion to the full church. He addressed the man's high stature in the community as a businessman, loving husband, doting father, and member of several prominent charities. He was a pillar of society.

The minister paused, as if to consider his next words. They came with a tremble in his voice.

"Even the mighty, even those who achieve great things here on earth, are in need not only of the grace of God but love and forgiveness from those they leave behind." He took a breath. "This man lived an honorable life. But as in all our lives, there are incidents, circumstances so grave, so serious, that not only God's love is needed, but the understanding of all. If God can grant forgiveness, is there any one among us who cannot?"

This seemed a dark turn, even for a funeral. It was a departure from the celebration of life and the commendation of a soul to a life beyond death. Alphaios could feel the congregation begin to stir with discomfort.

"As some of you know, though he never complained of it, our brother Jonas had a very serious heart condition. Just seven nights ago, he was driving home from a dinner meeting through the dark and a heavy fog. When he got home, he parked the car in his garage. That's where his family found him—on the floor, in front of his car. When the paramedics came he was near death, having suffered one more massive heart attack."

This really didn't explain the pastor's earlier, more ominous preface. Then, inexplicably, Alphaios began to feel the cold breath of dread.

"Jonas Treadway was taken to Presbyterian Hospital, where physicians determined his heart was hopelessly damaged. He was placed on life support."

The congregation was completely silent now. It was holding its breath, waiting for more.

"The tragedy goes on. Last Friday, a miracle seemed imminent. A replacement heart was found, and was on its way to him, literally on its way. It never made it."

Alphaios began to tremble. He looked at Inaki, whose complete attention was focused on the minister. He searched wildly about, and his eyes found those of Detective Rohn. Rohn closed his eyes. And nodded.

He felt physically ill. He grabbed for the wall and held on. How was it possible?

"We are at a loss for the why, but we know the how. The car delivering the new heart was stolen." The church erupted in nervous conversation. "The police searched for it, and finally it was found. But it was too late for the heart. Ten hours after the heart disappeared, our friend and neighbor Jonas passed away."

The minister paused to let the congregation digest this information.

Alphaios was dimly aware of a cry or two of outrage, but was consumed by his own fractured thoughts. "I've got to get outside," he whispered to Inaki. "You can stay here." He worked his way through the church doors and gulped in the fresh air. He leaned against a stone column and closed his eyes.

A moment later, Detective Rohn appeared beside him and gestured toward the steps. "Let's sit down." Alphaios nodded, and the two men, one in a rough brown habit and rope belt and the other in a fitted and stylish suit, sat down on the steps that faced the granite and glass towers of the city. Alphaios sat erect, tense. The detective leaned back and rested his elbows on a higher step.

"Do I have it right?" Alphaios asked. "Mr. Treadway had a heart attack in his garage after driving home on the same night Margaret Brown was hit by a car on the street?"

Rohn nodded.

"Was the car damaged?" Alphaios asked.

"The paramedics called it in. It wasn't hard to put two and two together. We don't know if he had the heart attack and then hit the woman, after he hit the woman, or not until he got home and realized the damage to his car. It was significant."

Alphaios took a minute to absorb this information. "But how could it be?" His emotions were roiling. "How could a heart from the victim of a hit-and-run, a sin and a crime, be sent to the very person who was driving the car? How's that possible?"

"Crazy, isn't it? Some kind of cosmic perversion."

Alphaios stared straight ahead.

Rohn sat forward and leaned his elbows on his knees. "I've had a few days to come to grips with it," he said to his clasped hands. "This is how it comes down. The organ transplant system is set up to avoid moral judgments. The sending hospital doesn't know the circumstances of the recipient, and the receiving hospital doesn't get any personal information about the donor. They keep the questions on a medical plane—blood types, compatibility, that kind of thing." He paused for a moment. "I suppose it could get very difficult otherwise. Who would make those kinds of decisions?"

After a moment, Alphaios nodded. He could hear and feel the big church organ begin to play. "When did you learn about it?"

"Not until after you found the heart and we did the investigation. It wasn't difficult, really. Just pairing the time of Mrs. Brown's death and the courier's pickup schedule with the time when Mr. Treadway's transplant surgery was supposed to take place."

"Who knows about it?"

"The police department, the medical examiner. The hospital transplant teams, I suppose, could figure it out. They didn't know where the heart was going, but would learn that it didn't survive. It could be that more people know but aren't talking." The detective pointed a thumb back toward the church. "Based on what he just said, my guess is the reverend."

"What about her kidneys, her eyes?"

"I don't know. I have no reason to know." The detective's voice sounded strained. "I don't need to know. I, for one, do not want to know."

The church doors opened and the congregation poured out. Chauffeurs emerged from their limousines and prepared to open doors for their employers.

"Two more things," the detective said. "You did the right thing, even if the heart died. You didn't make it die. And even if you'd known then what you know now, you couldn't have done anything different. The call of life and death wasn't yours to make. Not mine, not yours." He stood up to leave, and smoothed out his jacket and slacks.

"Second thing. The answer's no, we haven't found the guy who took the car. We're looking. I'd hate to be him right now. You think you're just stealing a car, and then discover you're carrying around a human heart. How could you know you'd be committing murder?"

The detective looked up at the sky. "So that's all of it, Brother. Just one more unhappy ending." He turned and went down the steps to the street. "See you around."

Alphaios was still sitting there when Inaki found him. It had gotten cold.

CHAPTER 28

ALPHAIOS BOUNDED UP the steps to the door. The day was bright and clear, and his walk from the monastery had been refreshing. The whole city seemed to be in good spirits today.

He entered the code rang the bell for entry and opened the door when the latch clicked. As soon as he entered the foyer, he found himself in an unexpected flurry of activity. Several workmen were setting up folding tables in the main hallway. Other men were bringing in portable lights on tall standards from the back entrance. XM and Kenny—Christopher was gone—were in an animated discussion just outside the scriptorium. The little-used front sitting room was open and being aired out, and a young man in a florist's uniform was placing large vases of flowers on its tables. A woman, a member of Cardinal Ricci's commission of scholars, was talking on a cell phone.

He'd never seen anything remotely like it in the reserved old building.

Up on the second floor, he could hear Inaki call out instructions, sounding unusually animated. He decided to go up and find out what was going on.

The archivist spied him as he topped the stairs, and waved him forward. "Cardinal Ricci is coming! I got a call late yesterday afternoon. He'll be here tomorrow. Wants to see the work we're doing and get a personal status report."

"Ricci? Here?" Alphaios felt a sudden rush of adrenaline.

"I'm told he flew in the day before yesterday. He's staying with Cardinal Fleet—they're old friends. I knew this could happen sometime, but figured we'd have more time to get ready. He also asked to use our sitting room to host a small gathering. Didn't say for whom."

"What exactly does he want to see?"

"That's for us to decide."

"Do you have something in mind?"

"I thought the two of us could figure it out today. I went ahead and made arrangements for tables and lights for the corridors. And his meeting. You'll need to work longer than two hours today."

"Okay, but we can't have bifolia out of the scriptorium overnight. Whatever we put out, it'll have to be in the morning. And then how do we protect them?"

"I thought of that. We can't have anyone touching the documents, so Cardinal Fleet agreed to provide full security for tomorrow. No one but our own staff will be allowed in the scriptorium except Cardinal Ricci and maybe commission members. So let's show the most valuable pages there. But we don't have enough room to show them all, so we'll have to use the hallways too."

Alphaios still felt wide-eyed about the turn of events. He needed to catch up with his colleague. "What else?"

"Only the scribes can handle the bifolia. And us, of course. Everything we display will have to be logged out and back in. I'll do that. The cardinal and his aides will be informed of these precautions when they arrive. We'll ask Ricci to keep his guests in the sitting room."

"I'll have the scribes put up some 'do not touch' signs, just in case," Alphaios said. "What else can I do?"

"Aside from choosing the pages to be reviewed, you and I'll be with the cardinal, answering any questions he has. Let me finish up a few things here, and I'll come down to the scriptorium."

Alphaios was both apprehensive and excited as he went back down the stairs. This would be the cardinal's first look at the book of hours since the copy had been started. He was confident of the quality of the work but was anxious now for the cardinal's approval. Would he find it as worthy in reality as he'd imagined?

He began to form an approach to the display. For each bifolium exhibited, they would show the original and its copy side by side. This would mean showing fewer bifolia, but since the new ones were to be an exact copy of the old, a side-by-side comparison would permit Cardinal Ricci to judge the faithfulness of

their work. He remembered a half-finished bifolium he'd rejected yesterday. It had his sweep of black ink across it but hadn't yet
been fed to the dragon. They could highlight the error and give
the cardinal an indication of their own critical review.

Speaking of errors, he would suspend all work by the
scribes until the cardinal's visit was over. Distraction caused
mistakes, and mistakes cost time and frustration.

Returning to his original line of thought, he considered
the problem of pages that were so damaged that they couldn't
be copied. The cardinal knew of the problem, but a sample of
re-created pages—either finished or in some stage of preparation—should be provided.

He would have to speak to Prior Bartholomew tonight; he'd
need permission to be at the library all day tomorrow. He
was not concerned about the prior's response, but wondered
briefly what trouble Brother Simon might cause, then set the
thought aside. He had more pressing issues.

When Inaki came into the scriptorium a half-hour later,
Alphaios had begun to list the pages to be shown. He described
his plan. They would start the cardinal's tour with three sets
of bifolia. One set would include a completed copy—both
old and new—one set with a mockup only, and one with the
rejected sheet. This would provide a basis from which the
cardinal could evaluate all the other pages on display. Inaki
agreed with the approach, but suggested two more pairs. A
fourth set would be a mocked-up page on which the scribes
had completed the text but which was awaiting Alphaios's
colors. A fifth would start with the severely damaged page

they suspected had contained the elaborate painting with the royal wink. Beside it they would place the medieval itinerant's description of the painting, along with the Jeremiah illumination Inaki had discovered in Uncastillo.

Settled on this plan, they began to select the samples. Though the highly illuminated pages were the most striking, they decided to include a proportionate number of the more ordinary pages, if they could be called that. Though it was all impressive, Cardinal Ricci should have a representative view of the whole book, not just its most spectacular aspects.

It was late when Brother Alphaios left the library, and the arrangements for the cardinal's visit were well underway. Floors were washed, furniture dusted and windows cleaned. Heavy black felt had been brought in for the hallway tables, and electrical cords for the lighting standards were taped down. He walked directly back to the monastery, still enjoying the air but his mind on the next morning.

As he hoped, Prior Bartholomew understood the circumstances and accepted with equanimity Alphaios's plan to go back to the library early in the morning.

Inaki and the scribes were already there when he arrived. Adrenaline was running high. The security personnel from the archdiocese arrived a few minutes later. They were businesslike and selected their posts quickly. The security personnel told Alphaios, Inaki and the scribes that no one but library staff was to touch the pages.

Together, he and Inaki reviewed the felt surfaces on which the bifolia would be placed. Finding them satisfactory, they went to the scriptorium, donned their gloves and began to lay out those to be placed in the corridors. Alphaios took the leaves from their wide, slim drawers, and Inaki carefully logged each of them as they left the room. The scribes took them to their designated tables and laid the pairs side by side.

The front doorbell buzzed repeatedly. A catering service arrived and laid out food and drink in the front hallway, and members of the commission gathered in a corner of the sitting room. Others came in who were strangers to Alphaios and whom Inaki did not know either. The scribes reported they were having to tell the visitors to remain in the sitting room. Inaki left the scriptorium for a few minutes to ask one of the guards to position himself at the entrance to the corridor.

When the bifolia had been placed in the corridors and checked, Alphaios took out the eight most colorful, lavishly illuminated pages. Even though they would remain behind locked doors, Inaki also logged these. Finally, he took out the five demonstration bifolia he and the archivist had selected the previous day. These also would remain in the scriptorium; it was not their purpose to give a seminar to a large group, but rather a private tutorial to the cardinal.

They were ready with fifteen minutes to spare. Inaki went back through the display, straightening pages imperceptibly, adjusting lighting, and fussing in general. Alphaios stood in the lobby, wondering how this day would go.

Shortly after the appointed hour, Cardinal Ricci entered. He was in "ordinary" dress—a black cassock with red buttons and piping, a wide red sash and a red zucchetto. With him were two priests. Both were tall, slender and smartly dressed in fitted black, floor-length cassocks. Alphaios knew that in comparison he looked beggarly. He was accustomed to the fashions of the Church, however, and had long ago concluded that such matters held little interest for him. His spirit was otherwise occupied.

The members of the commission and several others Alphaios didn't recognize swarmed out of the sitting room and crowded into the little lobby to greet the cardinal. He did not mind being squeezed out of the way, and retreated deep into the corridor where he watched and waited with Inaki for order to be restored.

Cardinal Ricci was tall, his flowing hair more silver than gray. He had urbane good looks, the bearing of gentry. More than any cardinal Alphaios had ever seen, he wore his garments lightly, as if they were not essential to him and gave him no more authority, no greater quality than he already possessed. His voice carried easily over the crowd.

Finally, the cardinal was ushered into the sitting room. One of his aides bent to ask a member of the group a question, then looked over toward Inaki. He separated himself from the group and approached.

"Are you the chief archivist?" he asked in accented English. Inaki nodded.

"I am Monsignor Continetti. Show me what you have for the cardinal. Immediately, please." He gestured toward Alphaios. "Who is this man?"

"Brother Alphaios, the illuminator. I'm Inaki Arriaga."

"Come along, then. Show me."

Inaki led the trio back to the scriptorium. He unlocked the door, and they entered. Going around the room, he outlined the approach they had planned for the cardinal. He explained to the monsignor that because of the fragility of the pages, only the cardinal should come into the scriptorium, accompanied by Alphaios and himself to guide his tour. Inviting others in would increase the likelihood of damage and unwanted leaks of information. The Monsignor frowned, but said nothing in response.

They left the scriptorium to make a quick tour of the tables in the corridor. As they approached the first display, the monsignor again knit his brows. "Take down the signs. They will insult the cardinal's intelligence."

Alphaios frowned. "The signs aren't for the cardinal but for the other visitors."

Continetti glared at him. "There won't be any others."

Inaki raised his eyebrows, but motioned Kenny over and, in an aside, asked him to take them down.

When they arrived back at the lobby, the front door buzzed once more, and to Alphaios's amazement, Prior Bartholomew appeared. Noting the look on the monk's face, he dipped his head and gave a small, knowing smile. "It's a nice day for a walk."

Before Alphaios could ask him a single question, the cardinal appeared in the sitting room doorway. "Bartolomeo! So here you are!" He wrapped the prior in a warm embrace. "We were schoolmates," he announced so all could hear. "The troublous twosome, they called us. For good reason. For my friend here, it was his skill with polemics, especially when in trouble. I'm afraid he had to use them on my behalf more than once. As for me, I'd rather not say." Laughing, the cardinal let loose of the prior and looked around. "All right, Bartolomeo, where is this painter of ours? Ah, here he is.

Alphaios. Greetings. And to you as well, Inaki Arriaga. So, you have some things to show me?"

Inaki spoke, clearly feeling his way. "Yes, Your Eminence. But I must impress upon you the fragile nature of our work. And we were given to understand that it was to be completely private until its presentation. All these people . . ."

"These people?" the cardinal said. "These people are here to see me, not the manuscript. If they think otherwise, they'll have to accept disappointment. Monsignor Continetti, please call and inform our next appointment that we'll be late. Then entertain our guests in the sitting room until we're ready." The monsignor glanced at Alphaios and Inaki, then bowed slightly to the cardinal and turned away to his task.

"Brother Alphaios, surely you do not mind if Bartolomeo accompanies us, do you? He is, after all, your host. I'll bind him to secrecy if you insist."

Alphaios blushed. "Yes, of course, Your Eminence. No, I mean not at all, Your Eminence."

The cardinal laughed aloud. "Well, let's go, then."

Inaki led them to the scriptorium and unlocked the door. It closed behind Alphaios and left them in silence. Blessed silence.

It was the book of hours itself, its beautifully illuminated pages, that guided the cardinal's visit rather than the plans made by Inaki and Alphaios. Upon entering the room, he was drawn immediately to the tables with the remarkable color and pageantry.

He heard a gasp from Prior Bartholomew, who crossed himself. The cardinal paused for long moments in front of the display, and appeared to utter a prayer.

Alphaios found himself affected as well. This was the first time their work had been displayed more than a few bifolia at a time. The richness, the cumulative beauty of the pages was indeed breathtaking. He stood by Inaki. Despite their efforts, they were content to let the book speak for itself. Even the sun seemed to conspire with them; today the scriptorium was infused with soft light.

Without uttering a single word, the cardinal, followed closely by the prior, moved slowly from page to page, peering at the new, then the old, then the new again. Once, when he looked up for a moment, there were tears in his eyes.

It was a long time before anyone spoke. When the cardinal finally did break the silence, it was to ask about the ruined page. "Have you been able to confirm whether the reputed painting with the wink belongs to our book?"

"Not yet, Your Eminence," Inaki said. "We're still tracing leads."

"Keep working on it. It's a delightful mystery." He turned to Alphaios. "If in the end there is no scholarly confirmation, Brother, we'll trust in your judgment."

Alphaios nodded and looked down at the floor.

The cardinal moved toward the door. "Now, let's see what else you have laid out for us." Inaki led them back into the corridor.

The chatter from the sitting room poured from its open door, and it was much less peaceful here. Nonetheless, Cardinal Ricci moved slowly from table to table, looking carefully at each page, bending forward from time to time to inspect some small detail. He uttered a few comments under his breath, but did not ask any questions. Alphaios wondered what was going through his mind.

When they had inspected all the work displayed, Monsignor Continetti was waiting for them. Cardinal Ricci waved him over.

"Monsignor, I must say I've found this work to be exquisite. I'm humbled by my small part in this remarkable project. But before I rejoin my guests, I find myself wanting a memento, some souvenir to take with me. Do you have a suggestion?"

"I'm quite certain you can take whatever you like, Eminence. Surely any one of these pages can be done over again with little trouble. Would you like me to select one? Perhaps more?"

Alphaios and Inaki exchanged looks of alarm.

"I'm sorely tempted, Monsignor, though you underestimate the time and enormous skill represented here. But I suppose not. I've set a rule, and if I don't honor it, others may not either."

Alphaios allowed himself a sigh of relief. As much as he was delighted with the cardinal's reaction, he did not want even the least of the pages to be taken.

"There is something else, though, that caught my eye," the cardinal said. "On the wall in the far corridor is a portrait of a monk in prayer. It too is remarkable. I believe our own Brother Alphaios is the artist. If he doesn't mind, I'd like to hang it in my residence. I'm sure I can give it a much more accommodating space than it's found here."

Alphaios was speechless. In the excitement of the cardinal's visit, he'd completely forgotten about the painting he'd so self-consciously hung there. Now it was to hang in the cardinal's palace?

Prior Bartholomew stepped forward. "I'm sure Brother Alphaios would be greatly honored. I know I would be. After all, it stood in my own cell for a brief time."

"Well?" Cardinal Ricci asked. "Can you bear to part with it, Alphaios? I'll give it a good home."

He was blushing, but managed to get out, "I . . . I guess I can. Yes, Your Eminence, of course. It would be a great kindness."

Cardinal Ricci turned serious. "Kindness is not my motive today, Brother. Beauty is. Insight is. I'm overwhelmed by what I've seen here. It is ineffable. I look forward to having time alone tonight to reflect on it more deeply."

Alphaios's eyebrows rose. This was a treasured practice of his own.

"Inaki, would you prepare the painting for travel?"

"Of course, Your Eminence."

"My brothers, I thank you for a remarkable day. Bartolomeo, my friend, I'm glad you're looking so well."

The cardinal turned to other matters. "Monsignor Continetti, let's see to our guests. How's our schedule holding up?" Alphaios could not hear the monsignor's answer as the two men turned and walked back to the sitting room.

Alphaios and Inaki would have time later to talk over the events of the day. For now, the archivist thanked Prior Bartholomew for coming and excused himself. He gathered up the scribes on his way back to the scriptorium; there were priceless pages to be logged back in.

Brother Alphaios and Prior Bartholomew were alone in the hallway. He didn't know what to say. The cardinal had invited the prior here today and had reveled in his surprise. For his part, the prior had never mentioned that he and the cardinal were friends. Had the prior told the cardinal of the portrait? How else could he have known?

Bartholomew smiled. "You can relax, Brother. Some answers are to be sought, some questions merely to be accepted. Spend your time on the ones that matter. Now, if you'll excuse me, this world of yours is perplexing and a bit overwhelming." With that, he started to leave.

"Prior," Alphaios said, "your being here today was an unexpected joy."

"Being here today, Brother, was to experience beauty like I've never before seen it. The joy has been mine. I will thrive on it for a long time to come." He let himself out the front door.

An hour and a half later, Alphaios helped Inaki finish logging the pages back into their drawers. One bifolium from the corridor tables had been slightly smudged, and was set aside for replacement.

It was an acceptable price to pay.

CHAPTER 29

MOSTLY, BROTHER ALPHAIOS felt humbled by the cardinal's visit. He spent that evening, even during compline, not in celebration—at least not quite—but trying to remember each part of the day. He sought to recall the cardinal's path through the display of pages, his posture, his expressions. He found that he cherished Prior Bartholomew's presence every bit as much as the cardinal's.

It was not about the portrait the cardinal had asked to take back to Italy; Alphaios still found himself embarrassed by that episode. Instead, it was the joy of sharing the beauty which had been a personal collaboration with Inaki, the scribes, and the master artists who had last put ink and paint to parchment nearly six hundred years ago. Today their work, all of their work, had been affirmed.

The next morning just after angelus, Brother Harold presented himself at the doorway of the kitchen. "Alphaios, the prior is asking to see you at once. John, he may not be back to assist with the noon meal." The two monks looked questioningly at each other, then Alphaios shrugged and removed his floured apron. He had no idea what might be coming.

He crossed the courtyard to the guesthouse. It occurred to him that he'd never seen it used for any visitors, though Brother Harold spent a fair amount of time keeping it ready. Prior Bartholomew was waiting for him. He seemed completely at ease.

"Cardinal Ricci wants to see you. He's sending a car to pick you up. The driver is to call me when he arrives."

Alphaios felt a pang of anxiety. "Do you know what it's about?"

"I haven't been told. Why, do you have something else on your schedule?" It was not a new joke in cloisters, and it cheerfully ignored their nearly inviolable daily calendar.

He relaxed a bit. "Aside from sext, only the kneading of the bread."

"Ah, yes, the bread. I've noticed some improvement in that area since you joined Brother John."

The telephone on the desk trilled, and the prior leaned forward to pick it up. He spoke briefly, then nodded to Alphaios. "The car's here. Go with God."

Alphaios went to the big door and opened it, uncertainty rising again. Had something gone wrong during the cardinal's visit that he'd missed? Was the cardinal displeased?

On the street was a large black sedan, its windows opaque. When the driver opened the rear door for him, he was both surprised and relieved to see Inaki in the car. He had just settled himself into the seat when his colleague asked, "What's this about, Alphaios?"

"I have no idea. All kinds of possibilities are running through my head."

"Me too. None of them good."

The sedan slid away from the curb and merged with traffic. Alphaios noted how much quieter the street was from this vantage point, and how much more distant the lives of the pedestrians. While they no longer appeared regimented, as he had thought on his first trip into the city, their individuality was much reduced. There was a sharp difference between observing them from a car and walking among them. He greatly preferred the latter.

Neither he nor Inaki was sure what he could say in the driver's presence, so they could not share their qualms during the forty long minutes before the car pulled up in front of an ornate metal gate. After it slowly opened, they moved up a circular driveway in front of an expansive brick house with a green lawn and towering shade trees. For one house to occupy so much land in this city was astounding. Alphaios could see an abundance of beveled glass set into dark wood. The house and the neighborhood whispered age and enormous wealth.

When the driver opened the door for them, Alphaios asked him where they were. "Cardinal Fleet's residence. The maid will let you in." When they were out of the car, the driver closed the door, got behind the wheel, and eased back onto the street.

Inaki led the monk up the stairs and onto a wide veranda, where he rang the doorbell. As promised, a maid greeted them.

She led them across glossy wooden floors into a large, sedate room with a very high ceiling. It was darkly furnished but well lit by the sun through cut glass in mullioned windows. Alphaios admired their effect on the quality of light.

The two men were still adjusting to their surroundings when Cardinal Ricci appeared. Alphaios was glad to see he looked affable. "Sit down, sit down. Make yourselves comfortable. Coffee?" He went to a wall and pulled at a long braided rope. Almost immediately, the maid showed herself in a doorway. The cardinal asked his guests if they preferred coffee or tea, then ordered a carafe of coffee, along with a plate of fruits and pastries.

There were many seating options available. They chose the ends of the same long sofa that might have been a century old. It was comfortably worn but looked like it would last decades more. He didn't know about Inaki, but if asked, Alphaios would have had to admit he sat there so he could be near his friend. This was foreign territory.

The cardinal sat in a large easy chair facing them. "So, gentlemen, here we are. I hope you'll forgive the inconvenience, but we didn't have an opportunity yesterday to speak privately."

"No inconvenience at all, Your Eminence." Inaki's voice carried a slight tremor.

"Anyway, I wouldn't have wanted one moment to be different. I was profoundly moved by what you showed me. I'm not embarrassed to say so in the frankest manner possible."

Alphaios sat as still as stonework. He looked at nothing. He had no idea what to say in response to such words.

Cardinal Ricci nodded. "Remarkable work, both of you. Alphaios, I understand you mix your own paints. Fascinating. I wish I had the time to watch you take a page—what did you call it, a bifolium?—from start to finish."

The cardinal shifted his gaze to Inaki. "Monsignor Continetti informs me you've been asking questions of the Vatican library regarding the fate of our book of hours when Pope Marcellus died. Your questions have been referred to me, for in the Church of Rome, even the slightest inquiry can draw great controversy. Even if it's about something that happened centuries ago."

The maid brought in a tray and set in on the low table between them. When she left, the cardinal settled back into the cushions. "I'm afraid those of us in the Church must both celebrate and suffer our history. We seem condemned to do so, for the fight between good and evil is not always between *us* and *them*—and there are always *thems*—but also among and within ourselves. We seem to have a devilish capacity to turn our faith in God into the service of our own personal interests, our own uses. Our own lusts, and worse. We have the opportunity to reject ugliness in all its forms, but often choose to accept it, or just as bad, to ignore it. We have the ability to create and treasure absolute beauty in the name of God, yet destroy it for the same reason. When we turn to God for guidance, we find that others have done the same, but with different results."

He leaned forward and poured three cups of coffee, picked one up for himself and sat back again.

"I've said more than I intended. But I'm sure you're quite aware that Church history is full of contradictions."

Inaki cleared his throat. "Yes, Your Eminence."

"So, my friends, it's fallen upon me to decide whether to share with you a part of our story. I've given the matter considerable thought, but my visit to your scriptorium yesterday settled my mind. You wish to know what happened to our book of hours when Marcellus died."

Alphaios was glad the conversation had turned to something tangible, but Inaki was the first to respond. "Yes, Your Eminence. Did Pope Marcellus really die of natural causes?"

"On this matter, Inaki, there's no good purpose for us to revisit anything but the official record. He died of an illness, and perhaps from the limited knowledge of medicine at the time. That is sufficient."

Alphaios cleared his throat. "Our interest isn't mere curiosity, Eminence. We're looking for clues that might help us understand why the book was hidden from public view, not just once, but twice. Learning that might assist us in determining what was on the pages that are so badly ruined. We have some suppositions, but information about why the book disappeared for a second time might confirm or contradict them."

"I can see your problem. Are you prepared to share your thoughts with me as well?"

"Yes, Eminence."

Over the next several minutes, Alphaios, with occasional interjections from Inaki, told the cardinal what they had learned and their theories: The book had been created at Leyre; Blanca

I of Navarre, still a young woman and under the beneficial influence of the Duke de Berry, had been its patroness; the horrible fire in 1419 and the reactions of the monks that had resulted in the deaths of its illuminators and placed the book, wherever it was, in danger of being purged; the 1448 mention of an exceedingly lavish book with a heretical wink; and the pilgrimage by Marcello Cervini to Compostela and the discrepancy in the records upon his return.

Alphaios voiced for the first time a theory that Marcellus had obtained the book in 1552, not from Leyre, but from Olite, from Blanca's descendants in the royal house of Navarre, for whom the book would continue to pose a threat from the Inquisition. This, he said, could also account for why Cervini had not recorded it upon his return to Rome.

Cardinal Ricci listened closely. When Alphaios was done, the cardinal asked several questions about Inaki's trip to Spain, how they had come by certain information, and how they had tied the pieces together. Alphaios found the cardinal's questions probing and germane, and felt their responses held together well.

"Remarkable," the cardinal finally said. "If nothing else, you've given scholars something truly monumental to try to debunk. And you can be certain they'll try." He seemed happy at the prospect. "Have you written this up? Documented it?"

Alphaios shook his head. "We haven't begun that work yet. For now, we're simply trying to deduce what was on some of the pages. Concluding that Blanca was the patron, for instance, gives us a perspective we didn't have before."

"I understand, but the two of you must make notes and be prepared to write up your work. It will become important, both to you and to me. Now, I suppose it's my turn to share some information with you."

He set his cup down, formed an open steeple with his fingers, and touched it to his lips. "First let me take you back to the Inquisition. Though it's not widely understood today, the Spanish Inquisition was as much a function of Spanish monarchs as the Church. In some areas, they used it to drive Jews out of their kingdoms and to target *conversos*, Jews who for convenience or even survival, had falsely converted to Catholicism. In areas of Spain that had been won from Muslim control, the targets were converts from Islam—*moriscos*. It is, however, the lesser but still significant repression of Protestants and witches and other blasphemers which is most remembered, at least in the western world. That and the horrifying nature of the punishments sometimes meted out.

"Your history of the fire suggests there was a very good reason for the book to be hidden. Long before the first inquisitor was appointed by a pope, the Inquisition was a broad and popular movement in many segments of the Church. In Spain, it was most active from around 1480 to 1530, but of course carried dread for decades before that. And centuries after. There were already lists of prohibited books in several other regions of Europe when the first one was published in Spain. That was in 1551. Our book of hours wasn't on it, but then it's unlikely the authorities knew about it, supposing what you say about its contents is true. As you know, this was just one year before Cervini's pilgrimage along the Way of St. James.

"It does seem likely that Marcello Cervini obtained the book in 1552. It'd be fascinating to know how that actually came about. I believe you've been made aware of the limits of the documentation. When it arrived in Rome, as you said, it wasn't catalogued into the library—even though the librarian there had personally directed the recataloguing of the Vatican's entire collection. It was apparently seen by only a few of Cervini's closest colleagues and staff. Whether he kept it in his personal quarters before he became pope, we don't know. We might safely conclude that he did. Parenthetically, I believe that many in Rome feared the Inquisition's corrosive effect on the Church as much as others cheered it on.

"It's a magnificent book, so for Cervini to hide it away, it must have contained serious controversy, even heresy. You're right, the first catalogue listing wasn't done until it reached his private chapel. Even then, it contains only its title, Book of Hours, and its size. No description of its contents or origin."

The food sat untouched, as did the other two cups of coffee.

"This is what we know. Marcellus brought with him to the papacy a secretary who'd been his personal aide for more than twenty years, Tommaso Parisi. He wasn't a member of the curia, from which most papal assistants are drawn. That was somewhat unusual and would have served to discomfit the members of the curia—who, if I may make a considerable understatement, like to remain informed. For us, what matters most is that his loyalties were almost certainly to Marcellus alone. After Marcellus's death, there's no further mention of this Tommaso Parisi in Vatican records. None whatsoever. That's unusual—most papal secretaries don't just disappear.

"As you know, Marcellus was pontiff for only twenty-two days. He was sick for several days before succumbing. Now I, too, am going to engage in supposition. Access to his quarters would have been even more restricted than normal, and the few aides permitted into the rooms would have been intensely focused on the pope's comfort and condition. Therefore, it's quite possible that though the book may have lain in plain sight, most likely in the pope's chapel, Parisi alone had any knowledge of it. Or knew where it came from and why Marcellus held it in such high regard.

"We believe it was Parisi who spirited the book away. If it had been someone else, say an inquisitor or some other zealot, the book might well have been destroyed. But since it was rediscovered in 1972, clearly that was not the case."

Alphaios and Inaki were completely absorbed in the cardinal's story.

"So how and when did it get into a storeroom on the Grand Canal in Venice? As you might expect, we traced the ownership of the palazzo where it was found. At the time of interest, it belonged to a patrician family named Barbaro. It was owned by two brothers. One of them, Daniele, was the Venetian ambassador to the royal court of England. The other, Marcantonio, was Venice's ambassador to France.

"The brothers had a new villa built on the mainland and moved into it in 1558. You must see it sometime. It's a remarkable building designed by Palladio, and it contains multiple frescos by Paolo Veronese. I'm sure you know the name, Brother. He was a painter of the Venetian School."

"I know him well, Your Eminence. He's considered by some to be an even greater colorist than Titian."

The cardinal sipped some coffee. "Now, we descend from supposition to mere speculation. We've found no connection at all between the brothers Barbaro and Tommaso Parisi. Nor between them and Marcellus's beloved sister Cinzia, nor any other members of his family. We can conceive that the Barbaros, with their broad view of the world and esteem for the arts, agreed to hold the book for safety. But agreed with whom? We don't know. The book wasn't taken to their new villa, but left in storage in the palazzo. Was it forgotten there? Abandoned as a still-troublesome artifact? Or was it slipped into one of their storerooms without their knowledge? Who knows? And as I said, the trail of Tommaso Parisi was lost."

He splayed his hands outward in an elegant shrug. "That's it. Except that the Vatican tried to reclaim the book after it was found in 1972. But given such limited documentation of its past, our claim wasn't strong enough to prevail. So in the end, there's still much we don't know. I'm sorry to disappoint you."

Inaki finally relaxed back into the sofa. "Fascinating."

"It's not disappointing at all," said Alphaios. Both Inaki and the cardinal gave him puzzled looks.

"No? I was sure you'd be unhappy not to get a complete history."

"Short of finding copies of the pages that were ruined, we have all the answers we can get. You've confirmed for us that it was probably some unorthodox, perhaps even heretical, aspect of the book that led to its disappearance. That guides our efforts to re-create the ruined pages. It's very likely they contained more evidence of freethinking by Blanca and her illuminators, even if it was only unconventional and not heretical, at least by modern standards. Who could know what would be considered unacceptable during the Inquisition?"

Inaki frowned. "But that means we have to invent several paintings. Even if we have some confidence in the topic and content, how will we ever convince the commission of their accuracy?"

"We won't," Alphaios said. He was speaking to Inaki but watching the cardinal. "But without them the book will be incomplete, and I don't think the cardinal will accept that."

Ricci nodded. "All but two of the other major paintings in the book have been done by Jeremiah, and we will assume that the ruined ones were done by him as well. Inaki, you and I have been living with Jeremiah and the others every day for nearly a year. We know them as well as if they were working beside us. They'll guide us. As for the commission . . ."

The cardinal picked up the cue. "With regard to these pages, I'll instruct the commission to focus on theme, consistency with other content in the book, and technique. Inaki will have to document the reasoning behind each painting. Having said that, I want to make one point clear." He leaned forward and held Alphaios's gaze. "This is not a time for radical invention."

Alphaios smiled at the thought. He felt a strong obligation, a compulsion, to be faithful to the convictions of Blanca and the work of the original artists. "No, Your Eminence, it's not. I'll have to save that for my own work."

CHAPTER 30

WHEN HE STEPPED through the big doors and onto Broad Street, Alphaios had to lean back into icy gusts of wind lest they push him into a run. The people around him were bundled up in heavy coats and caps, scarves wrapped tightly, faces tucked downward. He wished briefly for more than the old coat and open habit, then chided himself for a lack of gratitude. Many would fare worse this day.

Though the warmth of the morning's bowl of oatmeal was long gone, Alphaios could still taste it. Brother John, unbeknownst beforehand even to Alphaios, had slipped a dollop of honey and touch of cinnamon into the mix, sweetening it noticeably. Some eyebrows had risen in surprise, but no one had pushed his food away in objection or self-denial.

When he climbed the steps and entered the library, the warmth of the lobby enveloped him like an old friend. He went into the scriptorium, where Kenny and XM were hard at work with their quills.

The laboratory results on the paint scrapings had come back long before the mockup of the quire was settled. Alphaios found no surprises in the results; the severely damaged page had once been as vibrant in color as he had suspected.

He and Inaki took Cardinal Ricci's directive to heart. They knew that for this bifolium, and for the other badly damaged ones yet to come, it was imperative they have strong rationale to support their work. All of them had taken to calling the whole quire "the wink," not just the one ruined page.

They had decided to submit only one mockup to the commission. They wanted to be well prepared not only to support it, but to provide backup solutions should their judgments run into reasoned opposition. The last thing they wanted was other people designing the quire for them. And while Cardinal Ricci had given Alphaios extraordinary authority, bitter dispute with the commission or loss of support would be a serious setback.

While continuing their other work on the book, Alphaios and the scribes made several trial mockups for the quire, mapping the areas where text, pictures and decorated versals might go. They debated the matter extensively, and involved Inaki only after each iteration. By proceeding this way, Inaki could serve as devil's advocate, helping to inform their work and preparing them for the scholarly challenges they might encounter. They had not yet reached a consensus.

Though he didn't say so, Alphaios chafed at the idea of subjecting the painting itself to outside review. He knew that despite the cardinal's instruction limiting the group's role, members of the commission would wish to critique the specific content as well. Let alone the main idea of the painting, he could foresee arguments about every detail—the positioning of the figures, the setting, the background, the colors and styles of the clothing. Because there was no exemplar for this painting, every aspect of it could be subject to debate—especially what he had in mind for the wink itself.

Alphaios had been thinking about this page ever since he and Inaki had read the journal entry. Its central, provocative theme was well developed in his mind, but he needed to do more work on its setting. He studied all of Jeremiah's other paintings for an approach, and in doing so was reminded that the master illuminator's work varied tremendously. Some pictures had extensive natural landscapes behind the figures, some had architectural features, and some were so close, so present, that there was no need or room for a backdrop. Unlike most other early fifteenth-century books, there were very few contemporary figures such as nobles or bishops, unless their otherwise unknowable faces had been used.

Also, unlike many other books of hours, most of the scriptural scenes were placed in historically relevant settings rather than among medieval churches, arches and parapets. But as this painting with the wink was not explicitly based in scripture, a contemporary setting might be called for.

While the colors in Jeremiah's paintings were remarkably vivid, there was no dominant thematic color like the famous deep blue used throughout the calendar in *Très Riches Heures*.

In the one extraordinary case, the Expulsion, Jeremiah had even used bare parchment for effect. As much as he admired it, as audacious as it was, Alphaios did not plan to use the technique in this painting.

Given their recent conclusion that Blanca had been the patron, Alphaios wondered about the figural anomalies Jeremiah had portrayed in several of the paintings—the goiter, the shortened leg, grotesqueries of some kind or other. Were these from the mind of Blanca or Jeremiah? With their book of hours so controversial in doctrinal terms, one might expect them to have targeted only religious figures. Instead, Alphaios had found that both churchmen of high office and wealthy secular figures suffered under Jeremiah's brush. Both the devout and the noble could find something to object to in this resplendent book.

The book had been created late in the period of the Western Schism, but despite Blanca's father's known support for the Avignon papacy, Alphaios decided to give no indication whether this pope was from Avignon or Rome. The writer of the journal had not commented on the subject, and to include it would take the painting's message in a direction inconsistent with the rest of the book. This would not devolve into a debate about which pope the patron might have favored— or wished to deprecate.

Yet there would be much more to the painting than the journalist had commented on. One reason Jeremiah's work was so exceptional was his ability to engage the viewer in more than one thought, more than one aspiration, more than one sensation. Jeremiah had painted the original in a period when open or alternate interpretations could pose even the risk of death to the creators and owners of such art. The painting he intended to create would certainly fit in that category.

Its frame would be narrow to permit the largest field possible for the painting itself. It would be illuminated with crushed gold to create rich sparkles in the light. The royal retinue would not be large, not as large as he had first conceived. A winged angel in radiant white with highlights of crushed silver would hover above the pope's right shoulder.

The pope, of course, would be in resplendent white like the angel above him. He would sit on an ornate throne with golden highlights, papal cross in hand. Two crimson-clad cardinals would flank him, one bent down and leaning in as if to hear some private comment or request.

The king would have one knee on the ground, his head bowed in the universal posture of obeisance. His crown would lie on a soft amaranthine pillow to his side. His robe would be of purple velvet and lined with mink. Two noblemen, perhaps members of his family, would kneel beside him, their heads also bowed. One would wear a cape with alternating diamonds of leaf and forest greens, the other a cape of rich seal gray. The queen would wear royal red—deeper than the cardinals' crimson—and jewels on the points of her slender crown would catch the sun. Next to her would stand a young woman, head still up, grasping the sides of her dress and preparing to kneel. Its blue would nearly match the color of the sky at its apex.

She would have one eye closed.

At the edge of the group would be a knight, kneeling, holding the reins of an armored warhorse, only part of which would be in the frame.

There would be no heraldry to identify king or kingdom.

In the distance to the left, beyond golden fields rich with shocks of grain, he would paint a castle, tall-towered and crenellated, made festive with yellow banners flying against the cloudless sky.

In the near distance to the right of the grouping would be the unfinished frame of a small peasant's house. A man, a carpenter dressed in a simple brown shift, would be at work on its rafters while a barefoot boy offered water to a crippled traveler. The boy would hold a cup to the man's lips.

The pomp at the foreground would thus be rendered superficial, even trivial, by the simple scene of Joseph the carpenter and his young son. Who was Jesus helping? Perhaps a leper, or a Pharisee. Perhaps any simple sinner.

Alphaios did not need to sketch out the scene in detail, for it was already drawn in his mind. He and Inaki decided he would fully paint it twice: once for submission on a separate sheet of vellum, and once again on its proper bifolium when the scholars had accepted it. They wanted the commission to see the full force and energy of the composition and had agreed it would be harder for its members to debate a finished painting than a conceptual sketch. Submitting it already finished would also underscore the discretion Cardinal Ricci had awarded Alphaios.

Finally, they reached agreement on the mockup. Today was the day he would begin the painting.

Alphaios had been deflecting questions about the picture from the scribes and even from Inaki, so when he finally went to work with his brushes and pigments, it drew them away from their own worktables to watch. He chased them away repeatedly, but finally accepted their presence at his shoulder so long as they stayed completely silent and promised to get their own work done. This had been, after all, the most collaborative quire of the book, and the painting one of its most important illuminations. Questions and comments, stirring and shuffling though, he wouldn't tolerate. More than once he barked at them, especially Kenny, to settle down or go back to their own work. Inaki, though, was the one who seemed to have the most time to watch. Whenever he could, he observed intently, not letting a single brush stroke go unnoticed.

Ten days later, they were all present when Alphaios completed the picture by closing one eye of the royal princess. When this was done, there was a sudden release of constrained breath in the room and a burst of victorious energy. Alphaios was embarrassed at being clapped on the back and praised by his chattering, laughing colleagues. He allowed himself a smile, however, for it was indeed a beautiful work. He had accomplished nearly all he had hoped.

After the room quieted down, Alphaios slid the painting into its drawer to await the meeting. The angel gazed back at him.

~

FIVE WEEKS HAD PASSED since the meeting with the commission, and the scriptorium was again quiet, focused, intent.

As Alphaios had expected, the scholars had examined the quire with great care, and questioned both archivist and illuminator about minute details. Most of the questions were not about the wink, but about the carpenter and young boy, a period insertion into the otherwise contemporaneous illumination. They then debated strenuously among themselves about aspects of art history Alphaios considered to be of little importance. Once their energy had dissipated over minor points, they gave the painting an enthusiastic thumbs-up.

In their attention to lesser detail and awe at the picture's beauty, the members had ignored the most important element of this quire, perhaps of the whole book: What element of it, or what combination of its content and historical context had driven this book underground for nearly 600 years?

On the other hand, he wouldn't worry about their narrow vision. Their lack of curiosity about this point had given him far greater latitude than he would otherwise enjoy. From his perspective, the meeting had been a great success.

Inaki had the scribes embark on completing the quire as soon as the meeting had ended. They did not want to give members of the commission an opportunity for second thoughts.

Alphaios's second and final painting of the wink, on its completed bifolium, had been taken out of its drawer many times since the meeting. Inaki and the scribes had all done so. On these occasions, there was no joviality, no clapping as there had been when the first one was completed. Indeed, Alphaios noted that each of them studied it with great solemnity. When they again put the painting away, they returned silently to their own work.

CHAPTER 31

 EARLY ON A COLD but bright Saturday afternoon, Alphaios was in the scriptorium alone. The entire quire had been completed, and on his worktable, in full sun, lay Jeremiah's wink. If anything, this second painting was even more vibrant than the first. The whole of the quire had a kind of weight, a palpable presence in the room. Even when in its drawers, it possessed a magnetism they all felt.

Even so, a palette with dabs of paint waited at the edge of his table.

He heard the front door of the library open and close. Moments later, Inaki entered the scriptorium, still removing his scarf and coat. He greeted Alphaios happily, and began to talk about the cold wind outside. He stopped mid-sentence when he noticed the painting. He came to Alphaios and stood silently beside him for a long, reverent moment.

"It's truly remarkable. No one else alive could have done this. You have become Jeremiah—and added Alphaios as well."

"It's not finished, Inaki."

The archivist turned to search his friend's face. "Not finished? What do you mean? It's a wonderful painting. A masterpiece, and I don't use that word lightly. It'll be famous."

He stood motionless for a long minute. "I know it's good, Inaki, but do you remember that before the printing press, scribes and illuminators occasionally entered their own observations, their own comments into the works they were copying?"

"Of course. Often in error, sometimes deliberately. Why?"

"It isn't finished."

"I don't understand. It went to the commission, and they were nearly speechless. Cardinal Ricci will be thrilled. You've done remarkable work."

"It's not enough. The wink alone wasn't enough to compel Blanca to keep the book hidden. It's not provocative enough to enrage the inquisitors, especially against a powerful queen who was a devout Roman Catholic. It's not enough to drive the book underground twice. It had to be something more."

"What about all the other things we talked about, Alphaios? The feminine point of view, the breaks from artistic tradition, the audacity of Jeremiah, the fire at Leyre. Aren't you putting too much weight on this one picture?"

Alphaios reached into the slender drawer under his work-table and took out his finest brush. He dabbed it in the paint, and prepared to touch it to the parchment.

Inaki was alarmed now. "Alphaios, what are you doing? Put the brush down. Please. It's a magnificent painting. Don't! You'll ruin it!"

Despite Inaki's protests, Alphaios reached forward with the brush and delicately closed the right eye of the winged angel.

He spoke quietly. "If not for the angel's wink, the young woman's closed eye might be explained away as just another physical anomaly. Or just another sly but opaque trick by Jeremiah. When it's repeated on the face of the angel, Inaki, it's undeniably a wink between the girl and the heavenly host. Who can know who winked first? Was it the young woman or God's own angel?"

The archivist seemed to be in shock.

"Think of it, Inaki. Think of the sharpness of the journalist's protest. Talk about fallow ground for claims of heresy—this is no longer a simple suggestion of feigned submission to a pope. Instead, it suggests a joke, or worse, some kind of alliance between God's purest messenger and a young woman. Pope and king? Both of them are reduced to a sideshow, their pretense of power simply to be indulged? Or could it be a broadside against patriarchy? Queens commonly ruled countries, of course, but never has a woman been pope. Even a wraith of such thought would have been heresy."

Inaki seemed to have somewhat recovered and was now studying the painting with narrowed eyes, his lips pursed.

"Had it been known," Alphaios said, "such a painting could not have survived the Spanish Inquisition. Its owner and anyone else associated with it would pay an unbearable price, very likely thrown on the fires."

He took a half step back and looked at his work. "The angel is winking, too, Inaki. A joke? Or a pact between woman and angel? As for me, I'm going to get a cup of coffee. It's cold outside."

Inaki stood rooted to the floor, his eyes riveted to the painting.

Alphaios cleaned his brush and prepared to leave. He grinned at his disconcerted friend and let himself out of the scriptorium. He went to the lobby where the old coat awaited him. When a few moments later he left the library with it tight around him, he turned in the direction of the Green River Bar and Grill and grinned. Today he would be ready for Jess's gleeful repartee.

ABOUT THE AUTHOR

J. S. ANDERSON lives and writes in Longview, Washington. He has a lifelong interest in western religions and cultures. An aficionado of art, good food, and music (vocal music and the blues draw him most), he enjoys remarkable architecture and learning about the creative, artistic and cultural forces that contributed to significant buildings and their surroundings. An amateur photographer, he is drawn to colors and enjoys finding the odd picture and the unusual point of view. Find out more at www.jsandersonauthor.com.